DEMON IN THE ATTIC

NIGHT SHADES

BOOK TWO

T STEDMAN

DEMON IN THE ATTIC

A NIGHT SHADES NOVEL

CHAPTER 1

I'd been drawn to my old house again. It was just a small, slightly neglected, weather-beaten, white cottage that had a field of grazing sheep on one side and the forest on the other. It should be idyllic really, except the latticed windows made it look like it was crying and gave me a feeling of doom whenever I saw it. And the fact I couldn't put a single step over the boundary to look inside. No matter how often I try, day or night, I never get to see the place I was supposed to have grown up in and possibly died.

I have no memory. Although I'm not exactly alive. I'm a Shade. A being that lives in a small part of the earthly plane and never moves on. I am in between, you could say. The only thing I can remember is that my name is Samantha Payne and I don't know who I was or how I died. I woke up one day with my friends at Waxley-Black Manor. They were the ones that told me where I lived and where I went to school.

It was Tallulah and her boyfriend, Ollie, who first brought me back to the cottage. They filled me in with everything they knew, which wasn't much. A mum, Christine, a stepdad,

Graeme and sister, Trish. That was about it. Now I spend every day hidden, watching their comings and goings, yearning to know what happened. Tallulah explained that I saw my friends at school, but they never really knew me and no one had been to my house. Ever.

It had troubled me at first, but then I'd gotten swept up with all the mental stuff with Wax last year and by then we'd become inseparable. Now everything had settled down to a daily rhythm and my story had kind of been forgotten. But not by me. It was still a very real and heavy burden I carried with me every day. It was hard to be taken seriously in a paranormal world where you were a being that switched from being invisible to corporeal. Past lives weren't exactly a top priority.

All of us Shades ghosted out, only made real at all because of the magical properties of the water found in Wax's mine. It couldn't exactly bring a dead person back to life, but it allowed us to become solid at night and even sometimes during the day if you didn't stand in direct sunlight. So every chance I got, I came to the last place that connected me to the real world and when I'd been alive.

The others left me to it. They all knew how they'd died. It was just me who drew a blank. They all remembered us being at school, their accidents and incidents that caused their deaths and then waking up at Wax's huge old grey house – Waxley-Black Manor. Then soon after, I joined them. Ollie, Tallulah, Nicola, Archie, Joe and Josh. They were my friends, now my family, except I still felt the odd one out. The third wheel. The one that people kind of overlooked or took for granted.

There was Wax. Ollie's older, moody brother. He was a loner, too. Except he was alive and could see the dead. He looked out for us all and last year, found his Beccah. When they met, she had been something else. She'd been made a

Shade, temporarily, by Wax's evil uncle. Her spirit had been captured and brought here because she was the last Blackwood. That was a whole other story, but when we last saw her, she had in fact been in a coma in the United States. With all our help, Wax had broken the Blackwood curse and gone off to find the girl he loved, to wake her up with some of his miracle water. A real fairy-tale ending.

It made my heart ache to have someone that loved me like that. He was bringing her back to England today and everyone was so excited to see her for the first time in the flesh.

My rambling thoughts halted suddenly. The front door opened to my old house. The bearded, tall, wiry frame of my stepfather came out and slammed the door behind him. He looked around and strode in purposeful strides to his small white van parked in the black, tarmacked driveway, then opened the door. He paused and looked over the car roof right at me and I sank to the ground. He shouldn't be able to see me as I was ghosting, but my heart hammered as if I'd been caught.

I daren't look.

I stayed crouched, breathing hard, praying for the engine to start. I closed my eyes when I finally heard it cough into life. The engine revved and he pulled away.

I stayed put for a full minute, recovering. It always amazed me how hollow it made me feel when I saw any of my family. Him particularly. There was nothing left in me at all. No residual feelings of love. No emotion. No anything.

The wind whipped up the dead leaves and blew my hair into my face. *Sam ... Sam ... Sam* whispered past my ear. My breath hitched and I stood up quickly and looked around me. 'Who's there?' I said loudly. 'Ollie, is that you?'

Apart from the wind in the tops of the trees, I couldn't hear anything. 'Not funny, you know.'

I let out a slow breath, thinking that it was this place that sent me crazy. There was no point in staying, scaring myself half to death, gawping at my old life today. Nothing was going to reveal itself. I turned, heavy-hearted, and walked away. It always left me feeling sad. I pulled my coat tighter around me against the cold wind and looked up at the building clouds. The day would be short and I still didn't like being out here alone. After last year, I was never sure of what other beings lurked around.

I entered the shadowy footpath that went through the bare trees to the Waxley-Black place. I always took this route rather than the less scary road way. I couldn't afford the villagers seeing me alive and well; it could start a public outcry. I sped up my steps and my senses prickled.

I hadn't gone very far when a twig snapped a little way off. I stopped and turned my head sharply to the right, in the direction of the noise. My heart thumped. I listened keenly and scanned the grey-barked trees.

There was nothing there. All I could hear was my heart pounding in my chest and see my breath now coming in shallow pants. 'Who's there?' I called, in a far braver voice than I felt.

Still no movement or any further sound. In fact, no sound at all. Even the birds seemed to be holding their breath. There was a squawk a long way off, which brought me back to my senses. My mind was playing tricks. I continued my steps. A little more quickly this time.

The thing was, I'd felt like I was being followed ever since I became a Shade. Long before Beccah Whitely came. From the day I woke up. But no one else ever commented or seemed to sense it, so I kept quiet, thinking it must be me. Tallulah had laughed on the only time I mentioned it, saying there was nothing there and I just had a princess complex – something she'd read in a girls' magazine. It meant I thought

I was more important than everyone else. She'd said, 'trust me to think I had a stalker'. It was typical of Tallulah not to really listen and relate everything back to her.

My meandering thoughts had taken me all the way through the wood and I was finally back at Waxley-Black Manor. I looked up at the gargoyles and grey turrets. It was large and imposing, but it had become a happy place.

Wax and his parents had made a safe haven for us all. Their son Ollie was a Shade and we were his friends, so they loved us all being there together, under one roof, where they could be close to him. Plus, it wasn't safe to be spotted in the village or near our old homes with all our tombstones in the graveyard. Well, everyone's except mine. There had never been a burial for me.

'Come on!' Tallulah shouted, calling me from the front porch. 'They're on their way from the airport. There'll be home any minute.'

She was dressed smartly in her red tartan mini-skirt and black sweater, with her honey-blonde hair curled and a full face of make-up. I felt drab in comparison. I put up my hand and quickened my steps. I should change out of my jeans and old boots. I wanted to shake off my gloomy thoughts and make an effort. I should at least try to join Tallulah in her hyper-excitement. Today was a happy day. Wax had found his Beccah and as the youngest surviving Blackwood, she had inherited the creepy old house at the other side of the wood. Wax had called a few weeks ago and said she'd convinced her parents to move to England. He must be ecstatically happy. She was the one girl who'd gotten through his antisocial grumpiness and broken the ancient curse that had kept the families apart for more than a century.

I liked Beccah, but I wasn't sure what her parents would make of it here. They weren't exactly going to have Black-wood House to themselves. There were other Shades there too that had been there for years. Beccah's great-great-great aunt for starters. Then there was Tallulah's mum, Gerty, Burt the handy man and his dog, Brutus. Not to mention Wax's ancestors; the ghost Lucinda and malevolent spirit, Jedediah. That was a lot for any flesh and blood human to take. I wasn't sure how long they could keep them hidden or explained away.

'Hurry! Wax just texted. They're dumping their bags at Beccah's and coming straight over.'

Tallulah shot ahead to the kitchen and I headed for the stairs. 'I just need to change,' I said, to gather myself and escape Tallulah's overbearing excitement. Time at my old house always affected me strangely.

Joe and Josh passed me at the foot of the stairs, discussing their latest game. I waited, but neither of them noticed me, so I ran lightly up the grand, creaky staircase, that went up from the dark-red, gothic hallway. Past all the creepy faces of male Waxley-Blacks from past generations and the arched stained-glass windows, bathing the hall in much-needed light. Until I reached the long dark-red carpeted landing.

There were six bedrooms and two bathrooms behind the black doors on this floor. Wax had one at one end next to a bathroom and his parents had the master bedroom at the opposite end, next to the other. Ollie had the one next to Wax, then Tallulah and Nicola shared. Near Wax's parents, Josh and Joe bunked together and Archie had the smallest room alone. That just left me. I had one of the old servants' rooms in the attic. You got to it by a small staircase next to Wax's parents' room. There were two bedrooms up there, mine and the other one, just full of stuff. The rest of the loft space was open and an antique road show of furniture, boxes and trinkets, piled up on dusty floorboards.

My boots clomped on the bare wooden steps as I went up to the attic. I didn't mind being alone. I was used to it. I felt apart most of the time, anyway. That was when I wasn't feeling like I was being watched.

Like right now.

My foot creaked on the last step of the staircase. There was a shuffle and a scrape of wood against wood in the large loft space ahead of me. There shouldn't be anyone up here as everyone was already downstairs.

'Hello?' I said, edging hesitantly towards the small corridor to my room. Moving slowly with my back to the wall, everything in me screamed to run. My blood flashed around my body in fear and my eyes scanned the cluttered furniture for hiding places. The whole place was a hide-and-seek paradise. The small, dust-clouded window at the far end had been opened. Maybe a cat had got in. I couldn't see anything else out of the ordinary, so I hurried my last few steps and burst into the room.

I shut the door and vowed to get a lock on it for the hundredth time. I was shaking. I wiped my brow with the back of my hand and went over, sat on my single wooden bed and waited. For what exactly, I wasn't sure. I gazed around at the dark furniture. All I knew was that it was becoming a routine. After feeling I wasn't alone, I came to my room and a great tiredness came over me. It had happened ever since I could remember and was happening more and more. I hadn't spoken about it much because I was scared there was something wrong with me. Or even depressed, which seemed ridiculous for a Shade. I certainly slept a lot. The thing was, Shades weren't meant to get depressed, or sleep, or even get sick, but I certainly did a lot of it. It's all I seemed to do.

When I'd broached it with Ollie, he'd said it was probably to do with us all becoming more alive. I'd smiled and nodded, but I didn't really believe that. I'd been sleeping long before we drank the magical waters.

I attempted to rouse myself and get changed, but I slumped back down on the pale-blue throw and stared at my chest of drawers. The top left-hand drawer was a little open and I never left it like that. It was where I kept my diary and I made a particular point of leaving everything in a particular way so I could tell if anything had been moved.

I slowly got to my feet and approached the heavy wooden chest. It had definitely been opened. I slowly pulled out the drawer and peered inside. A huge part of me sagged in relief. My diary was still there. Although it wasn't how I'd left it. I always put it at the very bottom, next to the lining paper, on the right-hand side, at the back. Then I put four particular pairs of neatly balled-up socks on top of it. I did it on purpose for exactly this reason. Someone had chucked socks back on top, but they were haphazard and not the right ones.

My heart began to beat hard. Someone had been looking through my things.

I snatched up the diary, scattering balls of socks on the floor. I smelled the comforting leather and my blood seethed. Someone had read my diary. Who would do something like that?

I took out the pen hidden inside the spine and wrote furiously, *Leave my bloody things alone!!! This is private. How would you like it?*

Then a sudden thought made me hitch a breath. What if it wasn't one of my friends at all? What if it was the cleaning lady?

I dismissed the thought as nobody came up here. I was the quiet one in the background, nobody took much notice of.

Wax's parents? *No.*

Then the scariest thing occurred to me. Maybe it was someone, or rather something, I didn't know at all. Strangely, my recurring nightmare came to mind. The hideous, creeping goblin. But I dismissed it right away. No, this was real. This was no dream. No one believed me when I said I was being watched. This was proof. Now I could set a trap.

I was suddenly filled with an excitement I hadn't felt in a very long while. I could actually do something about it. However, as soon as I became enthused, the overwhelming tiredness came over me. I tried to resist. Analyse it. It was more than just usual tiredness. I felt warm and comfortable, safe and protected, like I was becoming wrapped in a soft cocoon.

I looked at my soft, inviting bed. *Maybe I was just tired. A little power nap wouldn't hurt.*

As I sank slowly into the soft, downy light-blue quilt, I must have fallen straight to sleep, because I was instantly dreaming. A blanket of beautiful feathers covered me and soft music played in the distance. *Piano.* Briefly, I wondered who was playing. Then a wonderful smell of winter spices, reminding me of Christmas, drifted all around me. My eyelids lowered and I succumbed to marvellous sleep.

Each time I slept it was the same. It took me down deeply so I couldn't move a muscle and what was more, I didn't want to. It was like I was given a sedative that made you contented and safe. Vaguely, somewhere, I did question how come my brain was alert enough to reason on all this. As if I was rattling around in a sleeping shell.

My heart felt like it was beating too fast for sleep. I was waiting. Waiting for something that always came. The wonderful weight that compressed on top of me. The final thing that tucked me into slumber. *Mmmm, there it was.* A pressure all around me that felt like tight swaddling. Always accompanied by a beautiful smell of jasmine and spice. The feel of feathers on my face. I always wanted to know what came next, but deep sleep always took me at that point.

I wanted to open my eyes so badly to see the soft feathers.

Black feathers. Somehow, I knew they were black. Then a softness passed over my lips.

THE COSY, safe dreams never lasted. At some point, I was left completely alone. I briefly examined that. *Who had I been with?* It always eluded me. It was struck from my mind by the awful feelings of abandonment that followed. I'd gone from a place of light and comfort to completely dark and alone. Always the same. Darkness. Strange ink-black, cloying darkness that pulled at my face and my neck, so I always struggled to get under the covers, but I couldn't move. My arms were stuck and my face was exposed.

I waited. Not breathing. Heart racing. Eyes unseeing. Ears straining for the minutest sound.

Then it came. *Thump, stomp, thump stomp, thump stomp.*

I gasped for breath, otherwise I would pass out. But the noise always came and was coming closer, closer, closer, and I couldn't hide.

Then like hopeful dawn, the wind came, carrying a thousand black feathers. It swept me up into a devilish smile and yellow cat's eyes.

CHAPTER 2

'Sam! Sam! Are you bloody sleeping again?'

My eyelids flickered open to Tallulah's booming voice. I felt bewildered. Lost for a moment, struggling to get my bearings. Until I came to and slowly remembered where I was. Tallulah was leaning in, glaring at me from the doorway, expecting a response. She huffed and stomped off.

I relaxed and looked up at the ceiling. My mouth was dry and I needed a drink. I must have slept for ages. No wonder my friends were getting fed up. It wasn't exactly normal and would anger Wax. He'd reminded us over and over to at least try to sleep at night. That way, we kept some kind of normalcy and he and his parents got their much-needed rest. But it was afternoon and I was in my bed and it was happening more and more frequently lately.

At least that was a good one. *Was it?* I felt momentarily confused. It started well. Some I remembered clearly, others I didn't. Most of the time, I was left with a feeling, rather than a visual. Fear and safety. Fear and relief. Protected and alone. It didn't make much sense. Although some were unbelievably real nightmares that left me reeling, in a cold sweat.

Logic told me I shouldn't want to sleep then, but I could barely make it through to night-time these days. The weird dreams happened every night and now, clearly, every afternoon, too. And it didn't seem to happen to anyone else. Something was very wrong with me. I had to be sick.

Then I remembered my diary and went to sit up suddenly, but I couldn't move. I had to fight off the sheet, quilt and blankets that had managed to wrap themselves around me. I wrestled with them for a couple of minutes until I escaped, slid off the bed and threw them away from me. Still preoccupied with how weird that was, I padded over to my chest and pulled open the drawer.

I sagged a little. It all looked the same. I swallowed, bitterly, and tried to get a grip and get my head on straight. Whatever this was. It was a state of mind. It had to be. *Wax was home. With Beccah. The real, alive Beccah.* I should go and see them. Be around people.

I was still dressed in my jeans and red plaid shirt from earlier, so I dragged my fingers through my hair and settled my brown waves into place. Then I looked down at my feet and saw navy-blue socks.

I wiggled my toes.

No boots.

I froze for a moment while I took that in. I hadn't taken them off. They were neatly placed at the foot of the bed. I began to feel my chest tighten. I just couldn't allow myself to think about this right now. I refused to. Otherwise, it would terrify me and send me into mad panic. Instead, I told myself I must have done it without thinking. I huffed, pulled on my soft trainers and marched out of the room.

I swept all the silliness from my mind. For the moment I would concentrate on feeling good. Sociable. Back to my old self. The real me. I went to turn down the staircase, with my back to the loft space and a whisper of something brought me round, sharply. 'Who's there?'

A breeze? The window was closed now. Nothing appeared out of the ordinary as I scanned the furniture and gloom, but something was there. Waiting. Watching. I could feel it. An overwhelming presence. 'I know you're there,' I said, hearing the wobble in my voice. 'You have to stop following me.' Then my anger overtook my fear. 'And stop reading my diary.' I suddenly felt better. Bolder. Whatever it was hadn't hurt me. With a loud tut, I turned and jogged down the stairs.

BY THE TIME I reached the large, modern kitchen, my grogginess had completely disappeared. It was miraculous. Luckily, no one noticed me slip into the room. Everyone had congregated around the island and were preoccupied in a bustle of happy greetings, hugs and kisses and Wax and Beccah were right in the middle of it.

Beccah hadn't changed at all. She was still beautiful with her long, straight white hair. She looked like a gothic doll in her long black shirt and jeans, but she had a rosy glow about her that she didn't have before and she looked happy. Blissfully happy.

She saw me and immediately drew me into a hug. It was warm and real and she wore expensive perfume. Something I rarely smelled since being a Shade. There was never anything new. We were in our own little world where few new people came into it.

A memory of Christmas spice stabbed me in the heart. I wasn't sure why I thought of it right then. Wax was there, frowning. Watching me. 'Are you OK? Do you need a glass of water or something? You look like you've seen a ghost.'

It was his idea of a joke and he was already smirking. Everyone else laughed and after rolling my eyes, I couldn't help smiling.

'All she wants to do is sleep lately. She's a right bore,' Tallulah chimed in.

Wax looked at me, puzzled. I shrugged. Then he was side-tracked into another conversation with his father, happier and more alive than I'd ever seen him. Although he was every bit as dangerous-looking with his tall, dark looks and head-to-toe tattoos. He certainly didn't look like an earl or a viscount, or whatever he was. He was so cool with his over-long hair swept forward and sparkling blue eyes, that seemed livelier than ever now he had his Beccah back.

I sighed and looked at Beccah, who happened to be watching me too. I blasted pink at being caught ogling her boyfriend. 'So you came back,' I said, to cover myself.

'I know, right?' Tallulah said, holding her hands out dramatically. 'Imagine leaving California for this dump.'

Everyone laughed. The Waxley-Black manor house could hardly be described as a dump.

Jed, Wax's father, was asking Wax about the trip and his mother, Olivia, was asking who wanted tea or coffee. The boys soon drifted around the kitchen island while we piled onto the leather sofa, under the window.

'So tell us everything,' Nicola said, flicking her shiny black hair over her shoulder.

'Yeah, did you forget all about us till Wax told you?' Tallulah asked.

Beccah ate up every question, not having a chance to answer before the next was thrown at her and I looked on dreamily. It was all so wonderfully romantic.

She'd helped us get rid of Wax's old uncle Ainsley and his namesake ancestor while she was still a Shade and finally her own ancestor too, the awful witch, Lila. 'I never thought we'd see you again,' I said. And I didn't. When she was trapped by the ancient curse Lila had set for her, I thought that was it. But Wax, the gorgeous, moody and scary as hell eldest Waxley-Black son, had fallen in love with her and promised to bring her back. And today he'd kept that promise. He'd gone to America with some of the special fountain waters we found in his mine, woken her up from her coma and brought her home, just like he said he would. It was a fairy-tale ending.

'I bet it was a shock when you first opened your eyes and saw the grouch,' Tallulah said, making us all laugh.

Beccah took it all in her stride and laughed along with us, then she frowned a little. 'I remembered it all, but it was in snatches. Like a jumbled-up dream. Wax helped me make sense of it and get back on my feet.'

'I bet he did,' Tallulah said, waggling her eyebrows and making us all laugh.

'So how long are you here for?' I asked, searching her face. I could only dream of escaping the borders of the village. All of us Shades were still restricted.

Beccah didn't understand the deeper significance of my question. 'Wax brought out all these legal papers proving Blackwood House is ours. Mum and Dad wanted to sell it, but I talked them into moving here. You know, after Pete and everything. It's the new start we all needed.'

We all remembered the story of the car accident that put Beccah in her coma and killed her younger brother, but Tallulah's excitement rode roughshod over all that.

'What! You're moving here for good?' Tallulah screamed, then threw her arms around Beccah's neck.

I looked on with tears welling in my eyes, while Beccah let her pull her about while she bounced and squealed. Nicola kissed her too, a little less demonstratively. I don't know why it affected me so much, but it did. I was so glad and I could only put it down to how lonely I always felt.

'Someone had to come and protect you from Wax's grumpy moods,' Beccah said, patting Tallulah's back to finally let her go. Her eyes fell on Wax talking easily with his brother, Ollie, the slightly smaller, skinnier version of him. I followed her line of vision. Wax looked nothing like the troubled recluse with anger issues of a few months ago.

'He certainly looks happy now,' I said, to cover my emotion. I was so unbelievably glad she was staying. I guess my world just got a little bigger and it was comforting to know.

'I know, right?' Beccah said, with eyes smouldering with love that made my own insides melt.

How I would love to have such a strong, gorgeous boy to love me like that. To go to the ends of the earth to save me like he did.

'So tell me the news. What's going on with all of you?' Beccah said. 'Come on … girl talk.'

We all hunkered down to dish the dirt. 'Me and Archie are still together, like an old married couple,' Nicola said. 'I wish he could be as exciting as Wax sometimes.'

'I've been creeping into Ollie's room at night when his parents are asleep,' Tallulah whispered, clamping her hand over her own mouth and widening her eyes with mischief.

We all laughed. She was such a drama queen. Everyone knew they'd left second base behind months ago.

Beccah burst into laughter with us. She looked so happy and glad to be back. 'What about you, Sam?' she asked, snapping me out of my laughter. 'Have you made out with Josh or Joe yet?' She sounded so American.

It was lovely that she pulled me into the type of conversation I was never usually included in, but the thought horrified me. I must have instantly pulled a face as everyone laughed. 'What? ... Yuk! It'd be like kissing my brothers.' The thought literally made me want to puke up my guts. However, despite the joking around, I felt a real pang of pain in my chest as the sudden realisation struck me. I'd probably always be alone. I'd be confined within these walls, within the bubble of the small village, never meeting anyone other than the ones present in this room. With the exception of Beccah's parents and a few creepy old fogeys with a collective age of about three hundred, at the Blackwood house. It was a bleak prospect.

Beccah had already gone on to talk about her parents and how great they'd been and how she'd have to introduce them to Aunt Sarah, Gerty and Burt, carefully. But my mind was already stuck on how my life was over. It all just made me so dreadfully tired. I wanted to sleep. I wanted the warm, cocooned feeling, the weight on my chest that comforted me and wouldn't let me move.

'What about us?' Tallulah was saying. 'When are you going to introduce them to us?'

Wax's mum, Olivia, had overheard and wandered over. 'I thought about asking your parents over for dinner this weekend, Beccah. What do you think? Give them a few days to settle in. Shall we say Saturday, here for seven? It will be dark enough for everyone to materialise and pass as alive, what do you think?'

We all looked at Beccah for her answer. It was bizarre to say the least. But she immediately smiled. 'Thank you, Mrs Waxley-Black. That would be lovely.'

'Fantastic ... and call me Olivia. It's the least I can do for bringing back to me more than one son.' She had tears in her eyes as she leant down and gave her knee a squeeze. It set me off and I had to wipe my eyes. Even Tallulah was a little affected. 'It wasn't just Beccah you know.'

Olivia rolled her eyes, smiled indulgently and pinched

Tallulah's cheek. 'You live here, Tallulah, so you're invited too.' Then she looked at us all. 'Everyone can come, it'll be like a party.'

It would be fun and exciting and my heart lifted a little. We did have something to celebrate. We had all come through the trouble of last year and Wax had definitely come out of it a happier, healthier young man.

Laughter came from the island where the boys were gathered as if to prove a point. Wax was there, chatting animatedly, a very different person.

'That settles it then. Dinner Saturday. Sit down at eight. Why don't we all dress up?'

Tallulah clapped excitedly, double time. 'I know, we could do a theme. Er … murder mystery, rock the casbah … tarts and vicars,' she said, wide-eyed, like a bolt of inspiration.

'Nooooo!' everyone groaned together.

Beccah looked particularly horrified. We all laughed, remembering the cruel trick Tallulah played on her last year. Getting her here to meet us for the first time in a tarty maid's outfit. By rights, Beccah should never have spoken to Tallulah again, but she punched Tallulah playfully in the top of the arm. 'No tarts, OK … my parents aren't ready for that.'

Everyone laughed, while I looked on. Grateful to have so many good friends, but feeling more apart than ever.

THE REST of the day wore on. My friends chatted and reminisced. How we all met, what we got up to and I remained quiet. The truth was, I had very little to say. They all knew who they were when they were alive and, more importantly, how they died and came to be a Shade. I didn't.

For some reason, that knowledge could not be called to mind. It was completely lost to me. I'd found my house. My steps took me there every day. Like an important piece of the puzzle. But the answer, the crucial piece, was always out of reach.

A wave of tiredness swept over me, so while Ollie was telling a very long and complicated joke, I made sure I slipped out before he came to the punchline.

I came out into the hallway and relief hit me like a blast of fresh air. Maybe if I splashed my face, I could liven myself up. The idea energised me enough to bolt up the staircase before anyone could spot me and call me back. I shot along the first landing and into the bathroom, nearest my staircase. I clicked the door shut and savoured the heady mix of soap and perfume and the feeling of seclusion in the warm, modern bathroom.

It was large, completely white and tasteful, with a huge tub, basin and a freestanding shower, still managing to keep a hint of antique charm with its hints of pastel colours in the many bottles, vases and candles. I walked quickly to the sink, turned on the tap and leaning forward, began splashing my face. I grabbed a hand towel with my eyes shut, then, letting out a slow breath, straightened, dabbing my face and examining myself in the mirror. I looked exhausted. As if the colour had been drained right out of me. I shouldn't feel like this. I shouldn't look like this, *should I?*

If ever someone imagined life after death, it wouldn't be this, I knew that much.

Something whistled past my ear and caught my eye. Just for a second, making me jump and turn around. 'Who's there?' came out as a squeak. My eyes were wide with fright as I scanned the room. There was nowhere to hide.

I jumped. The door handle rattled. I'd forgotten to lock it. 'I'm in here,' I called out, in case one of the boys tried to come in.

There was no reply. The door handle went down and the

door slowly opened. 'Did you hear me? I'm in here,' I called again, more forcefully.

Still the door continued to open.

The small hairs on the back of my neck began to stand up. 'Is anybody there?'

Something about this was boring into my consciousness on a much deeper level. My fear and dread a heavy weight, slowly descending my spine into the lowest part of my stomach.

The door was opening more and more.

My dream. This was my dream.

I attempted to swallow, but my mouth was too dry and I felt faint as my heart began to flutter out of rhythm. Then, just for a moment, I was sure I saw them: dark, shadowy fingers. But the door slammed shut, something squealed, like a rat or a wild animal and I was left breathing as if I'd been running for my life.

I looked down at my hands and they were shaking. I turned and looked back in the mirror and, just for the briefest moment, I saw the tall, dark boy. Serious face, black hair and those eyes. The eyes I would never forget. There was just a hint of a smile and then he was gone. I swung around and there was no one there. I leant back against the sink and rubbed my forehead. I was losing my mind.

I went to the door and cautiously peered out into the hallway. Of course, there was no one there. It had all been in my head. The dreams were just coming while I was awake now.

I came out into the hallway and ran up the small staircase, opposite. I didn't dare look out into the attic. I was too shaken up. I couldn't trust what I would see. I went straight to my room, closed the door and leant against it. I was breathing hard, but glad to be alone. I just needed to recharge. That was it. Being with people just sapped my energy.

After a minute, I felt slightly better and slowly opened my eyes. I felt it right away. Something different. I scanned the room. Bed still messy. Dressing-table on the far side of it unchanged. *There.* The tall chest of drawers at the foot of my bed. The left-hand top drawer was slightly open. After last time, I'd replaced it consciously. I knew I'd pushed it all the way in. I distinctly remembered doing it. I took hesitant steps towards the chest with my heart thundering, as if something would jump out and bite me. No one had left the kitchen, so I knew no one had come up here.

I carefully put my hand on the wooden drawer knob and slowly pulled, ready to jump out of the way. I almost fell over backwards as several of the most stunning blue butterflies fluttered out. They went up into the room and, one by one, they disappeared like popping bubbles. It was beautiful and unexpected and very definitely supernatural. But most importantly, no one I knew had the know-how to pull off a stunt like that.

I crept closer again to peer into the drawer. I breathed a little easier seeing my diary in place. It was flat and in the corner with three balled-up socks on top. *Three?* There should be four. However, something told me it was deliberate. Someone was telling me that they'd been in there.

I slowly pulled out the diary. A whisper-like wind whipped around me, like leaves rustling in a tree. Something shot past my ear and I turned around sharply, clasping my diary to my chest. My heart was galloping against it. 'Who's there?' came out a strangled croak. 'I know you're there. You've been following me.' But everything had gone quiet and still and all I could hear was the loud ticking of my alarm clock next to the bed.

When nothing else happened for a full minute, I opened

my small leather book with shaking hands and went to my last entry: *Leave my things alone.* Under it, in the handwriting of a small child was one new, incorrectly spelled word: *S O R Y.*

I stared at it, terrified. My mind scrambling, hoping, hating, longing, furious at who it could be. Yet exhilarated and more alive than I'd felt in living memory. I took the pen out from the spine and almost dropped it; my hands were shaking so much. *Who are you? Are you the one following me?* I quickly wrote.

A noise brought my head up sharply to look at the night-stand next to the bed. I couldn't see anything unusual, except a book I'd been reading lying on its side. There were four of my favourites that were meant to be standing and one had fallen over. Thoughts of ghosts and malevolent spirits sped up my heart. I thought we'd identified everyone last year, but maybe not. Perhaps they faded out like me or were permanently invisible. 'Are you here, now?' I whispered.

But there was nothing after that. Nothing moved. No whispers or sounds at all. The deathly sort of quiet that screamed in your head and hollowed your chest until it creaked in pain. Everything was telling me it was more than me going slowly mad. It was because I was doing it utterly alone. My friends in the house, who knew little more about me than I did, certainly couldn't relate. I was doomed to walk this tiny patch of earth, with no one special to love me or really care.

I slumped onto my bed and crawled under the covers, slipping my diary under my pillow. I wanted to dissolve and disappear in my misery completely. I hated being me. I hated this life.

Soon, my tears slowed and my whole body welcomed the familiar heaviness of calm. As if my punishing thoughts of being a lonely Shade, in a cut-off world, only weighed it down further and sped it along to oblivion. The wonderfully familiar warmth snaked around me, cradling me with the comforting confinement of sleep. The great weight that descended on my chest and the smell of dark spices that wafted under my nose, soothed and rocked me gently to dream.

I immediately recognised my soft, billowing dream world, where my eyes were always heavy. I could barely open them and always had to rely on my other senses. There, in the place of whispered, cherished words, I heard, 'Shhh, I'll always be with you, watching you … looking after you.'

I felt so happy and relaxed in the one place I always felt safe. I could never see much, but if I managed to crack my eyelids, I saw the yellow eyes of a big cat and black hair falling into a dark face in arrows pointing to red lips. Moving, saying comforting words. 'The darkness is now behind you and I will forever protect you from it. One day, I promise, you will be happy.'

The reminder of the shadowy figure from my nightmares threatened to take away my contentment. I tried to speak, but I was incapable. The thoughts, along with the words, just kept on falling away before I could say them. I was too relaxed. Although I was awake enough to feel soft breath brush my lips, that stole the last of my efforts to speak away. Yellow eyes – impossibly yellow eyes – and soft words. 'You belong to me and we belong to the night.'

Then I dreamed we were kissing. A beautiful boy was holding me. Stopping me from falling. Softly, drugging me into the deepest sleep I'd ever had. All I could remember feeling was that I wanted to. I wanted to belong somewhere. I wanted to belong to him.

CHAPTER 3

Something had woken me up. I was still in my room, but it was dark. Just the small lamp on by my bed. I felt groggy and confused. The room felt wrong. The furniture looked the same, but it was all around the wrong way. The door should be to the right of me, next to the headboard, but instead it was on the far wall.

I was scared. Something was coming. Something was always coming. I struggled and stifled a squeal, trying to pull my quilt over my head to hide. But that felt wrong too. They were blankets wound tightly around me. I was stuck. Trapped. My arms couldn't move. I was forced to look at the door in the far corner of the room. Footsteps. Clomps, as if coming up the stairs, but the stairs should be behind me. Then shuffling, like they'd reached the top and then stopped. Lost. No, deciding. Deciding whether to come in. My heart was beating so hard, it was making me feel sick. I'd forgotten how to breathe. It had gone out of rhythm or staggered. My mouth was opening to scream. The knob was different. Brass. Dull, loose. Noisy. Slowly turning. The door snicked open. Gradually opening every slow inch at a time. I wanted to scream my lungs out, but nothing came out. Nothing. Nothing worked.

I tried to turn to get my legs out of the bed to run, but I was frozen. Forced to look at the slowly opening door and the shadow. The grotesque slowly creeping shadow, edging, peeping around the door jam. The two long, bony, shadow hands, with extraordinarily long fingers, crawling along the wall to get me, like a crab. Hands that were followed by the shadow of an extremely long hooked nose and pointy chin. A goblin. A goblin. A terrifying, ugly goblin.

I screwed my eyes shut as tightly as I could and screamed. Screamed and screamed before those icy hands could touch me.

'Hey, weirdo, wake up!'

There was complete silence.

I swallowed and breathed. Feeling my chest rising and falling as my heart gradually stopped palpitating and slowed down.

I blinked and slowly allowed my lids to open, straight into Tallulah's coal-blacked eyes, about six inches from mine.

'Finally.'

'She's awake,' Ollie said from right next to her.

'This is too weird,' Tallulah said, getting up onto her feet next to the bed. 'She looks petrified.'

Beccah was pulling her by the arm. 'Wouldn't you be, finding all of us in your room? Give her some space, Tallulah, she just woke up.'

'But she shouldn't be sleeping like that.'

Wax came into view at the foot of the bed with his usual scowl. The others parted to let him get closer.

It was bewildering. 'What are you all doing in my room?' I said, trying to sit up, but couldn't because all my blankets seemed to be wound around me.

'You've been out for, like, twelve hours,' Nicola said.

'And you don't need much sleep. None of us do,' Archie added.

'Shouldn't do,' Ollie corrected.

Wax's frown deepened. And he shook his head. 'No … I think this is something else. Look how the bedding has been tucked in around her.' He came closer and pulled the quilt out from around me so I could finally move my arms and rest them on top. 'Who did this to you?' Wax looked scary, just like I remembered from last year.

I shook my head, but my mind went straight back to the hideous shadow. But I felt constricted before that. *Yes*, honey-yellow eyes, dark-caramel skin and whispered words of belonging to the night. That was a much nicer memory.

'She doesn't know anything, Wax, look at her,' Beccah said, pulling him gently by the arm so he wasn't crowding me so much.

He eventually let out a deep breath and nodded, stepping back. 'Are you OK?' he finally asked, sounding less forceful.

I nodded and sat up more easily now. 'I've just been tired a lot, lately.'

Wax looked at Ollie, who shrugged.

Wax pointed at me. 'Someone, or something, did this to her,' he said.

For some reason, I kept quiet about the diary and being followed. It felt private and mine and I wasn't ready to share. The nightmare was weird, but it was probably my over-wrought brain trying to process everything.

'Come down and get something to eat,' Beccah said, kindly.

I was relieved to get away from scrutiny and nodded. I slid out of the bed, realising I was still fully clothed from yesterday, keeping my secret close to my chest. I wanted to figure this out by myself.

. . .

EVERYONE WENT DOWNSTAIRS to allow me the space to get up, shower and generally get myself together. I sat in my towels at the edge of my bed and looked around me. I was bewildered and confused. They were right. I was sleeping too much. Even if I was alive, which I wasn't. Shades slept more out of habit and convention, not because they needed to, and I didn't think it was even possible to be sick. The only thing I knew for sure was that someone or something was stowing away in this house. It was following me and had written to me in my diary. There had to be a connection between the two. I didn't even want to think of my nightmare. All I knew was its appearance had to make me sleep. 'Are you there now?' I whispered.

I sagged, feeling ridiculous. If my theory was true, surely, I'd feel sleepy right now. I actually felt quite good. Rejuvenated, in fact. I shook my head and got dressed in some clean jeans and a stripey blue sweater. Then, pulling on my trainers, I went downstairs.

OLIVIA HAD JUST GOT HOME with all the shopping. It was Thursday, already, and she'd bought in all the food for the big dinner party on Saturday night. Wax and Beccah were absent, so they must be over at her place. Everyone else was helping Olivia put stuff away in the fridge, cupboards and pantry. To an outsider, it would seem like any other family home.

'What is it?' Nicola said, coming over to sit with me when I flopped into the tan leather sofa.

I appreciated her making the effort with me, but I shook my head. 'Honestly, I don't know,' I said, smiling at her wanly.

'Do you want a kick about before lunch?' Joe said to the other boys, tossing his football in the air and catching it.

'Do you wanna go for a walk?' Nicola said, next to me.

I shrugged and nodded. May as well. It was kind of her to ask and it wasn't exactly like I had anything better to do.

'Coming, Tallulah?' Nicola called over to her, putting the last of the fruit in a bowl on the countertop. 'Nah … it's too dreary out. I'm going to chill for a bit and watch TV.' She was already wandering off, putting her phone to her ear.

I followed Nicola out through the hall and we both grabbed a coat from the top-heavy stand by the door. Before I knew it, we were trudging the path through the woods in the direction of my old house.

'You always come this way,' Nicola said, echoing my thoughts.

It was a dank, grey day. I pushed my hands deeper into the pockets of my navy-blue puffa jacket and took a deep breath. The air smelled of damp earth and rotting leaves. 'Suppose so. Not many places for us to go.' I flicked my eyes in her direction and she looked like she was thinking about what I said.

'Do you think that's it, Sam; do you think you're depressed?'

It had occurred to me. 'Possibly … probably.' I was just about to ask her if she ever felt down, when a twig snapped not too far off from us. It was so loud that we both stopped in our tracks and looked in the same direction, to our right. The trees were quite bare and narrow, so we could see clearly in any direction. There were not that many places to hide.

'Someone's there,' Nicola whispered.

'I know,' I said. My heart was thumping hard, but I was thankful that, for once, someone else was with me to hear it. It made me feel a little braver and I started to walk in the direction of the sound.

'Wait, stop, Sam!' Nicola whispered loudly, as if whispering would somehow make a difference.

I felt her catch up to my shoulder. She tried to hold me back, but I shrugged out of her grip. 'It's OK, I just need to try something.' I took another step and examined how I felt. Then another and another. *Wait. There.* My head swooned. I took another step and a wave so strong made me almost sway off my feet. Nicola had to grab me quickly to steady me. I felt like I was carrying a great weight across my shoulders and needed to sit down. 'It's you, isn't it?' I said to the open forest. 'You do this to me.'

'What is it, Sam? Who are you talking to?' Nicola came around me and held the tops of my shoulders, giving them a little shake. 'Stop it, Sam. You're scaring me.'

I finally tore my eyes away from the forest and looked into her fearful face. 'You don't understand, Nicola.' I was already trying to step around her, but the strange feeling had gone. Whoever it was, had backed off.

Nicola was rattled and wanted to go back, but I ignored her and pressed on. The presence always followed me to my old house. We soon reached the perimeter fence and I stared at it, like I always did. Nicola came to a stop next to me.

'What is it, Sam?' I think you need to talk to someone. If not me then someone else.'

I nodded absently while I ran my eyes over the lonely cottage. 'Does it make you feel anything when you look at it?' I asked, more to myself. There was nothing remarkable about it. I didn't think anyone was inside. The small silver hatchback and white van weren't there and I didn't feel the painful bereft feeling I got when someone was in.

Nicola shrugged. 'It feels a bit creepy out here all alone,' she said, looking at it too.

That was an understatement. 'I don't think there's

anything anyone can do, Nicola, even if I did talk to someone.'

She looked right at me. 'Try me.' She had that determined look. I knew she wouldn't budge unless I gave her something. 'Sometimes just talking about things helps.'

I let out a long sigh. 'It's loads of things really. I guess it's mainly not knowing a single thing about who I am. And I know this house somehow holds the secret and I can't get in to see,' I said, nodding towards it.

Nicola immediately went to duck through the post and rail fence.

'Stop!' I shouted. 'Ollie said it's outside the envelope of the village and we can't cross it.' I sounded stupid saying it, but I was terrified something bad was going to happen to her.

She paused partway with her leg already through the gap, frowned and then ignored my warning and climbed through. She did a silly dance the other side on the grass to prove she was fine.

I watched fearfully, looking all around. Something wasn't right. She took a couple of exaggerated, huge steps towards the house as if to further prove her point and still nothing happened to her. 'Come on, it's fine,' she called over her shoulder. 'Let's go and be nosy.'

I'd stopped breathing, still waiting for her to combust on the spot, but when nothing appeared to happen, I let out a slow breath and dipped my head and went to follow.

My head hit something hard. Every time I went to push my body between the rails it felt like I came up against a wall.

Nicola was halfway across the lawn by the time I gave in, red and flustered. I straightened up and held out my arms in frustration. She was walking backwards, watching me. 'Come on, we haven't got all day.'

'I can't,' I said, kicking my foot against the barrier, making a dull thud.

Then my breath left me. My stepdad came tearing through the front door of the house, straight towards Nicola, casually walking towards me. 'Get out! Who do you think you are coming in here! This is private property.'

All I had time to do was open my mouth to warn Nicola and point, when something came at me so fast; a red and black blur of light. It grabbed me and I didn't have time to breathe. All I could do was scream.

I heard Nicola screaming, 'Sam … Sam!' over and over until it receded into the distance. Something had me tightly around the waist and was hurtling with me at break-neck speed through the wood. All I could see were flashes of mottled green and grey as the forest whizzed past me.

I'm not sure if it was because I could barely breathe, but despite knowing I was travelling motorbike fast, everything seemed to go quiet. I became aware of the noise of my breathing. My arms were around a strong neck and I began to smell the familiar smell of winter spice.

I was back in my dream. Clouds cushioned me and black feathery hair blew into my face. 'Who are you?' I managed to say, but I couldn't be sure it was out loud. I was no longer scared. Somehow, in my dreamlike state, I knew who it was. I was simply too tired to feel anything other than comfortable.

I focused on the soft, tanned skin and luxurious softness of his black hair brushing my face. I couldn't tell if any of it was real. 'Am I dreaming?' I said loudly, gulping air – I was travelling so fast. 'Please … tell me.'

Everything went darker as we flew into the house and up the stairs. Then the small flight of stairs to the attic. Before I could catch my breath, I was in my bed and the covers whipped up to my chin. Then, just as quickly, the warmth and the light disappeared and I felt cold and alone. Everything went quiet and I was confused. Nothing made sense and I began to cry. 'I'm going mad, aren't I?' I said it aloud, knowing no one was there.

I was about to lose all hope to the darkness when I caught a glimpse of a shadow on the far wall. Only a second and then it was gone, but just enough for me to see. The shadow of a creeping, beckoning hand. I pulled the cover over my head and went to scream. If the boy was real, then the goblin was real. Or none were real, and I was finally losing it and my mind was splintering.

Suddenly my world exploded into the brightest light. The covers were ripped off me and he was there, the boy, peering down at me.

I yelped in fright. Scrambled and cowered up at the headboard and screwed my eyes shut. My hands flew up to protect myself, as he was right there, floating in the air horizontally, inches away from my face.

Then nothing. I waited and nothing happened at all.

A long moment passed. I relaxed a little and slowly brought down my hands and opened my eyes. He was still there, hovering. Suspended above me. Watching me, carefully. Fully materialised.

I began to breathe normally again, allowing myself to focus on him. What he looked like and what he was. He looked quite young. I guessed not much older than me. Seventeen or eighteen. A strange and angelically beautiful boy. Like no one I'd ever seen before. He was fully visible as the bright halo subsided around him, leaving his skin with a ruddy, tanned hue and those unusual, mustard-yellow eyes like those of a lion.

He was watching me closely too. As if he'd never seen me this closely, either. The startling eyes were lively and inquisitive and set off perfectly by the soft black hair that fell forward into his face. He had high cheekbones and full lips.

And despite being a youth, he had strongly built shoulders that he would undoubtedly grow into one day. I would love to see the rest of him, but it was difficult because he hovered so closely. I guessed he had the body of an athlete, judging by his speed.

I soon began to struggle to keep my eyes open as sleep began to take me down. I wanted to keep looking at him. I whined 'No' in frustration. I was annoyed. He was controlling it, I just knew. I fought to stay awake. Restless and struggling. 'It's you,' I said, haltingly. 'It's you … you keep on … putting me to … sleep.' With one last-ditch effort, I said, 'Please … who are you?'

'Helix,' came back simply, like a whisper of leaves. 'Don't go to that house.' Then he completely disappeared in a flash of light.

The sleepiness immediately left me. 'Wait!' I said, scrambling to sit up straight. I was angry now. I had definitive proof it was him making me sleep all the time. He'd grabbed me from my old house, scared me half to death and then just disappeared, leaving me in shock. No explanation. No apology. Nothing. But as my anger subsided, I realised I'd learned something new; he'd told me his name.

'SAM! Sam! Nicola's voice came up from the stairs, followed by clomps of footsteps.

Shit! I'd forgotten. I'd just been abducted right in front of Nicola and left her in the woods. My stepdad had seen her. I hope she didn't get into any trouble.

She burst into my room, came to a sliding halt and stared at me wide-eyed. 'You're in bed,' she said, breathlessly. 'Are you OK? One minute you were there and the next you were gone. Something … something else was there.' She didn't even mention my stepdad.

'Sorry, I didn't think anyone was in,' I said. Hardly able to look her in the eye.

She frowned deeply as if she didn't understand me, but before she could frame a response, Tallulah was there at her shoulder. 'What is it?' she said, tapping her phone and putting it in her back pocket.

Nicola was still staring at me, searching my face, bewildered. 'We were at her old house and it was like something came out of nowhere and snatched her … I mean, she just disappeared.'

Tallulah looked between the two of us, comically, as if she didn't get something. I rolled my eyes and threw my legs over the side of the bed. I looked at the two of them, wearily. There was no way I was going to be able to keep this a secret any longer, not with Tallulah involved. 'You'd better call everyone together. I need to tell everyone something. There is someone else living in this house.'

Tallulah widened her eyes with excitement and rushed off shouting, 'Everyone! Kitchen … Sam's got an announcement.'

I felt disloyal. I had no idea why. It wasn't as if I owed the stranger anything. I didn't even know him. All I knew was he wasn't human, which meant he could be dangerous and so he couldn't stay a secret any longer.

I made my way down the stairs and arrived in the kitchen. Ollie was already there and everyone else began to filter in. I went and sat on the leather sofa and Tallulah began pulling cans of soda from the fridge and handing them out to everyone.

Ollie's parents were thankfully out and Beccah was at her own house. Just as I started to think it wasn't too bad, Wax stalked in, throwing me a dagger look at being interrupted from whatever he'd been doing.

I swallowed and accepted a can of Coke offered to me by Joe and waited while everyone pulled out a stool or leant against the island and looked at me expectantly. It felt doubly anticipated because I never usually said much at all. Wax was last to pull a chair from the table, with a scrape, and sat on it backwards, leaning with his forearms across the back of it. 'So let me get this straight. You and Nicola went to your old house and something came from nowhere, grabbed you, and brought you back here … and tucked you into bed.' There were a couple of sniggers, but Wax's face was stony as he looked straight at me.

Nicola must have felt sorry for me as she gave my hand a little squeeze. 'That's exactly what happened, Wax, and it *was* where I found her.'

He let out a weary breath and put his hand up through his hair as if he had little patience and no idea what to make of it.

'I climbed through the fence completely fine, but something was stopping Sam getting through,' Nicola went on.

I nodded manically along with her. 'It's always like that, like I just hit a wall,' I added. 'But then my stepdad came running out of the house, shouting. Didn't you see him?' I said, looking at Nicola, amazed she hadn't been more scared by it.

'Oh that … I took no notice. I just ran back to the fence when I thought something grabbed you. To be honest, I was more worried about you. Once I'd cleared the fence and dematerialised, he went back into the house, I think.'

'Did you see whatever it was?' Wax said, getting us back to the point. He let his arm fall, leaving his hair a mess.

'Not exactly,' Nicola said. 'It was just a gust of wind and streak of something black and white really. It was too fast. Then it disappeared and so did Sam.'

Wax looked from Nicola to me and I felt my cheeks go red under his scrutiny. 'Do you know what it was? You didn't just ghost?'

I shook my head and shrugged. I didn't think I had time

to think; let alone ghost out. 'I know who it was, but I don't know him … not really.'

Wax narrowed his eyes and regarded me closely, like he was mulling something over. I shifted uncomfortably.

'I think you'd better tell me everything you know,' Wax said, making me swallow. 'I don't want to frighten you, but none of you have been aware of it until today, so it means it's probably not a Shade. And I haven't seen it at all, which is a cause for concern.'

'Him!' I corrected, but I knew what he was driving at. Wax saw the dead in all their forms, shade, spirit, or ghost, 'It's a Him and his name is Helix and I really don't think he wants to hurt me.'

Everyone stared at me as if I'd grown another head. Like, who knew there was more to Sam than the quiet girl who didn't say a lot. Strangely, I didn't feel scared, I just felt relieved. I guess because now I finally had proof he was real, it helped me identify how I felt about my stalker. 'I think he's looking after me.'

'Looking after you,' Ollie repeated, loudly, sounding a little wounded. 'What from?'

I shrugged, feeling guilty. I knew it sounded far-fetched. Nothing bad had happened since we got rid of Lila and Ainsley last year. Then the familiar pain and upset surged up in me and I fought to contain it. 'Maybe he knows more than we do,' I said irritably. 'I can't remember anything about myself, remember?'

All eyes were on me, shocked, as if it was only just occurring to them. I would have cried if Nicola hadn't grounded me by stroking the back of my hand. I focused on it, unable to look at them for a minute. I didn't want to lash out or hurt anyone. 'I just know when he's near, I get sleepy. I think that's why I've been sleeping all the time.'

I warily looked up to see Wax raise his eyebrows and let

out a slow breath of surprise. 'I guess we need to find out who and more importantly, what, this guy is and what he wants from you,' Wax said.

'He doesn't want anything,' I said, anger rising to defend my mystery boy.

'They always want something,' Wax said, matching my tone.

I would have withered and died at his hard stare, but he was immediately onto business. 'Has anyone else seen or heard anything strange?'

Everyone shook their heads and mumbled, 'No.'

'Can you give us the room for a minute, please?' Wax said, staring straight at me.

My heart fell into the pit of my stomach. I was wary of Wax at the best of times. I don't think he'd ever spoken more than a couple of words to me directly before today. Being alone with him terrified me. I wasn't the only one. Everyone except Beccah and Ollie felt a little bit like that.

'What are you going to do?' Ollie said, looking between the two of us, nervously.

Wax looked to the heavens and then answered his brother evenly. 'We're just going to have a chat and then I'll start checking the paranormal forums for a clue of what we might be dealing with here.'

Ollie looked at me kindly and I knew he was checking whether I was alright with it. I gave him a wan smile and a little nod, which he took as a yes. 'I'll just go and make a start for you,' he said.

My heart pounded as Ollie walked out and I finally looked back at Wax, who'd been watching me the whole time with those steely blue eyes. 'So, you wanna tell me a bit more about this guy, Helix, is it? Do you have feelings for him?'

The shock of the direct and accurate question was like a stake to my heart. It was so ridiculous and yet so insightful.

I'd never even really spoken to him, but without Helix in my life, it would be a bottomless pit. Where everything was on a loop, with nothing to strive or look forward to. Until Helix had become real to me this world was somewhere I had very little interest to be. So I answered as honestly as I could. 'I really don't know him. It's only been over the last few days that I realised it was a person. Before, I just felt a presence.'

'And how did you do that?' Wax asked, shifting in his chair to get more comfortable. 'He must have done something.'

I instantly blasted red. I didn't know why. I guess it all felt so personal and about things I'd scarcely analysed myself. And it would sound silly out loud. 'He read my diary.'

Wax looked surprised and slightly amused.

Before he could make fun of me, I added. 'I always put it in a particular place, you see.'

'How did you know it wasn't one of us?'

'Because he wrote back in it, after I told him off, that it was private.'

'And what did he say?'

'He said he was sorry.' I looked down at my fingers, feeling like I wanted to cry.

We were soon all crowded into Wax's room, I'd labelled cyberpunk central. Kind of high tech mixed with gothic decor. It reminded me of last year when we were all fighting to free Beccah. We'd crowd around Wax and Ollie then too, while they searched all the paranormal forums and websites for clues. We had a common enemy then: Wax's uncle and the evil spirit of Lila. This time, when I sat on the foot of Wax's bed, I didn't feel good about it. Helix didn't feel like the enemy. I felt uneasy. Disloyal.

Thankfully, Tallulah had the attention span of a gnat and

soon grabbed her phone and went off to watch TV. The others gradually filtered off too. Even I found myself daydreaming. About Helix, mainly and who or what he could be. All the while Ollie and Wax scrolled endlessly, eventually switching to the Dark Web and the scarier sites on there. Their level of concentration was amazing.

Eventually Beccah appeared and stood behind Wax, playing with the small hairs at the back of his neck. I watched enraptured as he spun around on his chair and looked up at her and smouldered. It was a look I'd never forget because it sent a physical pain to my chest and lower abdomen. I could only imagine getting a look like that.

Wax's hands rested on Beccah's hips. His eyes dropped to mine and caught me staring. 'Get out,' he said quietly. Then he looked at his brother. 'You too. I'll continue this later and let you know what I find.'

Ollie rolled his eyes and stood up, stretching. 'Come on, Sam. Let's leave the lovebirds to snog.'

I got up, grateful he'd saved me from my embarrassment at getting caught ogling and followed him out. I turned and looked back as I closed the door, just in time to see Beccah close the gap and put her mouth on his.

Ollie's was a typical teenage boy's room and wasn't vampire-dark like Wax's at all. It was a smaller, brighter homage to his favourite football team in blue and white. The only thing similar was that he had a couple of screens linked up to his laptop on a desk. Other than that, it was plain, serviceable and messy, with cups and clothes strewn everywhere.

Tallulah was sprawled on Ollie's bed, messaging someone on her phone with a goofy grin on her face. I'd never asked who she actually talked to on the phone all the time. I really should, as all her friends were here in this house. Whoever it was, she always had loads to say to them.

'Make yourself comfortable, Sam. I'll just do a bit more, then I'm all yours,' Ollie said, waggling his eyebrows. Tallulah shook her head indulgently and patted the bed next to her.

I crawled onto the soft quilt and slowly lay down next to her. I felt her little arm movements as her fingers worked on her phone and listened to the lightning fast taps of Ollie's fingers across his laptop. I felt Tallulah giggle to herself a couple of times. It was kind of soothing really. I was just starting to slip down to darker, lonelier thoughts, when Ollie smacked his keyboard and said, 'Gotcha! Yeah, baby. There you are, you sly dog.'

'What is it?' me and Tallulah both said, sitting up together.

Ollie spun around on his chair, grinning. 'I think I've found our mystery stowaway.' He got up and was already making his way to the door. 'Get the others. I want to run it past Wax first … If he's finished "alone time",' he said laughing as he went out of the door.

Tallulah scrambled to her feet and followed him, now excited and not wanting to miss a thing. I got up more slowly, already apprehensive at what he would say and padded after them.

Ollie tapped on Wax's door.

'What?' came back moodily.

I held my breath as Ollie used that as his permission to enter. Tallulah giggled and my cheeks blasted red as Wax leant up from his pillow and Becca was in his bed with him. 'Remind me to get a deadbolt on that door,' Wax said.

It was too late. Ollie had already invaded his room and sat down heavily on the rumpled bed next to him, shoving his open laptop in his eyeline. Wax was forced to swear under his breath and sit up and take the laptop from him.

Beccah sat up with Wax, completely unfazed by the invasion, while Wax settled it across his lap. I couldn't help noticing all the tattoos covering his bare chest and that she was naked with only the sheet held tightly under her arms. She glanced at me and I smiled apologetically, but she just returned it, kindly, and pushed her hand up through her perfect hair, seeming more bothered about how she looked than the state of her undress.

'See!' Ollie said. 'It's him, isn't it?'

I was dying to look but scared at the same time.

Wax was speed-reading, scrolling page after page in silence.

The others began wandering in, lured from their rooms by the noise. Until they were all there, swarming the bed and Wax finally looked across at his brother and nodded. 'This is good.' Then his mood switched and he let out an impatient breath at everyone lounging on his bed, then his eyes rested on me, hovering near the door. 'Go downstairs. Let me and Beccah get dressed and we'll join you in five minutes.'

I turned slowly and went out into the hall. I was wary of what they'd found. I needed to go to my room and collect myself for this. I was about to move off when, 'Sam!' came from the room I just left. *Wax.* I turned back, retraced my steps and looked at him, now sitting on the edge of his bed, with his head-to-toe tattoos on full view. 'Don't go back to your room until I've had a chance to talk to you with everyone.'

I felt my cheeks burn at being so busted. I was surprised he knew me so well. I just thought I was invisible. All I could do was nod and turn and follow the others down to our usual congregating place: the kitchen.

Nicola had already put on a pot of coffee when I got there. I went over and sat on the sofa by the window with Ollie and Tallulah. Nicola came and perched on the arm. 'Tell us what you found?' Tallulah said, playfully shoving Ollie in the chest.

Ollie simply nodded at the doorway as Wax walked in holding the laptop in one hand Beccah's hand in the other. They were both fully clothed now, but Wax's feet were bare. The others perched on stools or simply leant on the island next to them.

I was glued to their joined hands and a pain twisted in my chest. For some reason, seeing them together did that a lot. I guess it was what they had. I wasn't jealous, like I didn't begrudge them, I just longed for a connection like that. Something to hold me up from the cloying weight of loneliness.

Wax walked over, poured Beccah and himself a coffee and opened the laptop on the black granite counter. Beccah hopped onto a stool and Wax's body encased her, while he looked over her shoulder at the screen.

My heart was beating painfully. Everyone was quiet, waiting, looking at each other nervously. Ollie hadn't said a word. The need to escape to my room was rising to fever pitch. 'Can someone please tell me what you've found?' I said, my voice going up an octave and cracking.

I looked at Ollie, but he deferred to his brother with a tip of his head.

Wax straightened and put down his cup. Then his eyebrows rose and lowered and he even smiled a little as if he was amused and didn't know how to put it exactly. It was infuriating.

Ollie grinned.

'For God's sake!' I shouted. 'Just bloody say it!' I was trying to get up, but Nicola put her hand on my shoulder to stay put.

'Hang on,' Wax said, holding up a hand and scrolling again.

I huffed loudly and glanced heavenward.

At last Wax looked at me directly. 'I'm not sure who he is, but I think I know what.' He turned the computer screen around to face the room. 'These are the terms I searched. I think he must be young by supernatural standards because he hasn't done that much damage yet.'

'What search terms?' I said, getting to my feet. I felt the others get up and follow me. Soon we were all crowded around the island and looking at the small screen.

There was a list of underlined, light-blue links on a strange-looking site with a background that looked like the reader was travelling through deep space. I could only guess it was one of those paranormal sites Ollie and Wax were always talking about.

Wax clicked one of the links that loaded and came up with a heading: List of currently identified demons. Just that word made me feel suddenly hot and my throat closed up. I wanted to argue that it was ridiculous and he couldn't possibly be, but when my eyes rose to Wax's, he was watching me closely and my protests died in my mouth.

I wanted to run away, but his direct stare riveted me to the spot. There was no blame or accusation in that look, just the analytical honesty of a brilliant mind. I lowered my gaze to look more closely at the list and went down it one by one. *Dream Demon or Energy Stalker* immediately made me pause. The title alone made me shiver. I already had the creeping feeling of recognition as I clicked on the 'read more' button. It came up with a list of names and areas of the world they came from. *Tokolosh, Incubus, Energy Vampire.* The list went on but my heart was already beating erratically in my chest.

'Click each one and see what it says,' Wax prompted. 'Does that sound like him?'

I did as he suggested with shaking hands. 'You think he's one of these?' I asked, barely able to speak.

Wax shrugged a little. 'I think they're all the same thing; just called something different depending on where in the world you are.'

I started to click more of the links, but my fingers all took me back to the same one. I was sweating and my blood was now throbbing in my temples. Each new piece of information I read was frighteningly familiar.

I could feel Tallulah mouthing the words as she read over my shoulder. Everyone had eyes fixed on the page. I stood up straighter having read enough. 'And what do we call him … here?' I asked looking directly at Wax, who was watching me knowingly. My throat was so tight I had to cough.

He bobbed his head. 'Incubus, I guess. I think he's young and hasn't come into his own.' His eyes bore into mine. 'He will be dangerous when he grows up, though.'

I was forced to look away and back at the screen. Wax wasn't mocking, he was deadly serious. I even sensed a hint of apology as if he knew he was giving me bad news and how much this had begun to mean to me.

The boys read on and began to snigger at all the sexual connotations.

'Why?' I said, barely able to speak. I needed it spelled out to me. 'Why is he dangerous?'

Wax let out a heavy sigh, pulled a stool closer and perched on it. 'I think he's fairly harmless at the moment, but he is sapping your energy. He might not even know he's doing it.'

Tallulah hitched a breath and put her hand over her mouth, dramatically. I looked into her wide eyes next to me. 'That's why you're sleeping all the time.'

It was kind of obvious. I looked back at Wax for him to continue. 'But then what?'

Wax shared an uncomfortable look with Ollie as if he

didn't know how to say it exactly. Ollie shuffled his feet and pulled the laptop around and began reading aloud:

'Incubus or Incubi, usually male … Succubus is the female,' he said, flashing his eyes at me. 'Been around for thousands of years … dah de dah de dah,' he said, skipping all the boring stuff. 'Ah, here it is: Subject case studies from around the world all corroborate similar characteristics. Extreme tiredness. Vivid, realistic dream states and waking with the feeling that a real sexual experience had taken place.'

I flashed an annoyed glance at Joe, who was grinning and messing about with Josh like immature little boys.

'Shut up!' Wax cut in. 'There is nothing to say he will limit himself to a girl?'

It was gratifying to see the grin fall straight from Joe's face.

Tallulah broke out laughing. 'Yeah, he could be bi-incubus.'

I rolled my eyes and pleaded with my eyes for Ollie to continue.

'OK … so yeah. They find someone. They seem to latch on or fixate on one particular person… often returning to the same human for their whole lives.'

Butterflies kicked up in my stomach at that, and I didn't understand why. I think it was the forever part. It sounded almost romantic.

'What do they do with them?' Joe asked, now looking a lot more sober and serious and his cheeks a bit red.

'They usually visit their chosen victim at night, often in their dreams. Case studies say they feel a weight on top of them – particularly their chest, when they're sapping their energy.

My chest was aching. I felt hot and claustrophobic. Suddenly there wasn't enough air in the room. It was only Nicola's steadying hand on my shoulder that prevented me from running away. I swallowed, blinked slowly and tuned back into Ollie's words. I had to listen to this. *I had to.*

'Witnesses all say the same thing, pressure, or weight on top of them, feelings of confinement and paralysis, often waking swaddled in blankets so they can't move.'

I felt the blood drain out of my face. It was exactly how they'd all found me earlier. I felt their eyes burning into me as they all thought the same thing. I kept mine glued to Ollie's. 'It doesn't make sense, though,' I said, my mind scrambling, buying some time. 'What does he feed off? What energy?'

Ollie immediately turned the laptop back around and worked his fingers over the keyboard again. I flashed a glance at Wax who was watching me closely.

'Looks like emotion, predominantly,' Ollie said, bringing my attention back to him. 'Witness accounts all say strong emotion, with one being the most dominant of all.'

I swallowed. My heart thrashed and I had to grab the countertop so I didn't fall. I knew what he was going to say. It was love. It had to be. Why would a being seek out one particular person if it wasn't?

Then Ollie said the absolute last word I was expecting. 'Lust.' His eyes flicked to mine, already filling with amusement. 'I'm not joking,' he said, half laughing as he looked up at Wax next to him.

Wax pulled the computer closer so he could see.

'I'm telling you that Incubi or energy vampires, predominantly feed from sex.'

I was stunned.

The room was stunned.

My mind went into freefall.

Tallulah giggled and slapped her hand over her mouth to stop herself at the stern look Wax gave her.

Everyone else looked at each other guiltily and was unsure how to act.

Wax looked at me, raising an eyebrow in question.

I couldn't believe that he – everyone. They all thought – 'No! But it's not. It can't be. I mean I haven't. I would know … wouldn't I?'

My head was spinning. They were wrong. I shook my head and pointed at the laptop. 'No … that's wrong. And I'm not really human, am I?' I said half-heartedly, remembering what the website said.

Wax shrugged. 'Energy is energy.'

Everyone started talking at once.

Wax stood up. 'Hang on … be quiet for a second,' he said, glaring at them all. 'Maybe he's simply too young. Perhaps he doesn't even know what he is.'

I swallowed hard and looked up into Wax's eyes. They were soft and soulful and the most sympathetic I'd ever seen them. 'He might be getting enough energy from you at the moment.'

I thought about the inference in those last words: that it wouldn't stay that way. I wanted to argue but every time I went to say 'but', it dissolved because it all made sense. All the sleeping, waking up restricted in bed clothes. Sadness was an emotion after all.

'You need to remember that he isn't dead. He's a demon. So he will grow up. And with that he will need more from you.'

There was a stunned moment of silence and then everyone erupted into chatter again. I stayed riveted to Wax. He was stern and moody most of the time, but he was straight-talking and honest and I realised that was what I needed. No flowering up of words. What he said was true.

Josh was saying they should take turns and stand guard over me, particularly at night.

I finally broke eye contact with Wax to join the conversation and shook my head. 'He can materialise and ghost out at will. Levitate. He's powerful.'

'And lightning fast,' Nicola added.

It sparked another round of competing ideas of setting traps and capturing him or scaring him off. None of which I had much faith would work and not convinced that I even wanted them to.

'What do you want to do?' Wax said, cutting over them all.

He spoke firmly but kindly. My respect for him grew. He understood, I could tell, that I didn't view Helix as an enemy. But I also knew that he would be thinking of the safety of our group most of all. 'He follows me everywhere. I sense him, but I think he lives in the open space of the attic.'

'Bloody hell,' Josh said, shivering as if the idea freaked him out.

'I think you're safe, Josh,' Ollie said, making everyone laugh and me blush.

My mind went straight to the memory of Helix's arms around me when he carried me. How tall and strong he felt. His soft brown skin under my hands. How he smelled of warm spice carried on an icy wind. His black hair flying in my face like soft feathers. The thought that Helix wanted to harm me in any way just didn't make sense. Just the opposite. He wanted *me*.

It certainly didn't scare me. I felt exhilarated. Alive. If I was being totally honest, it didn't bother me nearly as much as it probably should have.

Ollie, Wax and Nicola followed me back up the stairs. 'You sure you want to face him alone?' Wax asked.

I smiled weakly over my shoulder at him. 'I don't think he'll approach while you're there.'

'Yeah, but you've never known what he is before,' Ollie said.

I thought about that while we went the length of the landing and up the last flight of stairs. I paused at the edge of the open attic while the others gathered around me. Everything seemed perfectly quiet. 'You feel something?' Wax asked.

I shook my head. There was nothing there.

We reached my room. My eyes went straight to my drawer, which was completely closed. I sat on my bed bewildered. I felt like I was going mad, or at the very least making trouble out of very little. I felt exposed, embarrassed, disloyal, none of which was logical, but it was what I felt. I wasn't making any of this up. Nicola saw something. I had to keep telling myself that over and over.

Ollie pointed at the wall above the headboard of my bed. I turned my body to look. All I saw was the red board with the row of six bells that had been there since I came here.

'What are you thinking?' Wax asked.

'Shouldn't be a problem to reverse those,' Ollie said, moving closer to examine them.

I saw immediately what he meant. They were the old servants' bells. There would have been a pull rope in the kitchen, drawing room and several of the bedrooms.

'If it's OK with you, I'll rig up some sort of panic alarm system using those. He followed the wire down from the backboard to see where it went. I can put a call button somewhere here and we'll hear you wherever we are in the house.'

I looked on in a daze while he began to unscrew the board with something attached to his keyring. Wax was instantly with him, talking locations and circuitry. It was soon off the wall and under Ollie's arm. The mess and disruption made me want to cry. Ollie must have seen it on my face as he flashed a look at Wax. 'We can come back here later,' he said, lifting the board slightly, showing they had plenty to do.

I was grateful. I'd become exhausted around them and needed time alone.

'You sure you'll be OK?' Wax asked.

'I can stay with you if you want?' Nicola said, holding my hand.

They mistook my bewilderment for fear. I just wanted them to go. I needed time to think. To process all this. I nodded. 'Thank you, but I'll be OK.' Their intentions were good and I didn't want to hurt their feelings.

'At least keep your phone on,' Wax said.

I smiled wanly and watched as he walked towards the

door with Ollie following behind him. Both seemed reluctant to go. Nicola walked around the bed to join them, giving me a long aching look. 'Go!' I said, snapping, desperately trying to keep the irritation out of my voice and failing. I blasted red, feeling instantly guilty. They were only looking out for me, but honestly, they had no idea how strong the drowsiness was when it came over me. I had no more chance of dialling a number in time than I would if the ceiling caved in.

However, they finally got the point. After a final nod and sigh from Wax, all three of them left and closed the door.

I sat and closed my eyes, taking huge deep breaths for a full minute. Then I slowly opened them again and began. 'Helix … Helix … Come out. They've gone.' I was more worried that they'd scared him off, than what kind of being he was. I was convinced that if he intended to hurt me, then he would have done it by now.

Then I heard a whistle. A tune I didn't recognise. But it affected me somewhere deep down. A feeling of dread began to loom. I had no idea why. *Was it a distant memory?*

I turned my head sharply to the far corner of the room.

The door was back. The one that didn't belong there.

I got up and instantly felt different. I looked down. My feet were bare. Cold on the floorboards. I was in different clothes – a night shirt. Girly pink, with a rainbow and a white horse on the front. No, a unicorn. My heart thumped up into my mouth and I tried to swallow it down. I pushed on and tiptoed towards the door and tentatively put out my fingers to touch it. It felt real enough. I slowly put my ear to it.

A light chuckle made me stand bolt upright.

Then I heard the loud footsteps. *Clomp, space, clomp.*

Everything screamed for me to run out of the real door, but when I turned, it had gone. Nothing in the room looked right. Everything felt the wrong way around.

I stood rigid, straining to hear the slightest sound. The clomps grew louder, then stopped.

A loud shriek of laughter made me jump, then began to recede again.

My hand was shaking, but I had to see. I had to know what was really on the other side of the door. I slowly turned the rattling, brass knob, terrified what I suspected was right on the other side. The grotesque goblin from my nightmare. The long, bony fingers and the hideously hooked nose.

The door clicked ajar and I slowly began to draw it towards me. A little at a time until I slowly took a step backwards.

I fought not to slam it and stood my ground. With every part of me shaking I peered around the door. There, on the wooden landing of a place – I had no idea where – stood the ugly little man, grinning widely. He laughed and trudged back down the stairs as loudly as he could. Laughed again and clomped back up. His actions were exaggerated, very definitely deliberate and highly amusing to him. Until he got to the top; my jaw dropped open wide and he put his long fingers out to get me.

The door slammed in his face and I didn't touch it. I was left breathing hard. I took a long minute to gather myself. When I looked up again, the door had gone and my room was back to normal. I felt weak and shaky and stumbled over to my bed and sat on the end of it.

My mind raced at what it could mean. Whatever the awful thing was it was laughing at me. Maybe my mind was just overwrought at what I'd learned about Helix. *Helix*, I pleaded.

He didn't seem to want to appear. *Was that what seeing the goblin meant?* That nothing in my supernatural brain could be relied upon. My blood flashed around my veins at the thought that Helix wasn't real. Or worse still, that he might have gone because of what everyone thought of him and I'd never see him again. My life would return to the empty void of eternal days of hopelessness. But I couldn't afford to think that way, so I clung to the idea that maybe he was away or just making sure it was safe before he approached. 'It's OK,' I whispered, almost crying, willing, praying he'd appear.

Helix didn't come.

I had to get out of the house after that. I couldn't breathe. It felt too full of people. Everywhere I went, everyone took it upon themselves to check I was OK.

My feet seemed to follow their usual pattern and found the familiar path through the woods. I had to be losing my mind so much that I didn't know what was real anymore. My thoughts turned and churned over everything and what it could mean. Over and over, until I inevitably found myself at the perimeter fence of my old cottage. The beginning of everything. It all seemed the same as it always was. Quiet and still. The outside a little untidy, like it needed some love and attention. There must be people inside because the van and little silver car were in the driveway. Except there was a new dent on the car's wing.

I immediately dropped down as something was happening. The front door was opening and a woman – my mother – walked out with her head hung low. Her hair covered her face, so I couldn't see clearly what she looked like. She looked thin. Very thin. Next, a tall skinny girl came out. A teenager. *Trish.* My heart spiked. I knew so little of the people in that house. Least of all my sister. I saw so little of her. She never seemed to come out. She seemed extra skinny to me. I wondered how old she was. Tallulah reckoned about fourteen or fifteen. Younger than me, definitely. I was struck by how miserable she looked. More than that. An empty shell. Which was pretty harsh coming from someone who couldn't remember her. But that was how she looked.

They got into opposite sides of the beaten-up car and the engine chugged into life. They pulled away and out of the drive. I watched it all the way out, aching to know what their lives were. Neither of them had spoken, smiled or communicated at all. That seemed weird in itself. Everyone I knew, apart from Wax, spoke all the time.

I turned back and focused my attention on the cottage itself. The house of secrets. Even the building seemed lonely. Cut-off, closed down, as if it was waiting for something. With blank, staring black eyes for windows. My stepdad must still be inside but there was no further movement.

I turned and went to walk away, but halted suddenly at the quiet sound of voices. I was struck rigid, because a large chestnut horse carrying a huge man was a few yards away. I could see him clearly between the thin grey trunks of trees. The horse was standing relaxed and chewing on something, the man was leaning down talking to a tall dark boy, dressed completely in black. *Helix. Was he real? Was I dreaming? Was this the reason he didn't come?*

A hot spike shot through me and then my blood ran cold and prickled through my veins. I'd never seen anyone out here before. I quickly checked I hadn't forgotten myself and was still ghosting. However, the man on the horse sat up and tipped his head in my direction. The boy turned his head and looked right at me. For one spellbound moment, we held each other's eyes. I knew him. From more than just my dreams. From somewhere so deep and fundamental to me that it physically hurt and I had no idea why. He was a long way off, but he was clearly handsome.

Then in a single, split second, the two of them, horse as well, simply disappeared. One minute they were there and the next it was though they'd never been.

I swallowed hard and realised I had a dry mouth where it had dropped open for so long. My head swam for a moment. I had to gather myself together before I started back through the woods. I refused to believe I was seeing things. Seeing them like that, in a situation completely unconnected to me, seemed to prove that I wasn't. I'd simply happened upon them and they had seen me too. The one on the horse was a blur to me, but the boy, Helix, felt disturbingly familiar. Real. In the flesh. Not just a spectre in a dream. Somehow, I knew that he knew me too. The way he looked at me. That feeling he gave me that heated me up inside. And the way the two of them disappeared, just meant they were supernatural. *Were they demons?* They weren't human. Maybe Wax was wrong and they weren't even alive? Shades, maybe, like me. Who or whatever he was, I knew deep down that I should remember him.

I came out of the woods to the crunch of the shingle of the Waxley-Black's driveway. I was about to turn left towards the front door, when I caught a glimpse of red, disappearing up the driveway, towards the road.

I recognised that red jumper. 'Tallulah!' I called.

But she didn't seem to hear me.

'Tallulah!' I tried again a little louder.

She didn't even turn her head to see who was calling her. It was strange and unlike her. I jogged a little to try to catch her up, but after a few steps I'd lost her. I looked left and right, flabbergasted that someone could disappear that quickly. Well, someone I knew. I went the full length of the drive and as close to the road as I dared. Tallulah was nowhere to be seen.

It troubled me.

Still mulling over all the strange encounters, I went back slowly into the house.

.   .   .

I'D GIVEN up all hope of seeing Helix again, when the first wave of tiredness hit me in a shimmer from my head to my feet. I shook it off and sat up blinking myself alert. 'You don't have to put me to sleep. I know you're real and I know what you are.' As I said the words, I was already thinking that maybe he couldn't help taking my energy. Something about him always left me with a feeling that he was gentle and kind. Something I wouldn't have expected from a demon. It made me wonder what being a demon actually meant.

The following wave was strong, like I'd been physically hit. I felt soft quilt behind me as I landed on my back. The next thing I knew I was in my familiar dream. The cosy one with warm sunshine and fluffy clouds. I wasn't sleepy, though. In my dream I felt wide awake. I saw everything clearly for the first time. Birds chirped in beautiful green trees full of bright pink blossom. Nestled among them was a white gazebo completely engulfed in a mix of pastel-coloured flowers. It felt so alive and real, I could even smell their fragrance on a light breeze.

'It is conjured by your mind,' the whispering voice I recognised said. It brought my head around sharply. 'It's your safe place. The one you've come to since you were a small child.'

And there he was. The first time I'd seen him close up in his entirety. He'd always appeared in dreamy snippets before when I battled to stay awake. Earlier today was at a distance. Now I saw him clearly and he was beautiful. The last thing I would have called him was a demon. Angel more came to mind. I had to squint as he appeared in a bright halo that hurt my eyes. It slowly dimmed to reveal a dark-skinned boy with black wispy hair and those mustard-yellow lion's eyes, that I'd only glimpsed at before. 'Are you OK?' he asked immediately, his eyes running over me as if he was checking me for injuries. 'You were at the house.'

I closed my mouth, swallowed and nodded. I looked down at my hands to make sure I'd materialised myself.

'I can always see you,' Helix said, as if he knew what I was thinking. It also explained how he'd seen me earlier.

I looked at him warily. He stood perfectly still, as if he sensed my cautiousness and didn't want to startle me. It gave me time to really study him. He was really good-looking. Young, but already very tall and strong. He looked tense, like he was nervous and unsure of what I would do. I didn't want to run. I wasn't scared. 'Why do you follow me all the time?' I asked quickly. My voice sounded weird. Reedy and thin. Like it came from a computer game.

'You are my sacred duty. It has always been that way, ever since we were children.'

My heart jumped on that. 'Since I've been a Shade?' It hadn't been that long. No more than about two years. Unless — 'Even when I was alive?'

'Since my mother threw me from her horse on the Wild Ride and I landed close to your house. You were a small girl. We were the same age. I knew at once you were my responsibility.'

My mind was scrambling over the new information. *Wild rides, sacred duty.* What did come through loud and clear was that we were the same age and he had no family, like me. I clung to that, desperately trying to grab a single memory from before I was a Shade but came up empty. 'So you knew me from before?'

My mouth went dry and my heart began to thud. 'Do you know how I died?'

He hesitated before he nodded, slowly. He seemed to wither slightly, like he felt guilty and didn't want to have to deliver the answer to my next question.

'How? How did I die?'

$\mathcal{M}$y blood was racing through my veins as I waited, hanging on every movement of his lips.

He took another beat, then a breath as he adjusted his stance. 'Please know, Sam, that I have always been there to look after you. I *will* always look after you.'

Then it struck me that I'd died, so something didn't tally. 'You haven't answered my question, Helix. How did I die? They never found a body.'

Before I could take a breath, he was there, right in front of me, looking down into my eyes with his brows drawn together in concern. 'You died because of me.'

We stared at each other, eyes locked, while I took in the hopeless devastation in them. Real pain and hurt. 'I made a terrible error of judgement. You fell into the well and it was my fault.'

Tears were now filling his eyes while I was stunned into silence.

'I had to hide you. I didn't know you couldn't swim … Your father—'

My mind had already stalled on the well. What well? No wonder no one found a body. I must still be there and no one knew to look. 'Did you do something to my memory?' I asked as the thought suddenly occurred to me.

He froze for a moment, like he didn't want to say what he knew he had to say and he eventually nodded. A solitary tear rolled down his cheek. 'Yes. I needed to shield you from the pain.'

I took a step back, crying now as well. *What had he done? Why had he needed to do that? How could he?* I could only guess what he'd done to me, a young, vulnerable, underage girl. I'd had all these romantic notions about him, when in reality, he must have done something bad and hid me in the well.

My mind went to the crumbling stones of my lonely, dark, watery grave, that nobody knew existed and so nobody mourned.

Helix took an anguished step forward and I took another step back, determined not to let him touch me. 'What did you do, Helix? Get away from me!' I screamed when he tried to hold my hands to stop me moving away.

I dissolved into sobs and with one last, agonising look, Helix disappeared in a flash of light. I moaned and cried into the soft down of my quilt, now back in my room.

The door bashed open and all the boys came piling in. They were brandishing heavy weapons that I realised came from the fire tending stand in the drawing room. They were looking all around them for the intruder.

'He's gone,' I said, wailing anew, turning my face so my sobs were muffled by the bed.

'Carry her down,' Wax said.

Strong arms slipped beneath my back and legs, pulled me to the edge of the bed and then up into the air. My nose was against a wide, strong chest. *Joe's.* I could tell by the sports deodorant smell. My head bobbed up and down as he carried me down the small flight of stairs. 'Where to?' Joe's rumbly voice said, vibrating through his chest.

'Take her to mine,' Ollie said.

Joe laid me down on the soft quilt in Ollie's room, while all I registered were posters of several indie rock bands. I must be in shock.

Tallulah appeared directly in my face, looking concerned, but thankfully she kept quiet. Everyone was there and they were all subdued. Only Wax had the confidence to crouch at the side of the bed and ask outright, 'What did he say?'

I took in the directness of his blue gaze and the small star tattoos on his right temple that seemed to point right to it. The pale skin and stubbled strong jaw. Why couldn't I have a strong human boyfriend like him? My face went to crumple again when it hit me how deeply I'd begun to feel about Helix and now this. I was adrift, with my heart ripped open, dripping into the sea. 'He killed me. Helix killed me and I'm in an old well somewhere.' I couldn't hold it together and dissolved into more sobs.

I felt female arms come around me instantly and was grateful to Tallulah and Nicola. Without that, I would have fallen apart completely. I heard Tallulah's sharp intake of breath and a whispered, 'She's down a well. What well? I never saw a well at her house.' I couldn't hear what everyone was saying after that. I was drowning in my own misery. I'd been robbed of my human life, my memory, my family, who all seemed fine without me. I cried myself out until I lay there a quiet, empty void, completely unable to move, with my breaths coming in shudders now and then.

Tallulah moved out of the way and the bed dipped as Wax sat down to look at me. My eyes tracked to his without moving another single muscle in my body.

'Do you want to tell me what happened again? Slowly this time. Exactly. Word for word.'

He waited patiently while I studied his face and decided whether I had the energy or even wanted to. Then I gathered myself together with a ragged breath and gave him the whole story from start to finish. Strangely, the goblin no longer felt relevant. Just a silly, bad dream. So I stuck to the facts about Helix. How he'd been sending me to sleep and talking to me in my dreams. Always taking me to one particular place: my safe place. The one I'd been forced to conjure since I was a little girl for some terrible reason.

'What does he look like?' Wax asked, making me look at him more closely because of how kind he was being. I'd never known him be so nice.

I took in a deep fortifying breath. 'He looks our age. Dark. Handsome,' I said, my eyes darting away from his as I said that. 'Strong. Athletic-looking,' I said, flicking my eyes at Joe. 'And he has the weirdest yellow eyes. You know, like a big cat or something.'

I looked at Nicola guiltily, as I knew what she was thinking. What they were all thinking. That I liked this boy. Being. Demon. Energy sucker, *whatever he was.*

But I did. I did like this boy and my face began to crumple again.

Wax gave my shoulder a little shake and stopped me just in time. 'That's good, Sam. Now we know what he looks like. So can he go invisible?'

I immediately straightened, nodded and pulled myself together with a sniff.

'What did he say to you?'

'He told me he killed me.' I felt Joe shift his feet and say something angrily to Josh, but Wax held up his hand.

'What? He said those exact words? Think Sam. It's important. I need to know what we're dealing with.'

Misery washed through me. I was emotionally exhausted, but I tried to remember exactly. Gradually my brain fog cleared, so it replayed in my head. 'Well … he said he'd always looked after me and he would always look after me.'

'That's good. Go on,' Wax prompted.

'I shouted at Helix to answer my question because I knew he was stalling. He looked as guilty as hell. Then he finally admitted it was all his fault.'

Wax looked a little exasperated and I could tell he was doing his utmost to be gentle with me. 'What did he say, exactly?' he asked again in a calm and measured voice.

Everyone had gone completely silent, waiting on my every word. I couldn't bear it. 'He said I fell into the well and it was his fault because I couldn't swim and drowned. Then he went on about hiding me – something about my stepdad, but to be honest, I was too upset to take anything in after that.'

Nicola hugged me to her, but I continued to look at Wax from her arms, still absorbing what I'd said. Archie let out a noisy breath as if he'd been expecting worse and everyone else looked at each other to see what they'd made of it.

'What now?' Ollie asked.

Wax was still thoughtful. Then he nodded to himself as if he'd come to a decision. 'Well, the good news is, from the sound of it, he didn't mean to kill you, Sam. Did he say how long he'd been around here?'

I nodded. That was the thing that had stuck in my memory. 'A long time. Since I was a little girl.' I narrowed my eyes while I got it exactly right. 'Since his mother threw him from her horse on the Wild Ride, whatever that was.'

Wax appeared to freeze. Then he looked up at Ollie, who returned it as if they were having an unspoken conversation. 'Wild Ride. He definitely said that?'

I nodded, now alarmed, as I looked between the two brothers.

'That's not good,' Ollie said.

'No, not good at all,' echoed Wax.

CHAPTER 7

'What is it? I asked, my mind scattering, not only in fear at what it could be, but that its reputation was bad enough for Wax and Ollie to have heard of it.

Everyone stood straighter, more alert now, looking at each other for more information. Wax got slowly to his feet. His whole demeanour scaring me more than ever. 'We are going to need to speak to him. This changes everything.'

Ollie let out a slow breath solemnly. Joe and Josh stiffened as if they were getting ready to fight.

'Can someone please tell us what's going on?' Nicola said.

'We need to trap our resident demon and we need to keep him away from Sam before he does any real damage. We have to get some real answers out of him about the Wild Ride.'

'What about the Wild Ride?' I asked. Their reaction didn't seem so bad until I mentioned that. 'What is it? What is the Wild Ride?'

Ollie looked up at Wax who looked back stonily, then flashed his eyes at me. 'It's like a fox hunt that crosses over from the spirit world. It's supposed to be made up of all kinds of supernatural creatures, riding horseback, with a pack of hungry hellhounds at their feet. They hunt for souls, food, anything they need to take back with them. Beings join it and fall away all the time, but it never stops and it's always changing, until it returns to hell. Then it begins all over again. Some call it the Eternal Ride, but most call it the Wild Ride, because they don't care where they trample, what they destroy, showing no mercy to whom they take.'

My mind shot guiltily to Helix with the man on the horse in the woods. I frowned, deciding not to mention it yet. Instead, I looked up into Wax's worried face. 'I don't get it.' Then at the others all looking confused as well. 'That was such a long time ago.'

'If that was where Helix came from and his own mother dropped him off, then it was for a purpose and she will be back for him,' Ollie said, guiltily.

'The Ride's route is said to circumvent the earth, returning sometimes many years later. So if he came to you, at how old?'

'He just said I was small when he came … and the same age,' I answered with a miserable shrug.

Wax nodded thoughtfully. 'So that makes him around eighteen. An adult. Assuming his mother left him to grow up, then we don't have long before she returns.'

That thought terrified me for a number of reasons. Not just because of who The Ride might bring, but what happened when it left? Who might it take? Helix? One of us? Where would it take them? *Would it take them to hell?*

'We need to find the well to recover Sam's body,' Ollie said. 'It might tell us more about what happened.'

I scrambled to sit up, suddenly terrified at that. 'What would happen then? Would I stop being a Shade?' I asked, looking between the two brothers.

Nicola was immediately at my side. 'She's right. We need

to think about this. We don't know whether she will cross over when the mystery of her death is solved. We don't know why any of us are still here.'

'It's true,' Archie chimed in. 'Your uncle made us and we drink the fountain's waters, but we don't really know what we are or how long it will allow us to stay.'

Wax nodded, frowning. 'I hear you. Maybe not yet then. Until we know more. I don't want to get locked up by the authorities either. Supposing we find the well, it's going to be hard to explain how I knew Sam was there.'

The others all nodded and mumbled their agreement. I sank back down onto the bed and looked on in a daze.

Then Wax looked right at me with his no-nonsense stare. 'We do need to find out what happened in that house to make an Incubus demon feel like he needed to hide you in a well.'

I swallowed hard at that. I'd been so hung up on the whole Helix killing me thing that I hadn't thought about what happened in the lead-up to it.

'How can we do that?' Ollie asked.

'We need to make a plan. About the well, Sam's old house, The Wild Ride, everything. Because trust me, if it is coming back, retrieving Sam's body will be the least of our problems.'

EVERYTHING WAS a big anti-climax after that. I'd been on the periphery for so long that now things had started happening for me, I needed action. However, the more I purposely hung around my room to see Helix, the more he seemed to know and kept away.

It was Saturday and Beccah's parents were coming to dinner. Tension was building. Tempers were fraying with minor squabbles breaking out over the smallest things. No one could concentrate on doing anything. Everyone seemed on edge. We all felt it. I was becoming more and more terrified as my imagination ran wild.

Wax kept giving me questioning looks. I knew what he was asking: had I seen Helix? He was now becoming curious because I hadn't said a word. Ollie had rigged up his alarm system and I hadn't rung it once. I was supposed to secretly call them to come to my rescue so they could see Helix for themselves. But they'd lain dormant. The truth was, I was probably more scared of not seeing Helix again than what would happen if I did. I was scared that if they caught him, what they would do to him. And, more to the point, what Helix would do to them. He was a demon after all. I had no idea what that actually meant. No one knew how it would go with Beccah's blissfully ignorant parents. Would something happen in front of them? How would we possibly explain all this to them? The sitting tenants in their house and all the kids in this one. As time wore on, this dinner did not seem such a good idea. It was supposed to be an experiment. One where Ollie and Wax's parents could gauge what was safe to tell.

So I sat miserably in my room, an hour before they were due to arrive, not knowing what would happen after tonight. First Tallulah came and went, then Nicola and finally Ollie before I snapped. 'Oh for god's sake! I'm fine. Can you leave me alone to get ready?'

Ollie put up his hands in surrender. 'OK … just ring the bell then.'

I felt instantly guilty. He was just in the wrong place at the wrong time. He was only looking out for me.

At last I was alone. I went back to staring at my diary drawer, hoping something new would appear there. I stood up, went over and took out the book. I opened it at the last entry Helix had made. His handwriting was so childlike. The R even faced the wrong way. After all my anger at him for invading my privacy, it now occurred to me that he could probably barely read. Not with spelling and handwriting like that.

I sat down on the end of my bed. Guilty and frustrated, I suddenly wanted to write him a heartfelt message. Ask him all the questions that burned inside me. Instead, I simply wrote, *Helix, please come.* Then with my heart pounding at finally doing something, I put it neatly back inside the drawer.

I stared at it again. I'd told him off for going in there and now I wanted him to. I stood up and looked around for something to draw attention to it. I spotted a pink ribbon tied around a basket of bathing products on my dressing table. I quickly untied it and retied it around the wooden knob on the drawer. Then, after letting out a slow breath to get my heart rate down, I gathered my clothes and washbag and took one last look around. I sent up a silent prayer, and with excitement boiling up in my belly, I went and got ready to face Beccah's parents. Our circle would grow tonight. Eventfully or not, remained to be seen.

EVERYONE WAS in the kitchen when I went down. Wax had gone to collect the Whitelys and the rest of us helped with laying the big table in the dining room, reserved for special occasions. It was one of those you saw in old houses that felt a mile long. A room of polished wood, glass-fronted cabinets, filled with bone china, vases and figurines. The walls were red flock, hung with huge oil landscapes, at least a hundred years old. Then the magnificent focal point: the huge golden chandelier that hung spectacularly over the table. It really was a sight to behold. A real reminder that the family was really quite an important part of the peerage. Or they had been at one time. It was a step up for us, anyway. We usually just ate in the kitchen. Tonight, it looked like a medieval banquet. Bowls of salad, baskets of bread rolls, plates piled high with steaming potatoes, corn and chicken. 'I hope Bret isn't long. I can't keep everything warm in the Aga,' Olivia said.

It was always weird to hear Wax referred to as Bret. It was his middle name. I guess it was mildly better than Archibald Breton, which was his actual name. No one dared tease him about it though. Except Ollie. He got away with murder.

His dad, Jed, uncorked a bottle of red wine loudly. 'I'm sure it will all be delicious, darling.'

Voices and a loud boom of the large front door closing in the hallway signalled their arrival. 'They're here,' Olivia said with a sharp intake of breath. 'Now behave yourselves.'

Jed laughed and kissed her on the forehead, recognising her nerves. We weren't exactly a conventional household.

I had a sudden urge to run. I had to keep telling myself that they were just Beccah's mum and dad and she was really nice. But they were the first new people to come into our lives since Helix.

We all stood to attention in a row like cadets. I looked left and right at everyone. The boys had put on their smart trousers and shirts, following Olivia's orders. Us girls wore our dresses. Mine was a plain knit in deep burgundy. Tallulah helped me choose it from the internet, especially. It was a little on the short side, but it had long sleeves and nothing fussy about it. I liked it but felt a little exposed after a life in jeans and jumpers.

Seeing Tallulah in red, next to me, reminded me. 'Where were you off to the other day?'

She looked right in my eyes and frowned.

Ollie overheard and immediately tuned into our conversation. What felt strange was the look in Tallulah's eyes. It didn't change at all, not a tiny muscle twitch, frown, or anything. As if she was concentrating very hard on not reacting. She simply shrugged and asked innocently, 'When do you mean?'

'Yesterday. You were walking up the driveway to the road when I came out of the woods. I called you, but you didn't seem to hear me.'

Ollie's eyes narrowed as if he was trying to work out when that must have been.

'Not me,' Tallulah said with a shake of her head. 'I would have heard you, silly,' she said suddenly smiling, making me doubt what I'd seen, she was so convincing. I looked at her a long moment and her attention quickly fell on something else in the room. She didn't seem bothered about it at all. My gaze tracked to Ollie's. He was looking right at me less convinced. Like he wanted to question me further but ran out of time.

Wax walked in from the hall with Beccah and rolled his eyes at our line-up. The butler busily took everyone's coats as they entered. Beccah's dad came next, immediately holding out his hand to Jed. 'Good to finally meet you. I'm John.' He looked kindly, greying, probably in his fifties and was dressed in a well-fitted grey suit. He presented Beccah's mum. 'And this is my wife, Jean.' She was stunning, with her blonde mixed with platinum-grey hair pinned up. She looked slim, sophisticated and beautiful in a plain black Jackie O sleeveless dress. She certainly could have passed as a first lady or a movie star. I couldn't help staring as they shook hands with everyone, one by one.

'It's a pleasure to meet you,' Olivia said. 'Beccah has such a special place in our hearts.'

Beccah's dad, John, studied her quizzically, but smiled.

Wax rolled his eyes again, no doubt willing his mother to shut up. Beccah's time as a Shade was still unknown to her parents. She was supposed to be asleep in a coma.

'You have a very beautiful home,' John said, taking the heat out of the conversation.

'Thank you,' Wax's dad said, holding up two different bottles, one after the other. 'Beer … wine?'

John pointed at the beer and Jed took the top off and handed it to him. 'So you took on the old Blackwood place. Another great home, you know.'

'While the parents talked leaky roofs, dry rot and home improvement contacts, we gathered around Beccah and Wax.

'What do they know?' Tallulah whispered loudly.

After a wide-eyed, tight-lipped warning from Wax. 'Not enough,' he said, furtively checking his mother wasn't putting her foot in it again.

'Sorry, guys, the part where my spirit left my body during a coma hasn't exactly come up in conversation yet,' Beccah said.

I smiled. She'd so picked up Wax's talent for sarcasm. I felt sorry for her. This must be so nerve-racking. 'Have they met anyone at your house yet?' I asked, thinking of all the supernatural guests that came with the house.

She nodded nervously and looked up at Wax. He looked down at her adoringly and gave her hand a squeeze. My heart ached just watching them. 'They think Burt and Gerty are the gardener and housekeeper.'

'What about Sarah?' I'd be amazed if they'd managed to keep Beccah's Victorian aunt quiet. 'I haven't managed to pluck up the courage yet. Although she will keep ringing her damn bell for Gerty, no matter how much I tell her not to. She forgets.'

I couldn't help giggling. I could just imagine. 'How do you explain it?'

'Gerty keeps telling them it's her timer in the kitchen,' Beccah said, shaking her head wearily.

'What about Jed and Lucinda?' Tallulah said, shuddering.

Those two couldn't be explained away by anything less than a scary spirit and a ghost.

'Jed keeps wandering about at night, moaning of impending doom. Lucinda tries her best to quieten him, but I have to keep on getting up and steering him away before they wake my parents. It's exhausting.'

Wax shook his head. 'It's like bloody Night at the Museum over there.'

I burst out laughing, with many of the others. We couldn't help picturing that.

'Come on, everyone, let's eat before it spoils,' Olivia called out.

We all took our places around the table. Beccah's parents sat opposite Wax's so they could talk. The rest of us sat boy girl, like Olivia told us to. I sat between Ollie and Joe, waiting for the boys to pig the food before I picked up a cob of corn and a piece of fried chicken. I couldn't help studying Beccah's parents doubtfully. They seemed such a nice, straight-laced couple. I couldn't imagine them handling the truth. How do you start a conversation with someone that doesn't know? Especially at a dinner party.

'You OK?' Ollie asked, quietly, as he slathered butter on his warm roll.

I nodded, taking one from the basket for myself.

'So how did you come to know Beccah? I understand she had been talking to Wax online before the accident,' John asked.

The table hushed. Joe dropped his knife with a loud clink on his china plate. We all looked at Jed and Olivia. I held my breath. Olivia instantly looked at Jed to save her. It was so uncomfortable.

Jed immediately picked up the baton, smoothing the embarrassment over. 'We spoke over Skype or FaceTime, or whatever they call it these days, a few times, if Wax was out or asleep. Pretty soon it was a regular thing. She was so kind to us when she realised we'd lost our son,' he said, smiling.

I closed my eyes at the obvious blunder. Ollie was sitting right there and she wouldn't have known about her own brother before her coma.

Beccah's parents looked startled and looked at Ollie, the devastation clearly visible in their eyes. This party was not going well. 'Oh my, we thought you only had two sons,' Jean said.

Jed visibly cringed. Luckily Ollie saved them as if he'd been thrown a hot potato. He put his hands up. 'My bad, sorry. I went MIA. Teenage angst and all that. You know us teenagers.'

Wax glared at us all, shaking his head, while we all murmured and carried on eating our food. Catastrophe was averted, thankfully. Nobody could meet anyone else's gaze. Beccah's parents seemed satisfied and went back to eating their food. 'This is really very lovely,' Jean said, smiling brightly at Olivia.

'I'm sorry,' Olivia said, obviously understanding they'd pushed the conversation to uncomfortable areas of the loss of their own son, Beccah's brother, Pete.

'No, no,' Beccah's father said. 'It's been almost two years now.'

'We miss him terribly,' Jean said, putting down her cutlery and dabbing her eyes with her napkin.

I looked over at Beccah and she was looking down at her plate. Wax put a comforting arm around her.

It seemed so unfair. There we all were, with only six living heartbeats between us and Beccah had lost her brother completely, in the very same car accident she was in. It didn't make sense that we all came here and he didn't.

'Well, it's really lovely having you here,' Olivia said,

looking red and embarrassed at where the conversation had gone.

'Bet you find the climate a bit different,' Jed said, trying to lighten things.

John pounced on it gratefully, nodding and laughing ruefully, while he cut into a piece of chicken.

'These big old houses are certainly hard to keep warm,' Jed said.

'Yes, ours seems frozen in the nineteenth century.'

'Usually haunted too,' Ollie said, grinning, with a devilish glint in his eye. But I couldn't help detecting the hint of spite in it and immediately thought of my conversation with Tallulah.

Tallulah blasted red and kicked him under the table. I looked around nervously. No one seemed to pick up on the undertone.

Ollie went on mischievously. 'We have a few, what about you? Anything unusual at Blackwood House? Ghosts wandering about where they shouldn't?'

I closed my eyes at the obvious dig at Tallulah. If only I could rewind and erase my stupid question. There was clearly an argument brewing between them. However, in fairness, I'd never seen Ollie like this. He always seemed so good-natured and easy-going. But I guessed they were in a relationship and despite downplaying it, feelings would have to be involved.

Olivia glared at Ollie. He widened his eyes and held out his hands, still holding his cutlery as if to ask, *What?*

Despite what drove him, he had a point. Someone had to start off the conversation. It was what we were supposed to be trying to talk about, after all.

Wax was daring him with his eyes.

Ollie grinned and took a huge, ugly bite out of his chicken.

'What, even here?' Beccah's dad asked, seeming oblivious to the silent conversation of nudging, kicking and silent threats going on at our end of the table. 'I don't think we have … well not yet, anyway,' he finished, chuckling.

'I think I'd be terrified,' Jean said, smiling along with him. 'Although the wind can make quite a racket up in the eaves at night,' she added.

We all looked at Beccah, knowing that it could be the wind, or could just as easily be the spirit of Jedediah. I could tell by the looks on everyone's faces that this was so much harder than we first thought. I was more worried about Ollie fighting with Wax or arguing with Tallulah in front of everyone. Either way, we'd be in disgrace with Olivia and Jed, trying to make a good impression. They naively thought they could just invite the neighbours over and somehow welcome them into our paranormal family. Judging by the furtive and barbed looks we were all swapping, there would be no big secrets revealed tonight. I for one was relieved.

Thankfully, we finished eating soon after that. We helped Olivia clear away and a bottle of port and some cheeses were brought to the table at the parents' end. It allowed all of us to slowly drift off and escape to different parts of the house, leaving the parents to chat. I certainly felt about a stone lighter as I followed some of the others up the stairs.

Ollie ran past me, up the stairs after Tallulah. 'Wait!' he called

'I don't want to talk about it anymore,' Tallulah threw back at him.

They reached her room and Ollie barged right in as she went to close the door on him. All I could hear was raised voices after that.

Wax shook his head, bored with their childish argument already. His eyelids lowered and he pulled Beccah into his room with him. Joe and Josh, who were completely clueless to the angst of relationships, agreed on a dream team battle on their latest video game.

I was left standing there.

It felt weird. I looked over the balcony to check the coast was clear and crept down the landing to my little attic staircase before anyone remembered me. I suddenly realised I didn't mind being alone. Since coming to know Helix, I craved it.

I closed the door immediately and leant my back against it.

Then I saw it.

My ribbon. The one I'd tied neatly around the drawer knob. My definitely pink ribbon, to match all the pink toiletries in my gift basket, was now clearly blue.

My heart stopped painfully in my chest. I rushed over and snatched the drawer open, knocking my strategically placed socks all over the place. I didn't care. I swept them aside to reveal my diary. I picked it up with slightly shaking hands and went straight to the last entry.

Clearly, in large, smudged ink were the letters *O K*, the number *2* and a childlike drawing of a crescent moon. Tonight. It had to mean tonight.

CHAPTER 8

The loud rap at my door made me jump. I could barely breathe. My head was still reeling and my heart pumping from the concrete proof that Helix was going to visit me tonight.

'No lurking in your room,' Wax's stern voice came through the door.

I was a little surprised he wasn't still occupied. 'OK, I'm coming,' I said, my voice a little too high-pitched and scratchy. 'I'm just getting changed.' All the while, I willed him not to come in and scribbled a large *YES* under Helix's entry. Then I threw it back in my drawer, bundled the socks on top and scooped up the now-pink ribbon off my floor.

I looked at it closely. It was definitely pink and was blue when I came in. I let out a long breath of bewilderment as I tied it back on the drawer. Helix had magical powers, too.

'Sam!' Wax shouted, making me jump again.

'Coming!' I said, now panicking, picking up my dirty jeans and jumper from the floor. I yanked up my dress, pulling it painfully over my head without undoing the zipper, tugged on my jumper and stepped into my jeans.

My heart was racing, sure Wax would burst in any minute. 'OK ready,' I said, opening the door, looking up into Wax's shrewd gaze as he narrowed his eyes, weighing up my heated cheeks and my whisps of hair sticking up all over the place. I hurriedly smoothed them down with the flat of my hand and strode right past him, deciding to brazen it out rather than cave under his scrutiny. It worked because he didn't follow me.

I went back downstairs, getting myself together, not daring to look behind me. I heard the snick of Wax's door as he went back into his room. I walked back into the dining room and the parents were still sitting at the table.

'Ah, Sam, would you like some coffee?' Olivia asked. 'More coffee, John?'

But John was getting to his feet. 'No … thank you. We'd better get back. Trades people coming to give us a quote on a new kitchen in the morning.'

I briefly wondered how that would go down with Gerty. That was her domain.

Jean stood up with him. 'Thank you for a lovely evening. You must let us return the favour sometime.'

'We'd love that,' Olivia gushed, standing too. Jed got up and put his arm around her shoulders. It all seemed a little too rushed and strained.

'Maybe when our kitchen has been brought up to the twenty-first century,' John said, making them all laugh.

'You'll have to show Mum how to work it all,' Tallulah said, wandering in, texting. 'She still struggles with the dishwasher.'

I stared at her, still stuck on her recent argument and how quickly she seemed to have recovered from it. Then I tuned back in at the moment of silence that followed, while Jean frowned and looked confused.

'Gerty, your housekeeper. She's Tallulah's mother,' Olivia explained, slightly red-faced.

Jean's face brightened with recognition and then clouded again. 'And you live here?' she said, looking back at Tallulah.

I looked at Jed as a last hope to save the situation. I think we all did. Jed began herding everyone to the door, having finally had enough of the evening. 'You know … more room. Close to yours. Her father was ill. That sort of thing.'

'And Ollie was back,' Olivia added. 'And they were so close.'

My eyes found Tallulah's, which remained hard. Ollie hadn't reappeared.

'Seemed the right thing at the time,' Jed added.

Beccah's parents were literally bundled to the door. The butler appeared and held out their coats for them to slip their arms into. Goodbyes were said, cheeks were kissed and they were out of the door in no more than a minute.

Everyone slowly turned and glared at Tallulah, standing alone in the middle of the large hallway. 'What?' she said with a moody shrug. 'Nobody told me to say I was an orphan.'

Despite my dying to know what was going on with her, she was right. Every avenue had not been thought through before tonight. It had been a bit of a disaster on several counts. Jed tutted and walked past Tallulah with Olivia following, 'Jed, it's no one's fault,' and followed him in the direction of the kitchen.

Everyone filtered into the kitchen after them, now the imminent danger had gone. Even Wax wandered in with Beccah, looking like they'd just got out of bed.

'Your parents aren't going to be that easy to tell about any of this,' Jed said, moodily clinking cups into the dishwasher.

Beccah smiled wanly at Wax. I felt sorry for her. It wasn't her fault.

'I'm sorry, Beccah. I put my foot in it loads of times,' Olivia said, giving her a hug and a kindly smile.

'You weren't the only one,' Jed said, looking sardonically at Tallulah.

'Yeah, Tallulah,' Ollie said suddenly appearing next to her and poking her in the ribs.

She grumbled about not being told to lie, while I watched them closely. They appeared to be fine, but there was definitely tension between them.

Meanwhile, everyone helped tidy and the butler and the maid brought the last of the cups and dishes in from the dining room.

I finally let go of my fixation on Tallulah and thought about the rest of the evening. 'It is weird though, isn't it?' I said, thinking aloud.

Everyone went quiet and looked at me quizzically. 'What do you mean?' Wax asked.

My cheeks went hot as I felt everyone's gaze on me. 'I mean … we all came at the time Ainsley was using his spell. Even Beccah came all the way from America and she was only in a coma.' I gave her an apologetic look for bringing it up. 'So why did she come and her brother didn't? Just think it's weird, that's all.'

Almost everyone looked at me blankly. Some were stunned, others confused. Wax looked annoyed. 'What? It's true, isn't it?' I went on indignantly. 'Wasn't that why tonight was so hard? What can you possibly say to people that have lost a son when you know all that?'

IT WAS easy to slope off after my unintentional bombshell. They'd all been struck dumb. Everyone accepted that grieving parents were not going to receive the news well, that virtually everybody in the two houses had been saved from a real death, except their poor son.

I reached my room, closed the door with relief and instantly shuddered with a deep chill.

I looked straight at the pink ribbon and it was gone. For a moment, I stood frozen, heart thrashing. Then I walked quickly around the bed and saw it lying on the floor. I bent and scooped it up and pulled open the top drawer. My heart almost beat out of my chest and I was barely breathing.

Helix had been back.

My hands were shaking as I pulled out my diary and went straight to the last entry. Just two untidy words: T U R N – A R O U N D.

CHAPTER 9

I felt his warm glow on my back before I'd even moved. I slowly turned, keeping my eyes on the floor. My legs were already going to jelly and my head, swimming. 'Don't put me to sleep, Helix. Please!' I cried. 'Let me see you properly awake. I need to see you're real.'

The feeling of dizziness immediately subsided and I slowly raised my eyes to look at him. It was difficult to make him out at first because he was bathed in a brilliant light. It slowly dimmed to reveal the tall, dark, handsome boy from not just my dreams, but the one in the forest. Real. Except, close up he seemed taller. Stronger. Darker. Wider shoulders. Longer legs. He was dressed so perfectly, which I guessed was a surprise. Completely in black, with pressed trousers and a black T-shirt tucked into them, revealing a trim, athletic physique and arms covered in tiny glyph tattoos. His hair was long and wispy to his shoulders, just as I remembered it. And his eyes. Those unusual, mesmerising eyes. Mustard-yellow, like a large cat.

He looked right back at me, looking cautious and shy as if he wasn't sure of my reaction. 'Hi,' he said.

I couldn't help staring at his perfectly shaped mouth. Full, dusky lips against much-darker tanned skin than I remembered. Clear, glowing skin. High cheekbones. He was good-looking. Very. Stirring something deep down in my stomach. 'Hi,' I said back eventually, which came out in a croak. 'Thanks for coming … thanks for not putting me to sleep,' I managed to say after I coughed to clear my throat.

He clenched his jaw and seemed to straighten to look even taller than he was before. 'I don't think I can do it for long.' His voice sounded soft and echoey, like a loud whisper in a cave. Like it came from somewhere else. A device. Like a TV, or a radio, or something. It made me wonder if we were on the same plane. I'd learned that many supernaturals travelled between two. However he'd managed it, it was taking effort and making him sweat. Tiny little beads were collecting on his forehead.

Then a thought suddenly occurred to me. 'Is it because you need my energy?' I didn't know whether to feel angry or not. I didn't want it to be true. I wasn't disgusted by it. I guess I didn't want Wax and Ollie to be right and he was using me for something.

But Helix nodded. 'I'm sorry. It's just natural for me to take it from you. It's symbiotic. The way we're made. In return, I look after you.'

I thought about that for a minute. I wondered where he'd learned a word like symbiotic. I'd learned it in science. It's where two things rely on each other to live. 'Like clownfish and sea anemones?' I said, wrinkling my nose at the weird comparison.

He laughed a little and looked at me strangely.

It wasn't like we'd made a pact. I was just about to say he hadn't exactly asked my permission when he pinched the bridge of his nose and swayed like he would fall over.

'What is it?' I said, jumping forward to steady him. 'Do you need to take me to my dream place?'

He looked up at me immediately and nodded. His eyes looked bloodshot and glazed.

I looked deeply into them. He didn't seem dangerous, only lost. I took a deep breath and nodded. 'OK. Take me there. But we've got to talk. Really talk, I mean.'

Helix said nothing else. Instead, he swept forward like a swirling cloak that covered me in darkness and I was back there. Feeling soft grass under my back. Losing my fingers in the soft stems. Smelling the earth and all the green plants and flowers. It was so real.

With my senses alive, I slowly opened my eyes to see the blue sky, filled with cotton wool clouds. I turned my head and there he was. Helix. Lounging on his side watching me, leaning on his elbow, head on hand. He smiled a dazzling smile. He looked fine. OK. More than fine, in fact.

'Thank you,' he said, dreamily. His blink was slow as if he was half drunk on something.

I felt warm and fuzzy too. Maybe it was the warm sunshine in the middle of winter. Then a thought struck me. He was basking. Drawing the light from this place.

I sat up suddenly and hitched a breath when I fell in with what was happening. What always happened when he brought me here? 'Are you sucking my energy?' I said in absolute horror.

His eyes went wide, mocking my expression and he broke out into loud laughter.

'What? It's not funny. Stop it!' I wanted to smack him to make him stop embarrassing me. Until he finally held back his laughter with a hand and he pulled a strained and more serious face.

He tipped his head, looking sorry. 'Kind of, I suppose. I would get sick without you.' His brows drew together in all seriousness. 'I meant what I said. We are a symbiotic pairing. It's what I'm meant for. What we always seek.'

He seemed to know a lot for someone who'd been dumped as a kid and couldn't read or write.

'I have an uncle who visits from time to time to watch over me.'

The large man on the chestnut horse. I'd forgotten with everything else. That was a little more disturbing. I couldn't imagine an older, more powerful version of Helix. Plus, I was already dreading what Wax would say. Especially as I hadn't said anything earlier. Except the worry didn't stay with me for long. It slowly evaporated with the way Helix was looking at me. He was studying me like he'd never seen me properly before. My blood heated under that gaze. He smouldered. No one had ever looked at me like that in my life before.

I stiffened as he reached out a hand. He just tucked a stray curl behind my ear. His light, feather touch on my skin sent a shiver down the length of my body. 'What are you doing?' I said, alarmed, drawing back out of reach.

He frowned and looked a little wounded as he drew back his hand. He blinked his long lashes in disappointment. 'I would never hurt you, Sam. You're my life, my reason for being here.'

It felt like every small part of him was designed to tease or distract, lure me in and melt me. I couldn't give in to it. 'Aren't you one of those Incu-buses, Energy Vampires, or something? Don't you feed off sex?'

Something in him immediately changed and he was on his feet, scowling at me. I scrambled up, bemused, to face him as well.

'I am not the one who would hurt you like that,' he said, clearly offended.

Even though I didn't fully understand what it was I'd said

that had offended him, I did feel sorry. I never meant to hurt his feelings. 'I'm just trying to understand, that's all.'

'You really remember nothing from your life before?' he said, frowning and then narrowing his eyes like he was testing me.

It felt like something opened a dam and all my hopelessness flooded back to me. I could barely speak. I shook my head. 'Not how I lived, died, or anything.' I swallowed back angry tears. 'I don't even remember my family – I know who they are. Where they are. They can't see me, but I can see them and I know they didn't even grieve for me.'

Tears were streaming down my cheeks by the time I finished my tirade and Helix was holding my arms. Steadying me, grounding me. But when I looked up into his strange eyes, pleading him to reveal something to me, what I saw there hardened. He drew back as if he shouldn't touch me and I felt instantly sad. 'Tell your living friend to look on the lampposts of the village. Then, if you still want to know what happened, I will reveal it to you.'

My eyes widened in surprise and confusion and I wanted to pull him back to tell me now, but I felt sick and woozy. Helix was drifting away and I knew I was waking up. He was leaving and I was left angry, lonely and dissatisfied with my answers. 'Wait! Please, Helix. I'm sorry. I never meant to upset you.' But he'd gone and I was left in my usual tangled mess of sheets, more confused than ever.

IT WAS LATE when I crept back down the stairs and conventional night-time for the living. Most of my friends felt no difference other than it being dark, but Wax's parents needed their sleep, so we usually respected that and confined ourselves to our rooms. The house was silent and I was struggling with who to tell, knowing I had to confide in someone.

I stood on the landing and weighed my options. Then, admitting that there really wasn't any way out of it, I softly padded the length of the hallway, stopping outside Wax's door. I knew, although he was scary, he was the one Helix meant for me to tell.

I knocked softly.

'Go away. I'm asleep!'

'Please, Wax. I don't think I can wait until morning.'

The door was snatched open and Wax swept me with his eyes, checking me for any sign of damage. Then seeing I appeared to be in one piece, went to close it. 'Wait!' I said, putting my bare foot in the way.

He sagged in disappointment and looked at me blankly. 'What do you want, Sam?' he asked, pressuring me with his bored body language.

I couldn't help staring at the many tattoos on the top half of his body. Then dropping to track pants barely clinging to his hips on the bottom half. 'Can I come in?'

He let out a loud sigh and pushed the door open wide. He checked that there was no one else out on the landing and closed the door.

It always surprised me how dark his room was. He had on a bedside lamp, but the walls were a dark, flocked grey and black and his bed was black with a huge canopy above it. The family coat of arms stood proudly carved into the headboard. The room would be completely gothic if it weren't for the many screens on his computer scripting code.

I looked back at his bed and it was neatly made. It was clear he'd been working, not sleeping like he'd said. Beccah had often remarked that Wax rarely slept. It was because of the constant spirit voices that plagued him all the time. He would drink or work on his computer to take his mind off it when she wasn't around.

I sensed Wax's attention waning. 'Helix came to me tonight.'

Wax raised his eyebrows and without saying a word, cocked his head and conveyed I was alive to tell the tale, so get on with it.

'He said something I think you should know – well, two things actually.'

Wax walked over to his swivel chair and sat down heavily, giving me his full attention.

'He isn't abandoned here like we first thought. He has an uncle who visits him from time to time to keep an eye on him. I think I might have even seen them talking in the woods. It was at a distance, but I know one of them was Helix.'

Wax gave very little away of what he was thinking. He was quiet, processing, running through all the implications in his head.

I pressed on and started a slow pace up and down in front of him. It helped me get my thoughts in order and not ramble under Wax's intimidating stare. 'And we got to talking … and I asked him if he was an Incubus. He got kind of angry and said he would never hurt me like that. Then he went strange and asked if I remembered my life before. I said no and then he told me to tell you to look at the lampposts in the village.' I stopped pacing and looked at Wax in confusion. 'What could he possibly mean by that?' I sat moodily on the end of Wax's bed. It all sounded so silly and limp now I'd said it out loud.

Wax was very quiet, thinking carefully over what I'd said. I felt the first bells of alarm. He wasn't making fun or dismissing it out of hand. In fact, he turned around and rolled closer to his desk and began tapping fast over his keyboard. 'What is it?' I said, getting up to look over his shoulder.

'Well, for starters, it means he's not confined to the house or the land.'

That was true and hadn't occurred to me. Shades seemed to be limited to their houses or the borders of the original spell that brought us here. I couldn't even go home. 'Didn't we look there already?' My unease was rising in my chest in a hard, painful lump. We'd searched about me online loads of times and always came up with nothing.

'Only the obituaries,' Wax said.

Then my chest tightened further as I got what he meant.

He brought up a website with the heading, *'Missing Persons,'* and began typing my name in the search bar. He tried two different sites before my picture came up.

I felt empty and strange looking at a picture I had no recollection of even being taken. I looked young and not particularly happy. Just staring off into the middle distance as if even then, I wasn't fully there. My chest ached that I had no idea of the girl I was back then.

Wax was absorbed in the screen and he began reading aloud. *Samantha Payne, aged 16, went missing from her home in the village of Swineleigh Cross on Saturday, 31st. Her mother had gone to bingo and her sister had stayed at a friend's. Stepfather Graeme said she went to the village shop and never came back. An immediate search was launched in the nearby river and forested areas, but came up with no clue as to her whereabouts. Police were baffled with no leads.*

Two years on, to the day, and Sam's mother and father continue to paste her photo around the village where she lived in the hope it will jog someone's memory.'

I was dumbstruck.

Wax swivelled around to face me. 'That's why we could

never find anything in the births and deaths' columns. No body. No grave.'

'No death?' I finished for him. 'How can you be so sure I—'

'Died? Because of Ainsley's spell. Because you came here. Because I can see you,' Wax said as if my being dead was the most obvious thing in the world.

And it was. I *was* dead. I had to be. Beccah had been an anomaly because of being a Blackwood. There would be no such luck for me. 'And no mourning,' I added.

Wax nodded, now looking not quite so stern, as if he was feeling sorry for me. 'Because as far as your family is concerned, you could still be alive.'

I nodded, my gaze still on the stranger looking back at me on the screen.

'Your resident demon knew this all along. He knew your missing persons' photos were on the village lampposts. The question is, why did he not say anything until now?'

He was right. But Helix *had* told me and he had pointed me in this direction to join up the dots.

'Which begs the question, not what he told you, Sam, but what it is he's holding back and is reluctant to tell you.'

I swallowed hard and took my eyes off the screen to look at Wax's hard expression. His mind was a well-oiled machine, analysing all the angles, while my mind was stuck on a family who expected me to come home. 'But why can't I remember anything? Why?' Not my family. Not anything from before I went missing.

'I think you need to ask your friend.'

Even when I felt the words, 'What do you mean?' leave my lips, I already recognised the shift in Wax, referring to Helix as my friend. He was so clever; he knew he already meant more to me than he should. But I was grateful he wasn't calling me out on it.

'I think maybe he was more involved in this than he's willing to admit. Maybe *he* took your memories. And if he did, maybe he did it for a reason.'

I stared at Wax's unapologetic face for a long moment before I shook it from my mind. 'What, you think *he* abducted me?' My heart was already thumping, my mind warring with why he would or wouldn't do something like that. I refused to think he would see me so unhappy just to have me all to himself.

Wax just looked briefly at the ceiling and took a breath to gather strength at my raised voice. He held up his hands as if to say he really had no idea. 'Maybe you should focus on the last person to see you alive.'

I turned back to the monitor, but it was really to give me time to think. Time to gather up all my frayed emotions. Wax turned with me and homed in on the text: *Mother at bingo, sister at a friend's,* and he highlighted the last bit, *Stepfather Graeme was at home.*

An uncomfortable shiver went up my spine, like an icy finger. I felt an emptiness where that name was concerned and despite no knowledge to the contrary, I instinctively knew I didn't like him.

'And the uncle. If he visits, how often? Is he with The Wild Ride? He's an adult male incubus and this has a houseful of young women. Does that mean The Ride is due to come back again?'

That was too frightening for words. The man I saw *had* been on a horse, but I kept that bit quiet for now. I had too many conflicting thoughts to sort through yet to have Wax go all head of operations and have us under heavy lockdown. Instead, I looked out through the curtains that Wax hadn't drawn properly. The sun was coming up and the sky was pink. 'Shepherd's warning,' I said absently.

'What?' Wax said, his hands back to tapping across his keys.

'It's an old farmer's rhyme,' I said, letting out a ragged breath. 'Red sky at night, shepherd's delight. Red sky in the morning, shepherd's warning.' It felt very scary and prophetic right then. How on earth I could remember something like that and nothing at all that mattered in my life, I had no idea.

Wax's phone rang with a few bars of some screamo-death-metal song. It snapped me out of my depressing thoughts. He glanced at the screen and put the phone to his ear, suddenly alert. 'Beccah? What is it?'

My heart quickened, watching Wax nod and hearing Beccah's raised, emotional voice. Something must be wrong for her to call at this hour. Wax mm'd, at intervals, while he listened, rolled his eyes and swore. 'OK, I'll be right over,' he said, already getting up. He tapped 'end' on his phone and put it in his back pocket.

'What is it?' I'd already made up my mind I was going with him.

'Been an eventful night at Blackwood House,' he said, pulling a 'One Crow Left in the Murder' white t-shirt over his head and looking around on the floor. 'I take it you're coming?' he said, pushing his bare feet into white leather trainers, without tying the laces.

I nodded while he finished dressing in a plain oversized navy hoody, over the white T.

'You'll want a jacket,' he said.

'There's one in the hall.'

He nodded, grabbing his keys. He tapped his back pocket, making sure he still had his phone and we left the room.

My heart was beating hard with a mixture of excitement and trepidation. I'd learned something about myself tonight and not just the stuff about my un-death. I had to be doing something constructive. It made me feel better. I could no longer sit around and quietly mope. From now on that was over.

As we trotted down the staircase, I decided I liked Wax. He was moody and scary, but he was a boy of action. We trusted him and he got stuff done. This was the most time I'd ever spent alone with him and I trusted him implicitly. He was our leader and we all recognised something in him and it wasn't just that he was alive.

While I grabbed my black puffa jacket from the stand and followed him through the door under the stairs, my mind shot to Helix. He felt the antithesis of Wax. I guess I'd hoped to count on him in the same way, but I wasn't sure that was possible. He felt too unpredictable.

We were soon in the large tunnel that stretched between the two houses. No one knew how long it had been there, or who made it, but it was our secret way in and out. It was a huge, roughly hewn semicircle of black rock over our heads. A testament to the tie between the two families. It made me feel a pang of longing for the destined relationship Wax and Beccah had.

Wax was taller and his strong, purposeful strides bigger than mine. I had to skip to catch up with him several times. It suddenly occurred to me that the tunnel was lit by fiery torches held in brackets bolted to the rock. Before I could ask who lit them—

'Supernatural,' Wax cut in.

Leaving me mouthing the word: Oh. 'Are you going to fill me in on what the emergency is?' Speeding up my steps to catch up with him again.

We'd reached the small wooden door at the end of the tunnel that led into the cellar of Beccah's house. We got inside the dark room and Wax switched on the torch on his phone and put his finger to his lips. He pointed at the ceiling and I heard it immediately. There were raised voices coming from the room above. 'Come on,' Wax said, leading the way up the small wooden staircase.

It was obvious I wasn't going to get an answer to any questions, so I followed along quietly, staying as close to him as I could, through the dusty passageway to the next level.

Wax lightly tapped on a panel in the wall, but before anyone could open it, a gust of wind whipped past and threw me forward. I scrambled upright to see it was Lucinda, one of Wax's ghostly ancestors, who'd literally passed right through me. She stood directly in front of us, barring our way. She was a chalk outline moving constantly, seeming very agitated and upset.

Her voice was reedy, like poor radio reception, as she was an apparition that faded in and out. She was Wax's aunt, with so many 'greats' in front that I'd forgotten how many. In fact, she was a shared ancestor of Beccah's too. She remained roaming the two houses with her husband and malevolent spirit, Jedediah. Wax's scary uncle. 'What is it, Lucinda?' Wax asked.

'It's Jed,' she said, her voice crackling and breaking up. 'I tried to keep him quiet, but he was hellbent on wandering the tunnel and passageways, warning of impending danger. He's been doing it all night. I tried to stop him, but tonight he came right inside the house.'

'Lucinda!' the deep, bellowing voice echoed from somewhere deep in the walls.

The shouting voices started again and I could hear Beccah's among them. Wax wasted no more time and pushed open the panel into the room. A high-pitched scream pealed through the air as soon as we clambered out the other side, directly into the Victorian drawing room.

CHAPTER 10

*B*eccah immediately ran to Wax and he hugged her to him. Beccah's father, John, was holding Beccah's terrified mother up from a wilting faint.

I looked around me to get my bearings in the room. It was wood-clad halfway up the walls and was very old-fashioned. All faded sage green sofas, threadbare rugs and doilies. If you really squinted, you could get some idea of the old-world opulence of the place.

'Sorry, Mrs Whitely,' Wax said. 'It's a passageway between the two houses. It's the quickest way to get here, that's all.'

Beccah's mum, Jean, seemed to sag again with relief and Beccah's dad let her down slowly onto the sofa. He sat next to her and patted her hand. 'It's haunted. The whole house … it was awful. No eyes … no eyes,' Jean wailed to no one in particular.

She was rambling in shock. I looked warily at Wax, unsure of what I should do. He looked heavenward. We both knew she must have come across Jedediah.

Jean couldn't sit still and went to look out of the large sash window. It was light now.

Gerty came in wheeling a trolley with a teapot and cups on it. I was just about to thank her, thinking hot, sweet tea was a great idea for the shock, when Gerty launched straight in with, 'I can't have those workmen in my kitchen again today. How am I supposed to make Sarah's porridge? She'll come over with the vapours if her routine is changed for a single moment. And Burt needs his tea, otherwise we won't get an ounce of work out of him,' she went on in her tirade with her hands on her hips.

Jean looked over at us, bewildered, with her arm outstretched, as if it was the last straw and only proved her point. She let her arm fall to her side, resting her case: that the world had gone mad.

A perfectly timed call bell tinkled from out in the hall. 'Aunt Sarah, I believe,' Jean said, smiling maniacally and holding her hand up. 'You see what I mean? That damned bell goes off all hours of the day and night and Gerty won't allow us in our own kitchen.'

Gerty went to protest, but Jean was on a roll and her hand went up again to silence her. 'There's a darned dog in here somewhere that barks incessantly, as well, that I can never seem to find.'

John stood up and went to her, pulling her into his arms. It was all too much and she began to sob into his shoulder. I looked up at Wax, not having a clue what he could do about any of this.

He nodded and pointed for us to sit on one of the sofas. 'Please come and sit down, Mr and Mrs Whitely. It's time we had a chat. Gerty? Would you pour the tea please?'

She pouted, but did as Wax asked and the Whitelys came and sat on the sofa opposite Beccah and me. Wax picked up his cup and sat with us.

Jean took hers, china rattling, with shaking hands. She really was a mess. She finally sat and she and John looked at us warily as if they sensed something very big was coming.

'First, I want to apologise, Mr and Mrs Whitely. We had planned on bringing the whole thing up at dinner, but it was a hard subject to broach.'

'What subject?' John said, narrowing his eyes, cautiously.

Jean had now stopped crying and was looking at us with wide, bloodshot eyes.

'There are other people living here with us, Mum,' Beccah said, swapping a look with Wax, then back at her mother. 'The house kind of came with a few occupants.'

Beccah's mother's resolve to listen seemed to dissolve before our eyes. 'Well tell them to go, please ... Can't you see the solicitor for us, Wax?' she pleaded.

My eyes dropped just in time to see Wax give Beccah's hand a squeeze for the permission he needed, but it was Beccah who spoke up first. 'It can't be handled like that, Mom. These houses are very old and ... haunted.' She looked at her mother and father and let that last word sink in.

There was silence. Even Gerty looked dubiously between us and the Whitelys.

'The person you saw last night was Jedediah. He's a spirit and the great-great-great uncle of Wax's.' She looked up at Wax to make sure she had that right. He shrugged a little.

'And he's married to Lucinda, who's your ancestor too,' Wax said.

'The houses have always been connected, see?' Beccah said.

'The white lady in the long dress,' Jean said, looking off into the distance with a far-off voice.

'That's right, she's lovely,' Beccah said, brightly, encouraged by her mother not breaking down into hysterics.

'But that thing, that—'

'Jedediah,' Wax finished for her. 'My uncle. He's fine, he

protects us. He just takes some time to get used to. He's worried about something, that's all.'

'He's worried,' Jean said, rolling her eyes and shaking her head. 'What's he got to be worried about?'

'I'm not sure,' Wax said with a sigh. 'I haven't had chance to talk to him properly.'

'Who else is here?' John asked.

I so admired him, then. The whole thing must be terrifying for the both of them, but he was comforting his wife and asking constructive questions.

'Well, there's Gerty the housekeeper, who you know,' Wax said.

She bobbed a small curtsey and smiled wanly.

Both Jean and John straightened, visibly shocked.

'Burt the gardener and odd job man,' Beccah added. 'Oh, and his dog, Brutus, you keep hearing.'

The Whitelys just blinked, wide eyes, as if absorbing blow after blow.

'And there's Aunt Sarah, your great-great-grandmother's sister,' Wax said.

The bell tinkled again in the hall, making both the Whitelys look at the door.

'Would you like to meet her?' Beccah asked.

Jean looked up at John, alarmed, and his penetrating look directed at us, checked whether it was a good idea. Wax nodded. 'And they are all ghosts?' John asked.

'Of a sort,' Wax said. 'They're something a little more solid than a ghost.'

John turned to face Jean and dabbed her eyes with his handkerchief. 'What about it, Jean, what do you think? The locals don't seem to have any trouble with this sort of thing.'

Jean smiled a little at his attempt at humour, but she still looked unsure. John gave her arm a tug and the two of them slowly got to their feet. 'Lead the way,' he said, lifting his chin up and linking Jean's arm through his.

I thought they were being very brave. 'What about us?' I whispered to Wax as we got out into the hallway. He went up to Sarah's sitting room and knocked. 'One thing at a time.'

'Come in,' a croaky female voice came from the other side of the door.

Jean and John looked at each other with widened eyes. Beccah put her arms around both her parents and gave them a squeeze. 'I know this all seems mad. Don't be scared. She's an old lady. She goes on a bit and she's really forgetful, but she's harmless. I promise you.'

Wax was already opening the door as Beccah's mum swallowed and nodded for us to continue. We all traipsed into the long rectangular room.

If there was a photo in a Jane Austen novel, then it would be exactly like this room. It had two large, heavily draped windows in moss green on the left, with grand display cabinets, showing delicate china and glass in between. There was a large patterned Persian rug in the centre in a threadbare aubergine and cream. In fact, like the rest of the house, the whole room looked tired and worn if you took a closer look. As if its once grand shine had been polished away in the annals of time. Much of Beccah's house was like that. Literally frozen and not part of the real world, which I guess it wasn't entirely. No wonder the Whitelys wanted to decorate.

We edged forward at the Whitelys' speed across the rug, while they looked around fearfully at ornament-covered sideboards and cabinets filled with trinkets and followed the line of the many gilded romantic paintings of ladies of the time. I took it all in. Until we arrived at the dainty, yellow-flocked armchairs and mustard velvet sofa arranged around the lit fire at the furthest end. Beccah overtook us to face the chair with its back to us. 'Aunt Sarah,' she said, bending to kiss someone's cheek. 'I want you to meet my parents and friends.'

We all came to a standstill around a tiny old lady while she blathered and blustered about being woken up from her nap.

John immediately held out his hand and Jean stood there blinking in shock. I couldn't take my eyes off the translucent skin and doily hat that easily looked a hundred and fifty years old. I said, 'Hello', taking in the dark-green satin of her voluminous dress and her grey eyes, glazed white with advanced years.

Sarah reached for the pull cord of her bell and rang it loudly. 'Where's that Gerty? Dallying with Bert, I suppose. She needs to bring some extra cups. I ordered tea an hour ago. Sit … sit, so I can see you all. Stop crowding around me, I can barely breathe.'

I couldn't help the small smile as I perched on the edge of a footstool, while the others arranged themselves on the sofa and remaining chair.

'She's having trouble in the kitchen, I think,' Beccah explained.

Beccah's parents watched closely, faces blank and unmoving with shock. John looked straight at me, bewildered. 'How is she even here when I own the place?' he said.

I shrugged. I certainly couldn't explain. It beat me how any of us were still there.

Beccah stood up. 'Let me introduce everyone, Aunt. These are my parents, John and Jean. They recently moved here from America and live in the house and these are my friends, Sam and Bret, but everyone calls him Wax.

Sarah's eyes narrowed on Wax. 'Ah, the Waxley-Black boy. You went against my advice then,' she said, tipping her head sardonically towards Beccah.

'So … the curse didn't get you.' She spoke directly to Wax

and he inclined his head. 'We broke it, in fact, Miss Blackwood. It's a pleasure to finally meet you.'

'Mmm,' she muttered doubtfully. 'Maybe. Not completely as we're all still here.'

I looked sharply at Wax and he was frowning. None of us knew what she meant by that.

Sarah had already lost interest and moved on to Beccah. 'Not a cripple anymore, I see. You might salvage a good marriage.'

Beccah laughed easily with her aunt, stamping her foot. 'Good as new,' she said, making her aunt chuckle.

'I can see the family resemblance. Come closer, girl,' Sarah said, pointing a bony finger directly at Jean. 'You're definitely a Blackwood.'

Jean looked horrified and turned to John for help. He tipped his head for her to get up and approach Sarah. She swallowed and cautiously stood, then edged closer to Sarah as if she'd jump up and grab her at any minute.

Sarah held out a thin hand for her to take, which she did, barely holding the tips of her fingers. Jean was shaking. Sarah chuckled. Then her eyes glazed over and she froze for a second. Jean looked at Beccah in alarm. We were all about to jump up, thinking she'd had some sort of seizure, when she looked up at Jean again and tightened her grip. 'You got her back, my niece. She's a strong one. Remember that. But you have another. Weak. Lost. Tossed on the wind. But he is close, never fear.' Then she turned her head and looked directly at Wax. 'You!' she said, pointing her finger at him. 'Waxley-Black. Tell your clan to be ready. The Ride is on its way.'

'What? What, Sarah?' Beccah asked, but the old woman appeared to have lost her thread. The door at the far end opened, making us all turn and look. It was Gerty bringing in the tea.

'Bout time!' Sarah said, thumping her cane on the floor.

My mind was still reeling over her weird ramblings. The mention of The Ride definitely struck home with us all.

Gerty just tutted like she was used to being hurried. She put the brake on her trolley and began pouring the tea into cups. 'I can't find a damned thing in that kitchen.'

'What was Jed making all that fuss about last night?' Sarah asked her, while she picked up her cup.

'Do you know?' Jean said, surprising us all by joining the conversation.

'No, not really. He frightens the life out of me. He knows damned well he's not meant to come into the main house,' Gerty said.

'Precisely. Noisy fool. Enough to give a lady a nasty turn. You! Waxley-Black!' Sarah said, suddenly sharp again and taking Wax off guard.

He raised his eyebrows for her to speak.

'Get to the bottom of it. He's your damned uncle.'

He inclined his head, trying not to smile. 'I will. I promise.'

Everyone went quiet for a while then and drank their tea. No one knew what to say as Sarah had clearly forgotten her mysterious warnings of earlier. It was quite a shock after thinking she was just a sweet old lady. But she wasn't. I had to remember she was a Shade, just like many of us. And we could do things and feel things humans couldn't.

'So you all live here in my house,' Sarah said, eying Beccah and her parents shrewdly. 'And after you escaped the curse.' She raised her eyebrows and chuckled. 'Well done. Showed true Blackwood spirit, there.' She nodded, smiling at us all. Good to see the house filled again.' She sat back in her chair, taking her cup with her. 'I approve. It's nice to hear happy voices. And you can tell that uncle of yours that I will banish him to his estate if he continues to wake up the household. Am I making myself clear?' she said, glaring at Wax.

'Crystal,' Wax said, with a slow smile.

It was kind of funny that the Whitelys were sitting drinking tea with a Shade – well two, counting me, and talking about the malevolent spirit stalking the house like he was a wayward relative. They even seemed calmer about it, which seemed to make things better in a strange sort of way.

'You can all go now. I'm tired,' Sarah said with a flick of her hand. 'Oh, and before I forget. Before you threaten to banish him, find out the whereabouts of The Ride. That's what he's in such a tizzy about.'

We all looked at each other, surprised and got to our feet. It was a shock when she became so sharp. We all said goodbye and, one by one, left our cups on Gerty's trolley. We traipsed out in silence, back to the drawing room we started in.

I watched Wax closely. He kissed Beccah, touching her cheek and checking she was OK. I could see the pensive look on his face. The Ride was definitely coming, but he didn't say anything. I was dying to question him about it, but daren't re-ignite the Whitelys again.

Jean flopped down into a sofa, looking drained, with her normally perfect hair in wispy disarray. 'I can't believe it. How can it be possible?' she said, looking up at John, bewildered, who was watching her closely with concern.

He shrugged and shook his head as if he wasn't entirely sure it wasn't a psychotic episode and couldn't put it into words just yet. 'And you knew all about this?' he said, turning his head to Beccah.

'Wax has always been able to see them,' she said, putting her hand in his. 'Then we all came.' Thankfully, she didn't go into the magical properties of the water we all drank from Wax's mine yet.

'And what did Sarah mean about you coming back?' John asked. 'She knew you.'

My heart stopped, because now we'd entered truly woo woo territory and there was no other way of disguising it.

Beccah looked up at Wax for encouragement. He replied with a small nod.

'I'm not sure how, exactly, but I came here psychically while I was in my coma. It was how I first met Wax,' she said, looking up at him adoringly.

He bobbed his head. 'Technically, we did speak online first.'

She laughed and bumped into him playfully.

I looked over at the frozen, blank faces of her parents. 'What are you saying, Beccah?' John said, a little irritably, as if he had no capacity left for any more outlandish stories. Especially of the supernatural kind.

'I know it sounds ridiculous, but this place called me. That's why I wanted to live here. All my friends are here. It's magical.'

It was a gross oversimplification of what happened that couldn't be explained with physics, and she completely missed out the part where she almost got trapped in her coma. It was less about the place and more to do with Wax's evil uncle creating a spell to trap everyone, than anything else, but I guessed there was only so much her poor parents could take in one day.

Seizing the pause of John lost for words and Jean numb with shock, Wax cut in. 'Are you feeling OK now, Mrs Whitely? I do really need to find Jedediah and see what has got him so worried.'

Jean looked up at her husband fearfully. He put his arm around her shoulders and gave her a comforting squeeze into his body. 'Can't you tell him to just keep away?' she said, looking at Wax, with her lower lip quivering like she was on the verge of tears.

Wax's face softened. 'I'll try to tell him to dial it down a bit, but he does wander the halls to protect us. He's a malevolent spirit. It's very difficult to make him stop.'

Jean wasn't exactly comforted by that.

'I know it's a lot, Mom. Just try to go with it. For me. I love it here … and so will you. You'll see.'

Jean forced a smile that looked kind of pained and looked up at John doubtfully. Then she gave Beccah a little nod. 'I'll try.'

'If it gets too much, you can always come to us,' Wax said, not able to keep the devilish grin off his face.

Beccah playfully punched him.

I flashed my eyes at the ceiling. That was a whole other Pandora's box of crazy.

The Whitelys just looked on puzzled.

'It was hard for my parents too, but they take it as part and parcel of living here,' Wax said more seriously.

Jean took a ragged breath and nodded.

'I'd better stay here for a while,' Beccah said quietly to Wax as we turned to leave.

He kissed her on the mouth. 'I'll call you later.'

All the lovely tells of caring made my heart flutter. I sighed, put up a hand of goodbye, and followed Wax to the panelled wall, where he pushed the door section and it sprang open. I quickly ducked and went inside the secret tunnel after him.

The Whitelys watched with gaping mouths. I guessed they were wondering what else was right under their noses. It was a relief to escape them when Wax pulled the door shut behind us, closing us in the musty-smelling gloom. 'What now?' I asked, looking around me at the cobwebs and feeling very penned in.

Wax let out a long breath as if he was relieved too. 'Not sure. See Jedediah, I suppose.'

We didn't have far to go. The scary apparition was waiting for us at the far end of the tunnel, black robes swirling around him like constantly billowing smoke.

Lucinda was standing next to him, looking more worried than usual. Wax put up his hand and went right up to them, completely unafraid. Wax wasn't short by any means, but Jedediah towered over him at over seven feet tall. A hood covered most of his face, only revealing a pale-stubbled jaw. I'd only ever seen his eyes once and that was enough to give a girl nightmares. They were black skeletal holes that shone a light so terrifying it could burn right through you.

I swallowed, having to tell myself for the hundredth time that he was a Waxley-Black and on our side.

'What is it, Jedediah?' Wax asked right away.

Then he did something that literally stopped my heart beating in my chest. He raised a bony hand and pointed a long finger right at me.

CHAPTER 11

e? What did any of this sorry mess have to do with me?

'Sam? What about Sam?' Wax asked, looking as confused as I was.

Jedediah rarely spoke and when he did, he had a vocabulary of one word: Lucinda. So Wax switched his gaze to her.

'It's The Ride,' Lucinda said, her reedy voice quavering with fear. 'It hasn't been this close for many years. Jedediah heard last night that it's heading directly here.'

Wax faced Jedediah again. 'And you're certain?'

Jedediah nodded slowly, his robe now curling around him like snakes.

'The spirit world is alive with rumours about it. They say The Ride never leaves a destination without taking a soul.'

'Who?' Wax asked, frowning and looking suddenly angry.

'Me,' I said in a tiny voice that came out as a squeak. I'd cheated death once. It was time to pay the piper. My mind shot to Helix. He'd arrived by way of The Ride ten years ago. It stood to reason that he would leave the same way. I hated that idea even worse. I couldn't bear to lose him now.

'No one knows exactly,' Lucinda continued. 'Jedediah seems to think it's one of you.' She looked up at the spirit standing next to her and her face lit up with an eerie light as he looked directly at her. They appeared to be communicating without words.

'What is it?' Wax asked, clearly thinking the same as me.

Lucinda looked at me as she spoke and my heart froze again. 'He seems to think it is the one the Incubus has chosen.'

My heart sank so low in my chest it was painful. Part of me wanted to rail, why me? However, another part felt the inevitability of it. That nothing in this new life could be permanent. 'What use am I to anyone?' I asked, defeated.

'Because your Incubus cheated the Dark Angel out of a soul when you were children,' Lucinda said.

All the moisture had gone out of my mouth and I struggled to swallow. 'Dark Angel,' I repeated, barely able to breathe, my heart was jumping about so much. I dreaded to know but needed to at the same time.

'He is the Reaper. The one who takes the souls of the damned.'

A cold shudder went through me like an icy hand. I accepted it like the first fall of snow, but I didn't fully understand it. I was meant to die, but I didn't. Helix or Wax's evil uncle, whoever it was, had prevented me from going to the place I was meant to go. Suddenly, I needed to leave. I needed to go home. I needed to go to my safe place. To Helix.

'Can you warn us when it's almost here?' Wax said, stopping my thoughts spiralling down in my misery. 'How long do you think we have?'

Jedediah put up a bony hand and spread out his fingers.

'Five months … five weeks?' Wax asked, his lilt going slightly higher with alarm.

Jedediah hung his head sorrowfully and Lucinda stepped

forward, putting a translucent hand on Wax's shoulder. 'No, Wax. Just five days to coincide with the waxing crescent moon at the end of the month. Then it must leave before the first quarter moon. The Ride is very stringent on these things.'

I felt numb with shock. I'd wished to be anywhere else but here for so long. Now I'd have to leave, everything seemed so precious. My friends, this place. Helix.

My thoughts jumped to Helix. He must know all about this and he hadn't said a word. 'I need to go back!' I said in a strangled plea.

Wax took one look at my face and understood. 'Good idea.' He went to put his hand on Lucinda's shoulder, but it passed right through. He sighed to himself, nodded and walked out through the door to the long tunnel and in the direction of home. I trotted to catch up.

We were silent, lost in our own thoughts for most of the way. 'Does The Ride take people to hell?' I asked, having to skip again to keep up.

'Well, yeah. I guess… Eventually,' Wax said as if it was the most logical thing in the world.

'Well, what did they mean about cheating the Reaper? How does a sixteen-year-old girl cheat going to hell? And what could I have possibly done to make me end up there?' My voice going up a pitch with my indignation.

Wax stopped so suddenly to turn and glare at me that I bumped right into him. 'You didn't, Sam. Helix obviously stopped it. *He* cheated the Reaper. And as for what you could have done …' He let out an exasperated breath, turned and strode on.

I was left there reeling. I ran this time to catch up. I didn't say anything more. He was right. It all went back to the real question: what went on in that cottage before I died.

There was only one person I could ask who knew.

Wax and I walked back into the kitchen where everyone was congregated. Olivia was cooking a big English breakfast of bacon and eggs.

My stomach rumbled. I hadn't eaten since yesterday and it was my favourite.

'Ah, there you are. I was wondering where the two of you had got to, Olivia said.

Wax went over to the island, sat on a stool and took the cup of coffee Olivia held out to him. 'We had to go over to Beccah's. The cat is out of the bag about their house guests,' Wax said wearily on an exhale.

'Oh no!' Tallulah said, slapping a hand over her mouth, eyes wide, giggling

Everyone seemed to stop what they were doing to look at him. 'It's not funny, Tallulah,' Wax said, flashing her an angry glare. 'It's bloody bed knobs and broomsticks over there. Beccah's mother is one step away from the funny farm.'

There were a few more sniggers as everyone imagined disembodied objects flying all over the place. It was kind of funny. I took the opportunity to slip into the room and sit at the large kitchen table before I was noticed.

'Oh dear, what happened, darling,' Olivia said, immediately, while walking over and putting down a hot mug of tea in front of me. Guess I wasn't as unnoticed as I thought.

'It was Jedediah, and it was pretty serious really.' He looked straight at his brother, seated at the far end of the island. 'Remember The Wild Ride we were talking about?'

His brother frowned, 'Yeah, what about it?'

'Well, Jedediah found out that it's coming here in five days.'

'Oh my god!' Tallulah said, jumping to her feet from the sofa. She was always so dramatic. 'We're going off to hell. I knew it. We drank the waters. We're not meant to be here. That's it. We're so busted.' She began to pace erratically up and down. 'We need to get ready. Fight or hide or something.'

Everyone started to talk at once. Except me. I stayed an observer.

Ollie held out his arm for her to go to him for a hug. They seemed to have smoothed over their friction from yesterday. The indulgent smile he gave her melted my insides. She immediately flew to him and he arranged her snugly between his legs on the stool. She seemed immediately mollified as if that was all she needed.

'He thinks they want Sam,' Wax said, silencing everyone again.

They all looked at each other, then at me. It was a shock, as if I didn't even factor into the equation. 'What, Sam? She's too quiet and boring,' Tallulah said with her usual talent for tact.

'Thanks a lot, Tallulah,' I said, speaking up for the first time. But I hadn't taken offence. It was the truth. I really didn't do enough to be bad or offend anyone.

'This isn't Santa's naughty list, Tallulah,' Wax said, holding his head as if it hurt. 'But I agree. There must be some kind of mistake, or something we're missing.'

'What are we going to do? Because it will take someone. It won't go empty handed,' Ollie said, arranging Tallulah on his lap so he could talk around her.

Wax nodded thoughtfully. 'If we're not giving them Sam, then someone must go in her place.'

I sat there following the conversation as if I wasn't really there. Like I was above them having an out-of-body experience. I didn't believe for one minute there was anything anyone could do, but how I loved them all in that moment. Whatever had happened in my life before, the people in this room were my chosen family. Then I became aware that, one by one, all eyes drifted to mine. 'What?' I said, panicking someone had asked me a question.

Wax said one word. 'Helix.'

Helix was the obvious choice. He had come by way of The Ride; it made sense that he should go by it. But I didn't want him to go. The thought of my going to hell terrified me, but the thought of losing Helix and spending eternity alone scared me more.

My mouth had gone dry. I couldn't process this alone. 'OK, I'll talk to him. This afternoon, I promise.'

Wax gave me a single nod of respect. As if he understood what Helix meant to me. Then he turned back to his mother. 'And I think we need to invite the Whitelys back for dinner … probably tonight, Mum. They need your input to show everything can be alright.'

There were several groans from the boys and Tallulah hit her forehead with the heel of her hand. 'Oh no. They're so boring.'

Ollie gave her a little shake of reprimand and whispered something. She sobered immediately.

'Beccah's mum is a wreck, and her dad is only just holding the both of them together,' Wax continued.

As the only other people to have gone through something similar, Wax's parents understood. 'Of course, dear,' Olivia said, seeing it right away.

Jed, Wax's dad, put his arm around Olivia's shoulders and nodded too. 'We'll call them and invite them tonight.'

'Yes, as quickly as possible,' Olivia agreed, nodding, but looking far from happy about it.

'Do they know about your brother and everyone yet?' Jed asked.

Wax let out a long sigh and shook his head. 'I thought that was too much, what with everything they had to take on in their own house.'

'OK, well, tonight I think we have to tell them everything. What do you think, dear?' Jed said, looking lovingly down at his wife's adoring gaze.

'Should we come clean about all the goings on?' she said, turning to Wax.

Wax nodded. 'We'll play it by ear. But I think we have to one way or another. They can't take any more surprises.'

Everyone made their way over to the table I was already sitting at and ate a very late, sombre breakfast after that. I stayed as long as was polite, until I seized the chance, stole a croissant and headed for my room.

I was about to turn left at the top of the landing when Wax's voice rang clearly from the bottom of the stairs. 'Find out what you can.'

I stopped and looked down into his stern but expectant face and nodded awkwardly. He returned the nod and went back in the direction of the kitchen. My heart was beating hard at being caught escaping, but I swallowed and turned back in the direction of my room.

It felt cold and lonely after the warmth of the kitchen. I was coming to realise it was the lack of spirit energy. Helix was nowhere nearby.

The ribbon was still on the floor, so I picked it up and tied it back around the drawer knob. I checked my diary just to make sure there were no more entries and wrote: *Meet me in my dream please, Helix. I need to speak to you urgently.* Then I closed it, held it to my heart and put it back neatly in the drawer.

There was nothing else to do but go and lie on my bed and wait. I curled into a ball. It had been one hell of a night and day. Strangely, spending that amount of time with Wax wasn't nearly as bad as I'd imagined. Beccah was so lucky to have him looking out for her.

After wishing myself away from this place for so long, all

this had made me realise I didn't want to leave. I didn't want to leave my friends and, most of all, I didn't want to leave Helix. It seemed so unfair. Why did it have to be me or him?

Somewhere between one meandering thought or another, I must have dropped off to sleep. I was back in my sunny garden. Except this time, I felt more awake than ever before. Maybe it was because I was alone. I could see the vivid green grass clearly and not as a blur and the pastel gazebo was in fact made of white-painted wood and covered in flowers. The smell was heavenly.

I lay down on my back. There were a lot more clouds in the sky than I remembered and a rolling mist.

I leant up on my elbows. A creeping mist was quickly filling up the garden. This was new and my nerves prickled through my body as it got ready to run. It was getting so thick it was becoming hard to see more than a few feet in front of me. 'Helix, is that you?' I called out in a pathetic, small voice.

When no one answered, I scrambled to my feet and ran to the gazebo for cover.

And there he was.

Helix, walking purposefully out of the trees. He looked so different. Real. Strong. More serious. He was dressed completely in black, with a high-collared jacket done right up to his chin. It looked almost military, but without stripes. It was a snug fit, emphasising his trim physique and slim hips.

His hair was more striking too. Perhaps because when I saw it, it was always in a daze. Today it was falling forward in jet-black arrows down his face. He didn't stop until he'd walked right into the gazebo and was standing right in front of me, staring down with those golden, mesmerising eyes. His charisma was so powerful, I stepped back, bumping into the lattice wall.

He was so good-looking my insides swirled, so I couldn't make up my mind if I was excited or scared to see him. Either way, his effect on me was overwhelming. This was all so new. I'd never been this awake in his presence. It was hard to tell if I wanted to kiss him or run away.

He smiled a little as if he knew.

I narrowed my eyes. 'Are you using your powers on me, Helix?' I said, croakily, struggling to drag my gaze from his mouth.

He laughed and I loved the sound of it. 'Not consciously, no. Are you OK?'

I coughed to clear my throat, feeling a bit foolish. 'Did you know The Wild Ride was coming back in a few days and is coming for me?'

He stood rigidly still as if he had no idea. 'I knew it was passing nearby. How do you know this?'

'Jedediah, the spirit at Beccah's house, told us this morning.

He said something under his breath and went out of the gazebo to stare off into the distance. I followed him out and was surprised to find the fog had receded, but the sky was still full of clouds.

He turned around to look at me. 'We don't have much time. It will arrive before the first quarter of the next moon.'

'Five days,' I said, remembering Jedediah's bony hand.

Helix stalked closer until he was standing over me again, enthralling me with those eyes. 'I have a plan, but it means I will have to restore your memories.'

He touched my cheek and sent an electric current right through me. His frown of concern was the only thing stopping my bones melting in the heat coming off him. 'How bad can it be?' I said, hearing the tremor in my voice. 'I fell down a well. It was a tragedy.' I completely got that. I just didn't understand what he was reluctant to say.

He moved his thumb across my cheek again and a new bolt of electricity skipped through me. Every time he did it, my insides boiled up a little more. Like I was slowly dissolving. Melting away to soft dough in his hand.

'I took your memories so you could come to this house and live a life that was not burdened by them … scarred by them,' he added, his eyes dropping away for a second. 'I wanted you to have what was left of a normal childhood before adulthood robbed you of your innocence.'

His strange choice of words and worried, regretful expression pushed through his distracting electricity, leaving an uneasy weight at the bottom of my stomach. I had no idea what he could mean. What could possibly have happened that would have scarred me so much?

I shuffled awkwardly, unable to stay still. I was suddenly reminded of what kind of demon he was. Wax had reminded me never to forget that. He had already admitted that he couldn't help the strong attraction and drugging pheromones that were probably in his DNA. 'Did you do something more to me, Helix, than put me in a well?'

A wave of anger swept across his face in a whirlwind tempest, and for a moment I went to step back, but it went immediately. As if he was getting a hold on his emotions until he seemed exhausted, carrying an overwhelming sadness. 'No … not I, but another that should have been taking care of you.'

While my mind scrambled into a hundred follow up questions, he reached towards me and pulled me closer to him again. He gazed down at my hand that looked so small in his and gave it a squeeze. 'I wanted to protect you from it. But I can't hide the truth from you any longer. Tonight, I promise, I will reveal everything.'

He reluctantly released my hand and went to turn away. 'But how?' I said, lunging for his arm to pull him back.

He looked at me over his shoulder but continued to walk. 'Tonight. I'll take you on a psychic journey back in time. You will know everything and understand, but first we must go back to your room.'

'My room …Why?' I whined. The mist was already swirling around me. Helix was harder to see. 'What about the others. How long will I be away?' I was hanging back as if I could delay my return. Until a thick fog completely engulfed me.

I opened my eyes and I was staring up at the white ceiling of my bedroom. Before I could scream my frustration, the bed dipped and Helix sat staring down at me.

I was so surprised and pleased he hadn't left me, I grabbed onto his hand. But although I was awake, I could already feel my energy seeping out of me like sand in an hourglass.

He smiled a little and touched my forehead. It radiated heat through my whole body, but sped up the draining feeling. My eyelids were becoming heavy. 'I'm sorry. I can't help taking your life force from you. I must take more than usual for what I need to do.'

I fought the overwhelming wave of tiredness and struggled to sit up to face him, to prove I could be strong. It was so incredibly rare to see him real and in the flesh. I reached out a shaking arm that weighed a ton and pinched his cheek.

He frowned a little and laughed at the same time. 'What are you doing, silly?' he said, capturing my hand in his.

'Just checking.' I swooned, pinching the bridge of my nose. I couldn't pass out without at least asking. 'But why … why do you take my energy?'

I felt the bed move, forced my eyes open and hitched a breath of surprise. He was right there. Eyes, a few inches away. Golden, luring eyes. Lips brushing mine. Soft cushions. Tentative. Opening slightly, covering my mouth. My heart quickening so much, I thought it would beat right out of my chest. My breath left me. We were kissing. My first real, all-consuming kiss that I felt in my toes. Somewhere deep down, I was aware he was syphoning me. Like a plug coming loose in a bath and the water slowly seeping away. But it felt so good. Soothing. Blissful and I couldn't stop. I didn't want to stop. I wouldn't, until the last drop of life left me.

He left me hanging. Eyes closed and lips still pursed. I slowly lifted my heavy eyelids like a drunk and the look on his face would stay with me for ever. The seductive, half-closed citrine eyes. The way he ran his tongue over his lips like he'd slaked his thirst on a hot summer's day. He sighed contentedly and swallowed with a look of ecstasy. 'Mmm,' he sighed. 'You are even more beautiful than I imagined.'

I know I should have felt repulsed by it. Or at the very least scared. But I didn't. It was just who he was and he couldn't help it. 'So you *are* an incubus demon,' I said with a resigned sigh.

'And you are my Eitsvat – my chosen one.'

My heart stalled and fluttered. I didn't know where the word he used came from, but I knew what he meant.

'You are mine,' he clarified, kicking up my butterflies again like autumn leaves. 'I knew it from the day I came here.'

I swallowed, unsure what to say.

'Come,' he said, holding out his hand for me to take.

'Where are we going?'

'It's time to take you home.'

CHAPTER 12

There was no journey. No preamble or time lapse at all. The next moment, we were at my old house. The cottage on the other side of the wood I could never reach. Except this time, there was no barrier. After a brief pause to look at the tired, white pebble-dashed exterior and latticed windows, we walked right in through the gate, up the short driveway and up to the front door.

I was confused. 'How come?' I wanted to ask why it had been so easy, but Helix cut across me.

'We aren't here exactly. It's a memory. The day I came.'

I had no time to collect my thoughts to frame my next question because we were in my old room. I remembered it distinctly. Two single beds, pink-patterned duvets and a little girl fast asleep in one of them. Trish. My little sister.

It looked like any other kids' room. Closed curtains in the same pink cartoon pattern as the quilts, a toy box and a few posters on the wall of a couple of Disney princesses and popular TV stars of the time. I remembered them so clearly now. Trish, the cute little sister, who could only be about four or five. That made me about—

'Eight,' Helix said, following my thought process exactly. 'She was young. She mostly slept through it,' he explained.

I was about to ask what he meant when I heard the dreaded sound. My heart plummeted and my breaths went shallow.

A crash and then the shouting.

The wailing pleas coming from my mother. 'Graeme, please. We need to talk about it. Please don't go.'

'Stop nagging, woman. You're like an old crow. And would it hurt to put a comb through your hair once in a while? Why would I stay in and look at your tired old mug, eh?'

I was in the bed putting a pillow over my head. Eight years old and I was already so tired of living. I clearly remembered thinking, *I'm a little girl. This isn't right. He shouldn't be talking to my mum like that. I shouldn't have to listen to it.* God, I felt old, even then. Then would follow a bone-aching worry that Trish would wake up and be upset.

There was some more pathetic pleading from my mother, a door slammed and her crying by the front door. An engine starting on the drive and Graeme's car pulling off too fast.

It all came rushing back to me now like I'd never been away. My mum's sloe eyes. The stumbling. The unpredictable moods. Now, of course, I understood. At eight years old, I thought it was my fault. That having us kids was too much for her to handle.

She was an alcoholic. The strange bottles of clear liquid that turned up in the weirdest places. Like in my sister's toybox, the linen basket in the bathroom, or under the kitchen sink. All the places Graeme never went.

I remembered. I remembered it all.

He wanted me to call him Daddy, but I refused and always called him Graeme. He wasn't my father. My dad was a grainy memory in kaki with a blurred face. I remembered his smell. He smelled of fuel or oil or something when he hugged me and he had a tickly moustache. That was it. The sum total of my real dad.

Graeme and my mum argued because of her drinking and she drank because he didn't really want to be around her. It was clear as day to me now. Back then, he was the ogre that made her cry and I hated him for it. I barely slept because I lay awake listening for her rummaging in the house for bottles. Or the creeping in after a night in the pub. I had to be ready to cover Trish's ears for the inevitable fight to start. Sometimes, on very rare occasions, the bathroom light would go on and I'd see the orange glow around my door frame and I'd be filled with an overwhelming wash of relief. It filled every starving cell. Graeme either hadn't come home or they'd made it to bed without a shouting match. Then I'd sleep a dead and dreamless sleep that made me late for school.

Most of the time, I was just hungry. That memory over-shadowed everything else. Like a living thing of its own. Gnawing, grating, always on my mind, for me and for Trish. Shopping was forgotten more often than not and the cupboards were bare, except for little black pellets of mice droppings.

Hunger was usually the only thing that brought me out of my room, particularly at night. I watched my eight-year-old self slip out from beneath the quilt that smelled musty and needed a good wash and pad down the stairs, warily, to the kitchen. There were just two bedrooms upstairs. The stair-case came down into the living room. My mum was usually in a troubled sleep on the sofa with the TV left on. A flick-ering blue light. The only light in the room.

'Go on, she can't see you,' Helix prompted. Reminding me I was in a memory. I went over to look at her and stared down at her face. She seemed so achingly familiar now. The permanent frown. The shudder and whimper where she was crying in her dream. The black mascara tears that had dried on her cheeks, where she'd put on a full face of make-up before she'd passed out.

My stomach rumbled again and took me out to the messy kitchen. Bowls, pans and glasses were piled up in the sink of stale water. Something was hissing on the stove and smelled acrid like burning. I shot over to it. Something had completely boiled dry. Another boiled and spat. I turned off both burners, picked up a tea towel and pushed them off the heat. But my hands weren't my hands, they were the hands of a little girl. My hands at eight years old.

On the bright side, I guess my mum had attempted to cook something. Probably more for when Graeme got home than for either of us girls. She'd dressed up and then, when he didn't turn up, she drank and forgot all about it. About the pots. About us.

I took two slices of dry bread from the almost-empty packet in the bread bin and put them in the toaster. My staple diet. I remembered it all now. Breakfast crunchies for my sister. With or without milk, depending on the day of the week and whether my mother had been to the corner shop for cigarettes.

The key sounded in the door. The dreaded sound. My heart bolting up into my mouth. I sprinted from the kitchen up the stairs, taking two at a time. I shot back into my room before he saw me. Under the covers, shaking. Mouth dry. Listening. Straining for the slightest sound.

Graeme swearing. Stumbling up the stairs. His slow, drunken footsteps, *thump, thump,* halting the other side of my door. Breathing stopped. Sweat turning cold. *My dream. The Goblin.* Terrifying that I should be struck by that now. My subconscious had conjured it even without my memories. It was Graeme. I just knew. Reaching out for me into my cosy new life, without me even knowing it.

The door clicked and creaked open. I couldn't breathe. I daren't. There could be no clue I was awake.

Then a huge crash. Graeme swore and the door clicked closed again.

Danger averted. He'd gone.

I breathed. Huge lungfuls of glorious relief.

His footsteps retreated, bringing my heart rate down to far less painful.

That was when everything Helix was showing me began to make sense. I looked at Helix standing next to me and I was my older self again and he nodded, knowing I'd got there at last: it was the first time he'd protected me.

It all made sense. Each time was always the same. Whenever my mum was out cold, the door would slowly open and something would bang. A phone would ring. The TV would go on extra loud. Even a smoke alarm (when we eventually had one because of my mum's forgetfulness). Graeme would go off, investigate and the danger would be diverted. Graeme left me alone. For the time being.

But I never really felt alone again after that. A feeling of another person in the house was growing. I was completely aware of it. It felt comforting. Not sinister. Warmth. Sleep. I managed wonderful, restful dreams for the first time. My safe place. A young boy. It all appeared from that day.

I turned to look at Helix. His eyes were full of tears when he knew I'd remembered him. I saw him. The skinny black-haired boy with yellow eyes. Putting a finger to his lips and whispering, 'Shhh!' I was never scared of him. Even though I had no idea who he was or where he came from. He was not much bigger than me, but he was always close by, quietly being fierce and protective.

Some nights, if it was really cold – when there were no

coins for the electric meter and so no heating – the boy would hold my hand and wrap me in blankets and cover me with his body heat. 'Who are you? I whispered next to his cheek.

'Helix,' he whispered back.

WE WERE inseparable after that and he made my intolerable life bearable. However, I was getting older and my situation was changing. It all became very serious very quickly.

Suddenly I was there again. 'I'm just nipping out to the shop!' I heard my mother's voice call.

My heart sank. I looked straight into Helix's eyes. They softened immediately, like he knew what was coming. I didn't understand right away until I heard it. The key turning in the front door far too quickly to be my mother. Helix was pulling the loft ladder down. Except it wasn't Helix. Not at this age anyway. He was cute like an imp. Small with a mass of black curly hair, but the same lively cat's eyes. 'Come on, quickly!' he said.

Helix bundled me up into the loft and quickly pushed the ladder up after me. 'Hide!' he ordered as he lowered the loft hatch behind me.

I was terrified and alone. The loft was dark and confined. It was hot and the sloped ceiling was a low triangle bearing down on me. I couldn't stand up. There were suitcases and boxes everywhere. Then I heard it. 'Sammy … come here. I've got something for you.' He sang the words as if we were playing a game. He was never this friendly when my mum was around.

I put my ear to the hatch. My heart was beating so loudly, it felt like it was hitting the wood. Strangely, I never questioned why I ran. I trusted Helix implicitly. I just knew Graeme's motives for seeking me out weren't good. Then I heard the thumps on the stairs, just like in my goblin night-mare. Like he was deliberately trying to scare me. I closed my eyes and held my breath.

They came to a sudden stop right beneath me.

There was the agonising pause that always followed.

Sweat trickled down my forehead into my eyes and I could barely breathe. 'Where are you, you little minx?' he said from right underneath the hatch.

Then followed a crash.

'What the F—'

The TV went on. Then the bath in the opposite direction.

Helix. My wonderful, brave Helix. Running around the house like a whirling dervish. Throwing vases. Slamming cupboards and making comical ghost noises.

Graeme roared, 'Where are you, you little ba—'

I was immediately back in my own skin, staring up into Helix's eyes glassy with tears. 'You always knew, didn't you? What he wanted.' I said, tears falling onto my cheeks. They weren't tears for me, but for all the sacrifices Helix had made. His whole childhood had been spent protecting me.

He swallowed like it was difficult. 'It was why I lived here.'

Just like when we were small, I took him at his word. Everything made a dreadful kind of sense now. Graeme lying in wait. Seizing every opportunity when my mum was out. Coming home at odd times of the day just to look for me. Usually when I was home from school. It happened more and more, the older I got, and now I knew why. An electricity, an excitement, something was building to a fever pitch.

I remembered it all. Helix never gave up. He always found me ingenious places to hide. In the airing cupboard, inside a suitcase, but most often in the attic, where I'd seen his bed of old rags he'd stolen from the house that first time he'd hidden me there. It was where he lived. My heart ached at the poor, bareness of it. All those years and I never knew.

There was also my sister. I always felt bad for her. She would cry to come with me, but Helix would hold the tops of my arms and shake me. 'She is safe,' he would say. 'For now.' Then I understood she was too young. What Graeme wanted was bad and it was from someone a little older than Trish.

I could never let her know where I hid, but Helix explained her crying was the perfect distraction. I felt wretched and guilty, but it worked a lot, often pulling Graeme away from finding me just in the nick of time. It seemed to act like an alarm on his bad conscience. It deflected him. Snapped him out of it, to go back to his normal activities of the day.

I tried to act normal and go to school, but I felt detached from everyone around me. I remembered Ollie, Tallulah, Joe, Josh, Archie and Nicola. They tried to include me even then. I wanted to be part of them, I really did. However, no matter how I tried to act normal, I could never allow myself to get close. I had too many secrets. Terrible ones they wouldn't understand. My mind was always elsewhere. Trapped in this cottage.

I understood then. Everything Helix had freed me from.

I loved him. *How could I have forgotten?* He was everything.

The closeness of our bond. The strength of it.

With no time for friends, I'd rush home to begin the nightmare all over again. But Helix was always there. Waiting for me. Watching and waiting with those eyes, filled with love and longing for me.

WE ARRIVED BACK in my room at the Waxley-Black place. Helix looked grey. He had to be exhausted because we were sitting next to each other on my bed and I was still awake.

I jumped up, instantly concerned for him. He looked ill. 'Oh my god, Helix. What's happening?'

'Tired … that's all … just … need … rest.' He slowly lay back, flat on the bed, almost passing out.

I picked up his hands and tried to pull him back up. 'Helix! Please! What is it? What can I do?'

It came to me like a slap to the forehead. So simple, I don't know why I didn't think of it before. I shimmied down to lie next to him as closely as I could.

He was still there. Eyes barely open, he turned his head to face me. His sunburst eyes had dimmed to the colour of peanut butter. They looked so sad and soulful. Pretty ironic for a demon who was supposed to have no soul. 'What are y—' he tried to say.

But I put my finger on his lips to shush him. 'You were my best friend – *are* my best friend,' I corrected. 'You were my only friend, for so long,' I said, fighting back tears and pushing back the loose strands of black hair from his face.

'Forever,' he said, closing his eyes, savouring the light touch of my finger.

'Why did you feel the need to hide all that from me?'

His eyes flashed open and he stiffened right through the length of his body. My breathing stalled at the immediate change in him. 'Because of what came later. On your sixteenth birthday.'

The flash of anger in him subsided, as if he couldn't keep it up and his eyelids fluttered closed. There was no showing me what he meant today. He needed to build up his strength and I knew what I had to do. The very thing I'd done when he was tired ever since we were kids.

I edged closer and with my heart jumping and fluttering, I brushed my lips against his. It was miraculous. I felt the strength of his pull instantly. Like he'd literally lassoed my heart and was drawing on it in tugs.

His eyes flashed open again, but the feeling didn't stop. He couldn't help himself.

A wave of fatigue flowed through me and his eyes pulsed bright, headlamp yellow, then settled down to their usual colour. It was remarkable.

I felt OK again, but finally, I really understood. Any intense emotion was like oxygen to him. His body sucked it in and absorbed it without thinking. It filled his cells and nourished him. Like food. Something completely natural.

We were barely touching, but I could still feel a stream of my energy leaving me. He was quiet, just studying my face as he fed, as if he knew I was working it all out.

So Wax was right. 'You *are* an incubus – an energy vampire,' I whispered.

He closed the gap and brushed my mouth with his again. A stronger feeling swept through me. His eyes looking straight into mine, brightening again like a dynamo and settling down. I, on the other hand, began to feel dizzy.

He drew apart a little instantly. 'I guess that's why my mother left me to grow up with you. My kind can't grow up at home. We need to feed to become adults and there was more emotion radiating from your house than from any other around here. Sadness. Anger. Fear.' He paused. His body stiffening and his jaw clenching again. 'And lust – not the good kind.' His gaze dropped away and I wanted to ask him about it, but I was side-tracked by how he knew. I wanted to know how he got to know the unhappiest person in town was me?

'What did you see that pulled you to me?' I asked, my mouth suddenly tissue paper dry.

'You were like no one else I'd ever seen,' Helix said, searching my face as if it was a wonder to him. You have a glow about you. Like your love and joy is captured inside and seeps out in whisps of light. It lures and tantalises me even now. Whoever unlocks that will be a very happy male.'

I was initially surprised because he hadn't focused in on all the darkness that surrounded me, but my light. A light I never knew I had. And then what he'd actually said dawned on me, it heated my cheeks and kicked my heart against my chest. He'd used the word male. Not boy, not even man, but male. Him. I knew then that if it was ever anyone, it would be him. After everything. He'd given me his childhood, his whole life to protect me. After everything we meant to each other.

Before I knew it, we were kissing again. Except this was me. I was in control. I was rolling on top of him. Feeling myself weighing against his strong, larger body. His arms tightening around me, going along with me instantly. Squeezing me to him. Kneading, sending pleasure waves through my veins and reaching every part of my body. My tongue began to taste him for the first time and I was drifting. Falling ...

I landed heavily in the garden of my safe place. I was in the soft grass looking up into mischievous yellow eyes. I frowned, confused and went to push him off. 'What happened? Why did you bring me here? I want to go back. I was angry and disappointed with him. It was real and happening and I wanted to continue with the first real kiss of my life.

He laughed loudly and rolled, pinning me down with his body. 'I did nothing,' he said, continuing to laugh. 'You rejuvenated me and filled me with your strength, which means you fell asleep.' He rubbed the pad of his thumb across my cheek and smiled indulgently. 'Thank you.' His eyes dropped unmistakably to my lips.

I, on the other hand, did not find it funny. It was frustrating. 'So that is always going to happen?' I said, my voice rising to a squeak.

He shrugged a little. 'I guess … I mean, I don't know. I think we need to practice,' he said, his grin widening at his idea of a joke.

I scowled, but it was getting harder to stay mad at him.

He schooled his features. 'What I'm trying to say is, if we can get good at it, maybe I can manage not to take so much of your essence, so you can stay awake a little longer.'

I absorbed that. I knew he was trying to soften the blow that it was unlikely. Then it struck me. 'Are we still kissing on my bed?'

He bobbed his head while he considered that. 'Kind of, I suppose. Our mouths are joined while I syphon your energy.'

My eyes went wide and my cheeks flushed pink. I felt suddenly hot, like all my clothes were too small. I was reminded of Ollie's explanation that an incubus wanted sex. I swallowed. I just had to know. 'So where does the sex part come into it?'

Helix burst into laughter, as if I'd said the funniest thing he'd ever heard. He rolled off me but still kept hold of my hand. We both looked up at the white fluffy clouds overhead.

'Honestly, I'm not sure. I've never done it,' he said, turning his head to look at my reaction.

I did the same and studied those yellow eyes. I believed him. 'Neither have I.'

He grinned. 'I know … was there, remember.' He narrowed his eyes craftily and looked back at the sky. 'I would have drained any spotty teenager for daring to touch you.'

I don't know why that made my insides tingle, but it did. I studied his profile.

'My uncle said it will happen when I'm ready to be an

adult.' He faced me then and looked so childlike. So vulnerable. 'I am still a youngling.'

I couldn't break my gaze. I just stared into those wonderfully soulful, apologetic eyes and knew I had fallen for him and it had happened a very long time ago. He had been my only true friend. The one who protected me from a darkness so bad, I couldn't even go there in my mind yet. He hid me, comforted me through my tears when my own family couldn't. But I knew I could never fully let myself go around him until I knew the full and terrible story. 'What happened that last day?' I asked, my voice a barely audible croak. 'My sixteenth birthday. How did I end up a Shade, here, at Waxley-Black Manor?' Somehow, the two just didn't seem to mix in my mind.

Helix let out a long breath and looked up at the sky. His brow furrowed while he thought about that for a moment. He was gathering his thoughts and deciding on how he was going to begin something clearly hard to say.

'I need to know, Helix, otherwise I can never let go of the past.'

He sat up, swallowed and nodded, resigned. As if he knew this day was always going to come. He began plucking little tufts of grass with his fingers and letting them go. Then his eyes shot to mine as I slowly sat up to join him. 'You have to remember that this cat and mouse game with your stepfather had gone on for a very long time. Since I came when we were eight years old. I guess he'd pieced together there was another presence in the house. One that was toying with him to protect you.'

'What happened on my sixteenth birthday?' I prompted.

Helix rolled his head on his neck in misery. He didn't want to go on. His eyes looked dull and hopeless when he finally rested them on me. 'It started on the day before your birthday...'

Helix was pulling at the blades of grass again. 'I was getting nervous. I felt the excitement building in your stepfather – and not in a good way,' he said, flashing his eyes at me, guiltily.

My blood was rising to a dull thud in my temples. 'Go on,' I urged. Needing him to say it. I wasn't sure exactly, but I had a huge suspicion I knew what it was. Some masochistic part of me needed it spelt out. I had to know categorically. 'So, what happened, exactly, Helix?'

'He worked out that whoever was helping you lived in the attic. At first, he thought it was his own paranoia or the drink. But then I think he thought I was a ghost or some sort of poltergeist because he electrified the loft hatch to keep me there. He must have planned it for some time. Of course it only slowed me down, but it was enough.'

I swallowed down acid that had begun to come up in my mouth, dreading what he was going to say.

'I'd felt it building in him for weeks. I should have done more,' he said, shaking his head miserably. He looked at me and his eyes were full of tears. 'So I showed you the old well.'

He shrugged and looked away. 'It was completely overgrown and covered in brambles. The wall around it had long crumbled away, leaving just a hole. No one knew it was there. Still don't. The original house had been much closer to the woods and the old well had been forgotten when the new cottage was built.'

'Then what happened?' I asked, covering his hand in mine to stop him plucking the grass again.

He flashed his eyes irritably and I let his hand go. 'I found an old rope that could hold my weight, then I tied it around a tree and tested it. The walls were crumbling inside and had made a ledge to stand on. I figured with the rope and everything, it was safe. I planned to hide you in the well when I sensed danger, tie you properly with the rope and help you into the well down to the ledge. Then I'd come and get you out when the danger had passed, when your mother and sister got home.'

'But something went wrong,' I said, reading the bitterness on his face. It sounded like a good enough plan.

Helix nodded a little, living the misery all over again on his face. 'I should have seen it.'

'What, Helix? Tell me, please.' My heart was jumping and skipping and I was sweating with a white-hot fear.

'It came a day earlier than I thought. The day before your birthday. All along I'd sensed your birthday was some sort of feverish deadline that Graeme was working towards. I missed the change. I should have seen it.' Tears were now on Helix's cheeks. I wanted to hug him, but he had to go on.

'Your stepfather gave money to your mum and sent her out with your sister to get a birthday cake. Your mother was thrilled. Easily bought, that he would be there for a family party. They got up early, especially, and went while you were still asleep so as not to spoil the surprise. Your stepfather went along with it. Getting up too and working in his garage to hide his excitement and keep up the pretence.'

My mind drifted back. It all seemed so plausible. I suppose there were brief moments. Small snippets and hints that my mother could be loving when her heart wasn't overtaken by a constant, unbearable pining for Graeme. But my wistfulness soon hit a brick wall and my heart was beating at what happened next. 'Then what?'

'I felt his energy screaming at me, even from my loft bed. Filling me, lighting up my blood cells. He was feeding me, even from all the way out there, Sam,' he said, absolute despair in his eyes.

I just swallowed and nodded for him to continue.

'I tried the handle and a bolt of electricity sent me clean across the room and knocked me out. It must have only been for a few moments, but I woke foggy and uncoordinated. I used my weight and crashed right through the loft hatch, landing on the hallway floor. I felt stunned, but nothing was broken. I rushed to your room and he was there. Leering over you. You were crying. Pleading. And he was … he was …' Helix was openly crying.

I closed my eyes. Strangely, in my mind's eye, all I saw was the hideous hooked nose and the shadowy, crab-like fingers of my recurring nightmare. And with that, I took a deep breath and grounded myself. 'What did you do?' I asked in a cracked whisper.

I picked up your lacrosse racket and smashed him over the head with it. I told you to run. And you did. You ducked under his arm and ran out in just your nightshirt. Then I truly became what I am, as I smelled the badness on him. I absorbed him as much as I could, but I was still too young and weakened from the electric shock. I couldn't even materialise to scare him. All I could do was hit him with a barrage of things and hope that it gave you enough time to get away.

He began to search the house for you, ransacking as he went in his temper. Every time he went to give up and start to look outside, I would do something. Like turn on the bath. Throw pans on the floor.'

'What happened when my mother came back?' I asked. I couldn't imagine how Graeme could have explained away the mess.

'He blamed it on you,' Helix said in amazement. He said you'd had a meltdown because you wanted to go somewhere and he'd said no. Then, when your mother looked doubtful, he used the usual manipulation tactic; that she never backed him up and slammed out of the house back to his garage. I should have come straight out, but Graeme came back in to get rid of his evidence around the loft hatch. I waited to make sure he didn't go out to look for you. I figured you'd be safe,' he said, his eyes pleading with me to understand. 'I didn't come out to check on you till it was too late.' Helix put his head in his hands and sobbed.

I scrambled closer onto my knees and cradled him in my arms as he wept. Helix's heartbreak and the last revelation of what happened that day, forced the veil on my memories to finally drop away. I remembered every last detail perfectly. I remembered how I never wanted to be alone with Graeme. How I always had a weird sixth sense about him and that his intentions were never good. How he looked at me in a way he shouldn't and how it made me feel ugly inside. I remembered that last terrible day. *When he* – those dreadful, clammy, crooked hands. Always *hands hands hands*. I shuddered. My fear. Freezing me. I didn't fight. I never fought. I was unable. Until Helix woke me from my paralysis and screamed at me to run.

And I did.

I ducked under Graeme's arm and ran as fast as I could. Like a tornado propelled me, all the way to the well. Sharp stones, twigs and thorns cut into my feet, but I still didn't stop. I didn't feel it and I didn't look back. I didn't even breathe until I grabbed the rope and clambered down with no thought or hesitation. 'The ledge,' I said as the final piece of the puzzle came to me.

Helix nodded. He was watching me in misery as everything finally fell into place. His eyes were now red from crying. 'It gave way. You fell several feet down into the water. By the time I got there, you'd drowned … You'd hit your head … If only I'd got there sooner. Or strengthened the ledge.'

I had no memory of that. Just darkness, the smell of clay and slippery hands on the rope. I didn't blame Helix. In fact, I felt numb with realisation. 'But I didn't loop the rope around me like you showed me. I just panicked,' I said, as a flood of relief washed over me. The feeling was so strong, I laughed. 'It wasn't your fault, Helix.'

He sat up, faced me squarely and looked stunned.

All I could think was how much I loved him. I pulled him to me and kissed him hard. He hadn't killed me. It was just a tragic accident. 'It wasn't your fault,' I said again and again between kisses.

He simply kissed me back over and over in a daze. When at last I stopped kissing him, he stared at me in wonder.

'You did everything you could to help me,' and he had. 'You were just a boy.' Just an adolescent boy, left all on his own. He might be a demon, but there was only so much a boy of his age could do.

I finally let him go and smiled at him. He seemed bewildered as if my reaction had been the last thing he'd been expecting. 'So how did I end up here at Waxley-Black Manor?'

Helix shrugged. 'Luck … circumstance … fate. Not sure. The master of the house was practising dark magic that pulled spirits from this realm before they could pass over.'

'Shades,' I whispered.

Helix nodded. 'After I left your body, I wandered the forest in my grief, not knowing where to go. Pulled in the same direction, I guess. I found you on the path. I couldn't believe it. I was so happy at first. But then I saw that you were traumatised. That what had happened had been so terrible, your mind would have splintered if you faced it. So I did the only thing I could think to do, and that was to drain your mental energy. My uncle had taught me. I could take human memories to syphon their energy without them knowing. And apparently it worked on spirits too. Except with you, I had to take a little more,' he said, looking guilty. 'I took you to the brink and took them all. Even the good ones. I had to. They were so mixed in with the bad and there was no time to sift through them all, I figured a clean slate was best.'

'Even the ones of you,' I said, sadly, touching the side of his face. My heart ached at the huge sacrifice he'd made. He'd relegated himself to the shadows, to watch over me. Never to come near and show me who he was to me. A tear escaped down my cheek.

'I saw the others here recognise you right away. They took you in and I knew you'd be safe. So I rushed back to the cottage and put the barrier around it so you would never know the heartache that happened there.'

'But what about Graeme. The police. Didn't he get arrested?'

Helix shook his head. 'He said you'd had an argument and stormed out, and after a while it was assumed you'd run away.'

I remembered the missing persons' article. It had been a complete fabrication. It had happened the day before, for a start. 'Wasn't my mum suspicious?' But as I asked the question, I already knew. Graeme would have talked his way around it and my mother would have believed him. Because it was easier. Because it didn't make waves. Even with the reasoning behind why they should lie to the media.

Helix shook his head.

'My sister,' I said, quietly to myself. 'I prayed she would have known I'd never have just left her.'

'The police came and questioned everyone. They even scoured the woods, but they never found the well. Everything seemed to fit his story of a teenage runaway.'

Tears were now streaming down my face as I began to cry properly. It all started to hit me, one thing after another. 'Couldn't you have told someone?' I sobbed, hopelessly.

'Only you can see me, Sam, and even then, rarely in the daytime. I couldn't exactly walk into a police station.' He looked at me, exasperated. 'You have to remember that your old life had already gone. I needed to watch over you in your new one. That had to be my first priority. If I could have saved you from any of it, I would have done so.'

I felt instantly guilty. There was no point in directing my anger towards him, that Graeme had got off scot-free. 'You did … you did save me,' I said, pulling myself together. Despite how sad and tragic it all was, I had to remember that Helix had suffered too. He was just a boy, thrown away by his mother to fend for himself and all he'd done was worry over me. 'You were all alone,' I said, a sob escaping me.

'No I wasn't,' he said, pulling me into his lap. 'I was never alone and neither were you. We had each other … we'll always have each other. We are paired, you and I. It's the greatest gift my mother could have given me.'

I tried to argue and pull out of his arms, but he held me and kissed the top of my head. 'My uncle visits me from time to time, don't forget, just to check up on me. I'm not forgotten.'

I immediately stopped crying and thought about that.

'The man you were talking to in the woods?' Helix paused for a moment, then nodded. He was gazing at me lovingly. Every little thing about him was so distracting. Even pushing back stray strands of hair behind my ear. 'I am loved ... you are loved,' he said in a whisper.

We were kissing again. A deep, languid, drugging kiss that I never wanted to end. Helix eventually pulled out of it, breathing heavily. 'I must send you back to yourself. We've already been too long. I'm taking too much of you.'

I was about to dissolve into disappointment, but he held up my chin. 'Please listen to me, Sam. Danger is coming. The Ride will return. My uncle is with it and this time they *will* take a soul. They were cheated when you were made into a Shade. I kept you and a debt is owed.'

'But you didn't make me a Shade, Wax's uncle did. Surely it's not your fault.'

'It makes no difference to The Ride. And there's something else to consider. Your sister is getting older. The energy is building in your old house again, I can feel it. Your sister is no longer safe.'

My hand went to my mouth as a sob escaped me. 'Trish,' I whispered, remembering the cute little girl I looked out for as best I could. She'd been alone for almost two years. I wondered how much she'd grown and remembered the sad, skinny girl of the other day. No wonder she looked so unhappy. With me gone, there was no buffer. My mouth had emptied of moisture and my blood went cold. 'We have to do something.'

'We will,' Helix said, pulling me to my feet. 'We will think of a plan.'

I collapsed against him.

'Now we need to go.'

· · ·

WHEN I BLINKED AWAKE, Helix was gone and I was back in my bed. I sat up suddenly and looked around me. The lamp was on and the room was wrong again. The cold, creeping feeling slowly slithered up my spine because I knew and dreaded what was coming. The old alarm clock next to me clicked, making my eyes shoot straight to it. 1 a.m. As if the alarm was set but the little arm was across, stopping the bell from ringing.

Where was I?

This wasn't Waxley-Black Manor. It was more like my old bedroom at my old cottage. Except there was only one bed, but the room layout was the same.

My heart slowed a little and I attempted to swallow with an impossibly dry mouth. Maybe this was another dream place. Although somehow I knew that Helix was not responsible for this one.

Then came the first thump. Then another. I felt myself whimper and put my hand across my mouth to keep myself quiet. I wanted to pull the covers over my head, but I couldn't move. I could never move. It all became obvious to me then. I knew I'd been having this dream forever, or variations of it.

The clomping stopped and I held my breath.

I looked at the doorknob. The loose, jangling brass doorknob. That always came next.

There it was. A hand on it from the other side and the slow, dreadful turning.

It stopped.

There was always a pause. An eternity of silence to keep me guessing, whether he would creep in or slope away before the door slowly opened. Painstakingly, excruciatingly slowly, in case the door creaked. Then it all came back to me as if it was yesterday. Graeme constantly oiling all the door hinges. My mother thought he was crazy and OCD about it.

A vivid picture flashed into my brain of Helix reaching his hands up and hanging from the doors like some kind of bat. I'd thought it was some weird demon thing at the time. Now, of course, it made perfect sense. The wave of love I felt for him then physically hurt in my chest. Now I understood. He was pulling down the doors so they creaked again and I would have a warning.

The knowledge fortified me a little. I clenched my teeth and balled my hands into fists as the door began its achingly slow journey to open. My breaths went shallow, but I was ready for the goblin today.

The door opened to the angle of about six o'clock and I got the first glimpse of the long shadow of spindly, deformed hands. The way they moved looked like they were dancing. Like a puppeteer, deliberately trying to scare children. Like they were disembodied and had a life of their own. Scurrying a little. Index finger raised. Stopping to look around and creeping forward again. Closer. Skittering forward. Until the tip of the nose. The grotesque shadow, hooked nose, like every bad guy cartoon character I'd ever seen, peered around the doorway.

The urge to hide was unbearable. But I knew what this was. For the first time in my whole miserable life, I knew this was my fear's interpretation of Graeme.

He stilled

He knew.

My heart beat three painfully hard beats, like a punch to the chest.

One.

Two.

Three.

Until he flew.

CHAPTER 14

'Sam ... Sam, for God's sake, wake up!'

I was shouting and flailing. Batting grabbing hands away from me. Only gradually slowing when nothing bad happened.

I blinked, completely disorientated and out of breath, to see four pairs of startled eyes staring down at me. Archie, Ollie, Tallulah and Nicola.

I swallowed and gulped for air.

'Thank god. You've been out for hours and we couldn't wake you. Not cool, Sam,' Tallulah said.

I was still staring at them one by one, mixed up and confused, desperately trying to get my bearings.

The next thing I knew, Wax came bowling in as if he'd run all the way from his room, followed by Joe and Josh. The others hurriedly parted to allow him closer to my bed. His eyes skated over me, taking in my disarray. 'You OK?' he asked.

I didn't want to rake over the nightmare that just happened. I hadn't made sense of that yet. My mind naturally shot to the last conversation I'd had with Helix. 'It's Trish. She's in danger. We have to stop him.'

The others all looked to Wax to take the lead. 'Beccah's parents will be here soon. We have that fiasco to deal with first. Then we'll come up with a plan.'

I was grateful, but I itched to get going. It didn't help because Wax looked troubled. Like there was something else playing on his mind. Everyone began to file out of my door, leaving him the last to leave. He paused and turned. 'Are you OK for this? You look exhausted.'

I couldn't work out his expression. He was looking at me strangely. Calculating. Wary.

I nodded, anyway. Even though I had no idea really if that was true. I just wanted to get this over with so we could concentrate on Trish. It was something I couldn't do alone.

'Get ready,' he said and left.

I got up and took a quick shower, running everything over in my head. I squashed the goblin, immediately putting it down to processing my fear. I was satisfied, now I knew what it was. A nightmare. Real though it seemed, it wasn't nearly as important as rescuing Trish.

What I couldn't seem to get out of my head was living and reliving my encounter with Helix and Wax's troubled look, after. One heated my blood to distraction and the other was a bucket of iced water.

That was it. I had to find out. I slipped on my robe and tiptoed to Wax's room. I was about to knock when I heard whispered voices in the hallway below. I crept to the edge of the wall to peer over the carved wooden bannister. Wax was talking to Ollie at the foot of the stairs. It was in hushed tones, but the vaulted ceiling was like a church and meant I could hear what they were saying.

'You think she's making it all up?' Ollie said, sounding shocked.

My heart spiked as I strained to hear every word.

'No, of course not,' Wax hissed. 'I think it's real to her.'

Her. Me? Does he mean me?

I made myself flat against the wall as both their eyes darted up.

'Why would she do something like that?' Ollie asked. 'Doesn't make sense.'

I crouched lower and peered through the gaps in the balcony to see them. There was no way I could do the polite thing and walk away. My heart was now banging the walls of my chest.

'Think about it,' Wax was saying. 'Just suppose that her stepfather did something so terrible that her mind had to fracture just to cope with it. You hear of stuff like that all the time.'

'Yeah, in films, maybe. So you think she invented this Helix as a coping mechanism?' Ollie shook his head and turned away while he thought about that. 'We *are* a household of supernaturals, Wax. She could also be telling the truth,' Ollie said, turning back to face him.

Wax tipped his head at his good point. 'Think about it, though. An incubus, Ollie. Of all things. What does an incubus stand for? Everything it is. Everything it wants revolves around sex.'

Ollie looked stunned.

I felt stunned.

My face burned and my heart shuddered painfully.

'And now this thing has warned her that her sister is in trouble?'

In my dazed shock, I had straightened up to my full height and they both looked up at me. I was too completely shattered to attempt to hide. I just stared down at their busted faces. 'You're wrong,' I said after a beat. I wanted to cry, but I was still too shocked. 'You just can't see him that's all. Only I c—' I couldn't even finish my sentence because even I heard how weak it sounded. *No way. There was no way.*

By the time I came out of my trance, Wax had come up the stairs and was right in front of me. 'Sam, please. I didn't mean—'

'Didn't mean what?' I cut right over him. Suddenly I couldn't stand the sight of him. 'That I'm some sort of pathetic loser. So traumatised I have to make up an imaginary friend, even though I'm dead?' I ended up screaming at him.

I went to shove past him but he caught me by the arm and turned me to face him again. 'Wait, please Sam.'

The temperature around us suddenly dropped to minus twenty and we could see our breath. Wax looked down at the frost on the hairs of his forearm.

'I suppose I have the power to do that too.' I felt the power of Helix surge all around me.

Wax glared back at me. 'Perhaps, Sam. Perhaps the power is in you. That's all I'm saying.' His eyes were sad and full of sympathy. I couldn't bear the pity in them. I wanted to cry and rail. I was angry. Confused. But most of all, I was scared. Because a tiny part hid from the idea that he could possibly be right. Good and special things like Helix simply didn't happen to me.

I pushed past him and this time he made no attempt to stop me. I ran. All the way along the corridor, up my small staircase and straight into my attic room. I slammed the door and threw myself face down onto the bed, where I screamed, kicked and punched out my frustration. I didn't stop until I felt myself falling, falling, falling into my vortex of sleep. Landing eventually into soft grass.

I was immediately hoisted up into strong arms and he held me. Helix gripped me tightly, surrounding me in warm comfort and the smell of winter spices. My nose burrowed into his chest to get more of him.

This couldn't be in my head. He was holding me. He was. His hand gently passing over my back to soothe me. I wasn't imagining it. I wasn't making it up. I took a huge inhale of his scent. 'You are real, aren't you?' I said, slowly pulling my face away from his chest to look up into deep citrine eyes.

He dipped his head and planted a slow, lingering kiss on my lips like warm honey. 'Can't you show yourself to them?' I asked, my voice gone to a croak and my eyes still on his mouth.

He shook his head sadly. 'I think only you can see me because of who we are to each other. There are strict laws. Humans would soon wipe out younglings before they could grow up.' He thought about it for a beat while I studied his smooth, dark skin in detail. I'd never had the opportunity this close before. I was lost in his long, dark lashes and stunning eyes, when he continued, 'Maybe when I'm an adult, for a select few. I'd need to ask my uncle.'

I was disappointed and frustrated that I had no way of proving I was telling the truth, but I guess I understood.

'I can't afford to get pulled out of here because of some misdemeanour.'

I saw the sense in that. My blood ran cold at the thought.

He smiled his crooked, small smile that melted my insides. It always made me wonder what devilish thought he was thinking. 'Come on, temptress. I must get you back to your room. You have a dinner party to attend.'

My heart sank at the thought of a whole evening with Wax the doubter and the traumatised Whitelys when all I wanted was to spend more time with Helix. 'How am I a temptress?'

. . .

THE ABSOLUTE LAST thing I felt like doing was sitting at a table with two humans on the edge of a nervous breakdown, when I was only just holding it together myself. I was still furious with Wax. Yet here I was. Hair combed, same dress – as it was the only one I owned – scowling at Wax across the big dining room table.

If last time had felt awkward, then this one was excruciating. No one had hardly anything to say because all the surface chat had been said at the last cringeworthy dinner. It had only been two days. Everyone was being cowards, frightened to start a conversation in case they put their foot into danger territory.

Wax, I realised, was very good at having a conversation without words. He flashed his eyes at me a few times. Once guiltily, then with annoyance and, lastly, get over it. I wanted to catapult my mashed potato at him. But I didn't. His real focus was on Beccah. She looked miserable. Jean, her mother, was sitting next to her, looking bewildered in a catatonic daze. Her father, John, the other side of her, looked like he hadn't slept for a week. Probably hadn't.

The rest of us coughed, fidgeted and told Olivia how great the food was at least five times each.

Then, after I'd almost given up, Jed cleared his throat and decided to speak up.

Tallulah whispered, 'Finally,' far too loudly.

'Bret said you had quite the night the other night.'

Jean responded for the first time since she arrived and actually moved her eyes to look at her husband. John bobbed his head and raised his eyebrows. 'You could say that.' He put his knife and fork in the centre of his plate and pushed it away from him. 'You know, Jed, we haven't been here that long, but Jean and I have been talking and I don't think we're cut out for life in rural England.'

There was stunned silence as everyone tried to process the last thing they'd expected.

'What's that supposed to mean, Dad?' Beccah said, in a high, squeaky voice.

'What I mean, darling, is, I don't think we will be able to stay.'

'No, Dad!' Beccah shouted, throwing her cutlery onto her plate and going to stand up, but Wax kept her in her place with a hand on her arm. It was loving but firm, knowing this needed careful management.

'I'm sorry, Beccah, but it's just too much for your mother.' He looked at Olivia and Jed apologetically, who hadn't said a word and he went to get up, bringing Jean with him. 'I'm sorry. We shouldn't have come, but Jean needed any excuse to get out of that house.'

Olivia and Jed were soon on their feet too. 'No, no, it's our fault. So insensitive of us to expect it so soon. Why don't you stay here? At least while you sort everything out,' Olivia said, with a hand on Jean's arm and the other gently rubbing her back. We'll put the boys in the Attic with Sam. That'll be alright, won't it, boys? … Jed?'

Joe and Josh shrugged, too sucked into the drama to think up any reason to argue and Jed inclined his head. 'Of course, dear.'

John looked across at his wife, whose eyes were glassy with tears, then at Olivia. 'Thank you. That is very kind of you.' He guided Jean back to her seat and everyone sat down again, danger averted for the time being.

'Let's just finish our meal and Wax can go with you to pick up some of your things.'

Jean grabbed onto John's arm as if she would be dragged off there and then.

'I'll go. You can stay here,' John said, soothingly

It was a real indication of just how fragile Beccah's mum

was. Jed laughed a little nervously and exchanged a worried look with Olivia. 'Yes, stay here in the warm. We'll play cards … Fancy Rummy, darling?'

Olivia smiled a little too brightly. 'What a great idea. We haven't all sat round for a game of cards since Christmas.'

It all felt absurd to me under the circumstances. There were real issues going on here that everyone was skirting around with their nicey-nice, sing-songy conversation, just covering everything up with manners. I felt nauseous. Bringing up the subject of Shades was going to be impossible like this. The meal. Us here. All around this table. It was unbearable. Like pulling teeth. On top of what Wax thought of me, I wanted to explode. I wanted to lose my mind. 'What is it exactly that is scaring you so much?' I piped up loudly.

Everyone looked at me in shock with an audible intake of breath. 'Sam?' Olivia said warily, her eyes pleading for me to tread carefully.

Someone dropped their knife on the floor.

Tallulah giggled nervously.

I looked at Wax defiantly. His face was blank and his eyelids low as if he knew exactly what I was doing. 'Let her carry on,' he said, raising his eyebrows in a silent dare. I could tell by the narrowing of his eyes after that he was surprised but knew as well as I did that proceedings needed a nudge. He smiled a little, proving I was right. He was quite OK with handing the baton of bad guy over to me for the evening. I was too angry to get side-tracked by his amusement that I'd done him a favour.

I tutted and focused back on the Whitelys. 'I mean, is it the unwanted house guests? Is it that they're all dead? Or is it that life here isn't all cosy and conventional like back at home?'

'Sam!' Olivia scolded. 'I don't know what's got into you.'

John put up a hand to say to Olivia it was OK and looked right at me. 'All the above, young lady.'

I shrank a little under his mildly annoyed gaze at my rudeness, but I'd started now and my own sanity had been called into question tonight. Apparently having an incubus demon as a boyfriend was too weird for this household. The very place Olivia was offering safe haven.

'Are you saying we have no right to be scared?' John said, getting more annoyed by the minute.

I felt my face flush red.

Wax looked to his father to diffuse a growing situation. 'John, please,' Jed said. 'She meant no harm by it.'

I was sick of being quiet little Sam, who everyone ignored and just assumed I was happy with it. Well, I wasn't. I stood up, scraping my chair. 'Actually, I don't care … Sorry, Beccah,' I said, watching as her jaw dropped open. I turned to Tallulah, Ollie, Joe and Josh and pointed at them one by one. 'She, him, him and him, dead. All of them. Killed in a minibus crash.' Then to Nicola. 'Dead! Suicide from pills.' Archie: 'Dead! Hanged himself. Oh and don't forget me. I died in a well, hiding from my paedophile stepfather.'

I took a last, triumphant look at Wax, who sagged wearily. I kicked my chair out of the way and flounced towards the door. I stopped, remembering just in time, 'Oh, and Beccah got trapped here while she was in her coma. And didn't you know, I have an imaginary incubus demon to cope with it all,' I ended shouting, directing my gaze deliberately at Wax. 'So fill your boots,' I said, snatching open the door. 'You have every right to be scared because Hell's gates have opened and The Wild Ride comes in five days.' I took one last look over my shoulder at the astonished faces with open mouths. 'But hey, it's OK. I'm just mad and seeing things,' I said matter-of-factly, stomped out and slammed the door.

CHAPTER 15

It wasn't until I reached my room that the tsunami of emotion came pouring out. Because the flood gates opened. Tears of frustration, anger and self-loathing, fear; all became jumbled, mixed-up and tumbled out in a torrent.

I threw myself on the bed, cried until I cried myself out, then I rolled over and blinked up at the ceiling. Helix didn't come and neither did Wax. He was with his first priority, smoothing over my insensitive outburst downstairs. Maybe he was right about me. I was a loose cannon and couldn't be trusted.

Turning my face into my pillow, I cried bitter tears.

I was so alone.

It was Nicola who eventually came to check on me. She gently knocked on my door. I'd finally stopped crying but made no effort to answer her.

When I didn't answer, she peered in and came and sat with me on my bed. She gave me a sympathetic smile, picked up my hand and just sat there. I was grateful for that.

'Are Beccah's parents OK?' I asked, with a voice gone hoarse from crying.

Nicola nodded and shrugged, threading her fingers through mine. 'Well, after the bomb you dropped, Wax is down there explaining everything.'

I inwardly flinched. Now I'd calmed down, I felt awful for the way I'd done it. Everyone must hate me. *And why not?* I'd gone from saying barely anything at all to— 'I ratted everyone out. I'm a horrible person.' I felt my emotions welling up in me again. My face creased and my eyes stung with fresh tears.

Nicola gripped my hand tighter and gave it a little shake. 'Don't, Sam. Please. You're not a horrible person. You did everyone a favour, really. We would have skirted around it for weeks left to our own devices. A little blunt and unortho-dox, maybe,' she said, with a bob of her head. 'But it's out of the bag now. At least they can get used to the idea and learn to deal with it.'

A sob left me and I shuddered. I tried to calm down. 'Have you heard what Wax is saying about me? He thinks I'm imagining Helix to cope.' I held a fresh sob in my throat before I started bawling all over again.

Nicola tutted and shook her head. She shifted and faced me squarely. 'Listen to me. I was with you that day at your house, remember? What I saw grabbed you and it happened too fast to be you on your own. You were there and then you were gone. Like a streak of light. Can't you talk to Helix? Get him to show himself? And if he can't, get him to show you or tell you something only someone outside would know?'

My spirits immediately began to lift. She was right. 'What about the pictures on the lampposts? I couldn't have seen them.'

She pointed at me, smiling. 'There you are. That's one thing.'

I sank a little when it occurred to me. 'Yeah, but anyone could have told me, I suppose.'

'Don't focus on that. Wax likes you. You're family and he only wants to help you. '

My emotions were so raw and exposed, I could only accept that to a point. 'He hears spirits all the time, why does he find it so hard to believe in Helix?'

Nicola let out a slow breath while she thought about that. 'Maybe it's not a case of not believing you, but more about what you went through being so bad, anyone would struggle to process it.'

I blasted red. 'He told you,' I said flatly. My humiliation burned a slow path through me from my head downwards.

Nicola hurriedly shook her head. 'Barely anything. You know Wax. He's not about to gossip. He cares about you. We all do.'

I shifted and shrugged begrudgingly. I wasn't about to let go of my anger that quickly.

Nicola released my hand and got to her feet. She bent over and kissed me on the forehead. 'You know we all love you and are here for you, don't you, Sam?'

I looked up and studied her dark-mahogany eyes, let out a huff and nodded. 'You're a good friend, Nicola. The best.' I instantly felt disloyal. *Helix.* A lump lodged in my throat. Apart from Helix, I'd never had a proper friend growing up. A sob left me and I was crying all over again.

Nicola's soft arms wrapped around me. 'It's OK. I don't mind being second-best friend,' she said, pulling away, smiling.

I laughed between breaths and sobs as she straightened. 'It's not that,' I said, sitting up straighter with her. 'I'm scared, Nicola. All the time. I'm scared for Trish … Scared The Ride will take me away and I won't be able to look after her.'

Nicola nodded along with me, getting it right away. 'Well,

you have us and as long as we're all here, we won't let anything happen to you.'

I STAYED in my room after Nicola blew me a kiss from the doorway and left. Everyone came and checked on me, one by one, except the one person I was waiting for. *Helix.* He didn't come, no matter how much I tried to fall asleep. The last person to visit me before bed was Wax. He knocked. 'Can I come in, Sam?'

I nodded, no energy left for conversation.

He came in as if he'd heard me and stood next to the door. 'You OK now?'

'Are the Whitelys OK?' I asked.

He shrugged. 'As well as can be expected for a middle-aged couple who just found out they were in the middle of dinner with a bunch of supernaturals.' The corners of his mouth gave just a hint of a smile to show me he wasn't angry.

I relaxed a little. 'Sorry.'

'Look,' he said, closing the door properly and putting his hands on his hips. 'For what it's worth, I'm glad you have Helix. Whether he's real, in the flesh, or not. He got you through a really difficult time.'

I stared at Wax, sifting through the apology that didn't commit to believing me at all. 'He is real. You'll see,' I said, my blood rising again.

Wax just inclined his head. 'Goodnight, Sam.' He slipped out of the door quietly, leaving me more frustrated than ever.

MIDNIGHT and the house was quiet and there was still no sign of Helix. I was getting really worried that something had happened to him. Then, following the worry came paranoia. That maybe Wax had been right. That now Helix had been identified, he would no longer come to me. The thought was terrifying. I had to get up out of this bed. I had to do something. Stay active. Otherwise I'd go mad, for sure.

Then another thought suddenly struck me. *Trish.* Helix had taken me there the other night. Maybe doing that meant the barrier was now down. I shot out of bed and pulled the dress I was still wearing up over my head and changed back into the jeans and jumper I'd worn earlier. I crept out of my room carrying my heavy boots and went as quietly through the house as possible. Until I reached the end of the hall, where I slipped the boots on, grabbed my coat and silently slipped out of the front door.

I zipped the collar up on my coat against the cold, still night. The air smelled crisp with frost. The quarter moon lit the way enough to see the mist-covered path that billowed and cleared as I walked. The whole forest seemed more alive at night; the torch on my phone reflecting back pairs of small eyes that scurried away. The further I got, the more the air smelled of the rotting decay of old leaves and bark.

I jumped at a squawk, but it was only a bird who'd decided to warn its friends I was coming. I swore under my breath and continued on. I was grateful it was winter for the lack of leaves, meaning the path wasn't as dark as it could have been. I cracked branches underfoot, making things flutter or scurry away. My heart was thudding, calming and spiking painfully again, all along the route. Until my old house finally loomed into view. It looked like a dark ogre crouching, waiting for me at night. I made my way around to the front driveway and stopped at the boundary line of the gate.

A shiver went down the length of my body. There wasn't a single light on inside the house. Not even in the porch. *Power cut? More like meter unfed.*

I swallowed. My mouth was unbelievably dry. I dematerialised and looked down at the invisible line between the gate posts. I lifted a foot to test my theory and slowly put it across the line.

Nothing happened.

I was right.

Now I knew my past, the barrier had disappeared. I cautiously approached the door, my heart pounding. Small steps, straining my eyes and ears, half-expecting Graeme to jump out and grab me, even though I knew I was invisible. I looked up at the bedroom windows above the door, my mother's room. In the dark, the black frames looked down on me like sad, smudged eyes. Then lastly at the black front door.

I hadn't thought about how I would get in in the middle of the night.

Then I remembered like a bolt of inspiration. If Graeme hadn't come home yet, then there was a chance there was a key left outside in the flowerpot. It was something he insisted on in case my mother was too comatose to let him in. He mislaid his keys, often leaving them in his van at the village pub.

The pot I remembered was still there. Blue, painted with flowers. A mother's day gift from us when we were kids. Now it had a chunk of pottery broken out of it. I delved my fingers into the damp, loose soil. My fingers brushed the small piece of metal. My initial relief didn't slow my heart for long as I approached the front door. It fluttered up into my mouth. I pushed the key into the lock as quietly as possible, but it still clicked and crunched deafeningly loudly.

At first I thought it didn't work. I pulled it out and wiped any residue of mud on my jacket, panicking that it was an old key and the locks had been changed. Finally, it went in the whole way and turned the lock.

I silently pushed open the door, ready to grab it in case it creaked. 'Is that you?' A croaky voice came from the living room.

My heart stopped. *My mother.* She must have fallen asleep in front of the TV. I cursed my stupidity, I should have known. I considered running back out but remembered that was silly as I was invisible. I quickly slipped in and closed the door.

I stood my ground. Barely breathing as my mother shuffled out into the hallway, holding her head.

I was shocked.

She looked so old. So tired and used up. She'd aged so much over the last two years. Or was it because the memory I had of her was from when I was a kid? Before the drink took its toll.

Part of me wanted to hug her. A huge part. She was my mother after all. But the rest wanted to slap her and scream into her face to pull herself together and be a parent.

Instead, she looked right through me, swore under her breath and headed for the stairs. She went up slowly as if she was counting steps. I followed behind, carefully matching her footsteps in case of noise.

Every now and again she stopped and listened. She looked behind her and stared right at me. It was as creepy as hell. All I could do was freeze and look into her wide, unseeing eyes and not move a muscle. 'Is there anyone there?' she called out in a tiny, strangled voice.

A solitary tear rolled down her cheek. 'Is that you, Sam, come home to haunt me?'

Her sensing me there stopped my heart and almost broke me. My confidence was shaky anyway. All I could do was hold my breath and wait until she finally gave up and continued up the stairs. By the time we reached the top, I felt sick from the strain.

My mother stumbled off to her room and I waited on the

landing until she disappeared. I didn't move until I heard the bed creak and knew she'd got onto it.

I stood on the threshold of my old room. The one I shared with Trish. My heart broke when I imagined the poor young girl possibly lying awake, listening for every noise and footfall, just like I used to do.

I hoped. No, I prayed that Graeme hadn't started his old games yet. Helix had been right to warn me. Trish must be coming up fourteen now and no longer looked like a child.

I swallowed, took a deep breath and slowly turned the brass doorknob. It made exactly the same loose jangle noise I remembered. Just like my goblin dream. My dreams had kept the fear alive, even if my memories didn't. I cursed Graeme for the terrible fear Trish must be living. Night after night. The anticipation. The noises she must be dreading. I opened the door just wide enough to squeeze through and closed it as quietly as I could.

Inside, what was left of my broken heart completely shattered to pieces. Her bed told me everything I needed to know. She was cowering, completely under the dirty covers. She had clearly heard me come in the room and was pretending to be asleep. She was trying not to breathe, but the slight tremble was impossible to hide. Tears filled my eyes. I hurriedly wiped them away with my fingers. I had to do something as I was prolonging the agony.

I crept closer to the bed, trying not to scare her but knowing that was impossible until she knew who I was. I bent over so my face was close to hers. 'Trish. It's me, Sam. Don't be scared.' I quickly materialised so she could see me.

There was a brief pause, where she was obviously deciding whether she'd imagined it. Then she slowly pulled down the quilt and was looking right at me. For a moment, I thought she still couldn't see me, until, 'Sam?'

I was on the bed in a flash, pulling her up into my arms. She squealed.

'Shh,' I had to say between laughter and sobs. 'Don't wake Mum.'

'Sam, Sam,' Trish said over and over. 'You came back.'

'I would never leave you. I told you.'

We both hugged as tightly as we could, frightened that the other would disappear. Murmuring how much we'd loved and missed each other. Trish pulled apart first. 'But you did leave me, Sam. You did.' Her eyes were filled with hurt.

'I couldn't help it, I promise.'

'Where did you go all this time? We looked everywhere.'

Then I looked her deeply in the eyes, gathered myself together and opted for honesty. 'I died, Trish … I died.'

Trish didn't say anything. Just blinked. She frowned and then drew back with a scowl as if she was furious with me. 'What are you saying, are you making fun of me?'

'No, no, of course not.' I felt wretched that she thought I could do something like that. So with nothing else to convince her, I dematerialised. 'See?' I said, getting up and watching her eyes search the room for me.

I stooped and switched on the lamp, which made her squeal.

'Shh!' I said, quickly making myself visible again.

Trish covered her mouth in an attempt not to scream. 'Sam. Am I finally going mad?'

I immediately sat back on the bed and scooped her back into my arms. 'Don't be scared, please. I'm telling you the truth. I've come back to help you.'

Another noise brought both our heads up sharply. The crunch of keys in the front door. 'Turn off the light,' I said, my voice gone deep with menace.

CHAPTER 16

Thump, thump, thump. I knew that sound well. It was drunk, belligerent Graeme, as opposed to slimy, weaselly Graeme.

Trish froze. My mind scrambled. Panic, gnawing at the edges of my conscious thought. But I only allowed it for a moment. I shoved Trish over and got in the bed with her, pulling the cover back over our heads. 'Don't be scared,' I whispered. 'If he comes in here, he won't see me but I'm with you, OK?'

Her body was rigid with fear, but she jerkily nodded her head.

'Just follow my lead.'

Graeme's labouring steps reached the top of the stairs and halted, just like I knew they would. It was 'make-your-mind-up-time'. A time warp from when I was last there. I could literally hear his brain working. Deciding on whether to chance coming in. Whether my mum was asleep enough. Trying the door.

Then the sound I'd lived a thousand times and always dreaded. The slight jangle as he gripped the wobbly brass doorknob that he could never quite fix. The door silently swung open and clicked as he closed it quietly behind him. He'd been busy oiling the hinges.

Trish's fingers squeezed into my bicep. I vaguely registered it because I was back there. A sixteen-year-old girl, trembling late at night in her bed. Unable to run. Nowhere to go. Terrified to move. Cold sweat. Shivering. The smell of stale beer, desperation on his breath and diesel oil in the creases of his hands.

All the things I'd planned to do evaporated and, for a moment, I was petrified.

Trish whimpered. 'Sam. Sam. *Sam!*' The last one a squeal as the covers were slowly drawn back. Graeme's dark, bearded, transfixed, ugly silhouette came into few.

'There you are,' he said in barely a whisper.

He was drawing back the quilt further, further.

Trish was quietly crying into my shoulder and I couldn't move.

The hand was coming closer. Weird, long, bent fingers. My nightmare. They were always in my nightmare.

I wanted to slap it away. Bite off a finger. Anything. But I was fossilised with fear.

Then, like a ray of sunshine breaking through clouds after a storm: 'Graeme, is that you?' My mother's voice came from behind him.

For a moment, it was his turn to freeze. His hand was mid-air. He didn't so much as move a muscle. Only his eyes darted to the side. His mind working. Waiting. Listening. For my mum to give up and move along.

Then I saw it. Over his shoulder. The white ball of light slowly building. A wave of nausea, following with fatigue. I laughed with relief. I couldn't help myself.

Graeme jolted, registering the laughter didn't come from Trish. He felt it too. He staggered and brought his hand up to hold his head. While he staggered and tried to stand up straight, I pulled Trish with me out of the way. We scrambled right up to the headboard.

Helix was lighting up and drawing everything from the room in his terrifying glory. He was a beautiful angel.

'What the f—' Graeme said, staggering around in shock and backing away to the door.

'The boy,' Trish whispered next to my ear.

I tore my eyes from Helix to look at her expression. She was gazing right at him.

'You see him?' I asked, amazed.

She nodded, transfixed.

I couldn't process it and had to face Helix again.

Graeme was crumpling to the floor as Helix slowly inhaled his energy. It was our chance. I pulled Trish with me off the bed and sidestepped until Helix was between us and Graeme. 'Stop now, Helix,' I whispered, gently touching him on the shoulder. I could literally feel the power pulsing through him. 'We need to go before you kill him.'

There was no further discussion. No preamble, plan, or anything. The light dimmed like the power was cut. Helix swirled around and a huge black cloak swept us away.

The next thing I knew, I was in my bed, in my attic room, back at Waxley-Black Manor. However, this time, I wasn't alone. Trish was sleeping soundly next to me. I wanted to cry with relief. I was so happy she was safe. Helix was standing, watchful, at the foot of the bed. There was something different about him. Something new. He seemed older. Stronger. His expression more serious. His eyes, concerned.

'Can we go to my dream place?' I asked, as my eyelids began to feel heavy. I just couldn't leave things as they were. I had to at least talk to him. Thank him. Let him know what a wonderful thing he'd done and how grateful I was for it.

But he shook his head. 'It's not safe for me to be alone with you tonight.'

I fought to keep my eyes open. I was annoyed at my weakness to stay awake. I didn't understand what had changed.

'I shouldn't have brought you here,' Helix said, nodding his head towards Trish.

'I know, you saved her, thank you.' I felt so much gratitude, but I battled to stay awake. Instead of succumbing, I struggled and got out of bed and approached him.

He seemed to tower over me as he looked down intensely with his mesmerising eyes. They seemed feverishly bright today. His hand came up between us to stop me getting any closer. I felt it keenly where it burned an imprint over my heart. I frowned up at him, confused. 'What's the matter? Whatever I've done, I'm sorry.'

For a moment his face flashed with frustration and then softened into sadness. 'It's not you. Something changed tonight. It's the reason I wasn't with you right away. I had to go and see my uncle.'

I felt my throat instantly constrict in panic. A terrible premonition that I was losing him. A heart-stopping fear he was going away.

His hand moved up to my shoulder, where he gave it a squeeze. 'He said it's time. The Ride is almost here and I must go with it.'

And there it was. My worst fear realised. My face crumpled. I couldn't help it. 'No, Helix … you can't … you can't leave me.' I covered my face with my hands and started to cry.

His arms were instantly around me, blissfully surrounding me in warmth and gorgeous winter spice. His mouth was tantalisingly close to my ear when he spoke. 'I have to, Sam. I am about to change from a youngling into a grown male. I can feel the changes coming upon me, especially tonight when I syphoned energy from your stepfather.'

I didn't understand everything he was saying, but I knew enough to know that Graeme's energy wasn't good and was like no one else. It was a dark, unhealthy strength that Helix would undoubtedly detect.

I gripped onto him as if he'd fly away and burrowed my nose into his neck. *Oh that smell.* I was already falling. Falling, falling into soft feathers.

WHEN I AWOKE, my heart fell. I wasn't with Helix. He was gone and I was slammed with memories of the night before. My eyes flashed open with a start and I turned my head to the pillow next to me. Then exhaled with relief as there she was. Trish, still sleeping peacefully.

Then it was all true. As much as I wouldn't swap having her there, it meant everything else I remembered couldn't have been a dream either.

Graeme had been left in a heap on my old bedroom floor and Trish had gone. That would be a matter for the police and posed a problem of epic proportions for us.

Wax would have to know.

The Waxley-Blacks would have to know.

And the most heart-wrenching of all, the last thing I remembered: Helix said he was leaving. I wanted to curl into a ball and cry, but I couldn't crumble. I needed to speak to the others. I also couldn't leave Trish to wake up alone, so I gave her a shake.

Her eyelids flickered open. She hitched a breath in surprise and stifled a scream, slapping a hand over her mouth. Then she yanked me to her with a strong arm around my neck. 'You're real. Everything was real. I can't believe it wasn't a dream. You're here. I missed you so, so much,' she said, beginning to cry.

I laughed a little. 'Come on,' I said, patting her back to release me from her chokehold. She did slowly, allowing us both to sit up and study each other's faces. Her blonde hair was a wispy bed-head mess and she was studying me intently with big cornflower blue eyes. She was growing into a beautiful young woman. 'Are you really dead?' she said, poking my cheek with a finger. 'How come I can see you?'

I laughed at how wonderfully childlike she still was and then smiled sadly. 'It's a very long story, one I will definitely tell you, but, first, I need to let everyone know you're here.' I got up off the bed and held out my hand. 'Come on. Let's go and get you some breakfast.' I couldn't help take in the thinness of her arms.

She got up slowly, looking bewildered. I realised we were still in last night's clothes. Hers, nothing more than a nighty, revealing just how terribly thin she was. I went to my chest of drawers and threw a pair of jeans and a sweatshirt at her. She caught them, grinning happily. We were instantly sisters again. We both registered the wonderful moment of ordinary, then quickly changed our clothes. We both looked less rumpled, so I took her hand and led her out, wide-eyed, through the attic, along the hallway of black doors. Down the majestic staircase and into the warm and modern kitchen, the size of the whole ground floor of our old cottage.

Everyone was there; we must have slept late. They went silent, one by one, as they noticed us. Olivia almost dropped the pan she was holding. Tallulah giggled nervously and Wax swore. Even our newest members, the Whitelys, were openly staring at us from their seats at the kitchen table.

'Morning,' I said as brightly as I could. 'This is Trish, my sister.' Their faces remained shocked and questioning.

'I know who she is,' Wax said, dumping a loaf of bread on the table. 'What is she doing here?'

'Wax!' Jed barked. 'Would you like something to eat dear?' Jed said a little more kindly.

I looked sideways at Trish as she hadn't answered. She pointed in astonishment at Ollie, then Tallulah and the others. 'You're all dead. I know you are. It was in the papers. We had an assembly about it at school and everything.'

I briefly closed my eyes and opened them to Wax's terse look. Of course she would remember the tragic deaths. The whole village would.

'Oh dear,' Mrs Whitely said, shaking and grabbing her head. Trish saying it out loud seemed to compound it all over again. I guess it did make it all seem a lot more real.

Wax sat heavily in his chair as if his day just got better and better and looked daggers at me. I sat with Trish, next to Nicola, unfortunately right opposite him. I smiled gratefully at Nicola's welcoming smile. 'I went back to my old house,' I started to explain. My gaze fell on Wax. It would be him I'd have to convince.

'Clearly,' he said.

'Wax!' Olivia reminded. 'Let her talk.'

'My stepfather, Graeme … he almost.' My gaze dropped to my empty plate. Trish gently squeezed my shoulder. 'My dad is a bad man,' Trish explained. 'But the boy came. The one from when we were small. He brought us here.'

My eyes flashed to Wax's. His widened and he nodded, thoughtfully, but with a new respect. I'd forgotten, with everything else, that Trish had proved Helix's existence. I should have felt vindicated, but quite honestly, I just felt relieved. I think I'd started questioning my sanity myself in the end. Then I remembered our last conversation and a huge knot appeared in my throat. I took a sip of juice that Olivia passed me to shift it. 'He'd just got back from seeing his uncle.' My voice felt tight as I attempted not to cry. 'He will be leaving with The Ride soon, so you don't have to worry.'

There was a collective exhale of breath and everyone broke out into conversation. It did seem to solve all our problems. However, when I flicked a glance at Wax, he was watching me closely. He knew. He knew how devastated I would be.

'So how did you leave him? Your stepfather, I mean?' Wax asked.

I put my head up defiantly, 'In a heap on the bedroom floor, I think.'

Joe laughed. 'Go tough girl, Sam,' he said, reaching for a slice of toast.

I smiled shyly. Tough was a word never associated with me.

'So Trish is now missing?' Ollie said, bringing everyone back to the point. 'We'll need to work out what to do with her.'

The police will surely be looking for her,' Olivia said.

I sank back into my chair, deflated. I hadn't had time to think things through to that extent.

'This needs to be handled carefully,' Jed said, agreeing with his wife.

'Can't we just get him arrested?' Tallulah asked, biting off a huge mouthful of croissant. 'Surely if Trish explains, they'll have to listen and lock him up.'

I was nodding along at the valid point. Then everyone chimed in, some agreeing, some with reasons not to. Trish gripped my hand under the table. It was hot and sweaty from nerves and excitement. I knew it was because she sensed her life was changing, permanently, and she wanted that, whatever was decided.

'Then what?' Wax's voice cut over everyone else's. 'She ends up in the care system. Is that what you want?'

'She certainly can't continue with that man,' Olivia said, to murmurs of agreement.

Wax inclined his head as if that was a given. 'That's true. But what we need to do is find a way where Graeme goes and she gets to stay where she is.'

My head hurt with all the conflicting arguments. Wax was right. It wasn't going to be that easy. Trish needed to be safe and I had to learn how to let Helix go.

I SPENT one lovely day with Trish after that. It was wonderful to see her act like an ordinary kid of her age, instead of carrying the weight of the world on her shoulders.

She joined a game of basketball with the boys outside, scoring baskets through the hoop fixed above the garages. She played makeovers with Nicola and Tallulah, until she more resembled a pantomime dame. But the best time of all was when the two of us just lounged on the sofa in the sitting room and watched cartoons. We cuddled and laughed like we used to. Better than we used to, as we didn't have the constant threat of being interrupted by our mum waking or Graeme coming home. My heart ached at the sharp memory of it falling like a boulder of dread, hitting the bottom of my stomach. Our childhood had been lousy, neglected and dirty. I kissed Trish's head. Her hair smelled like it needed a good wash as a stark reminder.

That evening, I made sure she had all the luxuries of a good bath: scented bath salts, coconut shampoo, deep conditioner. The works. It was the best day of both our lives as sisters. I could tell it in her rosy glow and bright, smiling eyes.

Bedtime came and Trish sat on the end of my bed

wearing one of my nightshirts and soft, fluffy, pink dressing gown. She was pink and clean and smelling scrumptious. 'I can't stay here, can I,' she stated, sadly, playing with her fingers in her lap.

I shook my head and sat down next to her. 'They'll be looking for you. But we'll get rid of Graeme, you'll just be on the other side of the wood and we can see each other all the time.'

Her face brightened, but her smile was weak. 'Mum's not well, she doesn't mean to be forgetful.'

I nodded, remembering Trish had always been fiercely protective of our mother. She looked miserable. I knew what she was thinking. The thing that had nagged at me all along, that it was unlikely she could look after her. It was more like the other way around. 'You never know. It might be OK. You're older now,' I said, trying to pull her out of the doldrums. 'I read somewhere that they don't like taking kids away from their natural habitat.'

Trish rolled her eyes and looked at me sardonically. 'I'm not a polar bear, Sam,' she said, making me tickle her in the ribs. Still, she had a point. Despite the laughter, she seemed unconvinced.

A soft knock came from the door. 'Sam!' Ollie's voice came from the other side.

Frowning, I got up to answer it. 'What is it?'

'Family meeting in the kitchen, now. Can you come down?'

I looked over my shoulder at Trish, watching me carefully. 'Her too? It does concern her.'

Ollie shrugged and nodded. He turned and was already walking away. 'Right now though, Sam.'

It seemed serious. I let out a ragged breath and motioned with my hand for Trish to follow me. Her smile fell away with understanding. Her little holiday was over and she'd have to go home and face the consequences.

My heart ached. I put my arm around her shoulders and kissed her cheek as we walked. 'It will be alright. You'll see.' I had no idea if that was true and swallowed down a huge lump.

When we walked into the kitchen, there was a lively debate going on. Everyone was animated and loud, making me squeeze Trish's hand to calm her frightened expression. Beccah was there, but her parents had, thankfully, retired to their room.

I sat with Trish next to me at the kitchen table watching avidly, trying to gauge the direction of opinion, when Ollie cut the air with a loud, 'Shh!' He had to do it twice before everyone finally stopped speaking.

Bang! Bang! Bang! Came from the hallway. It was the front door knocker. Then came the loud bell. 'Someone's at the door,' Tallulah said, eyes wide with fright.

My heart thrashed. Trish whimpered and gripped onto my arm with both hands.

Olivia looked at Jed fearfully. He was already on his feet, making his way towards the noise. 'You all stay here and don't make a sound,' he ordered before he disappeared into the hallway.

Wax followed his father.

'Bret!' Olivia hissed.

'I'll stay out of sight,' he said, disappearing out into the hall.

'Stay here,' I whispered to Trish.

She refused to let go of my arm. 'Don't leave me.'

'I'll be invisible. I just need to see who it is, OK? I'll tell you after.'

Trish reluctantly let me go. I dematerialised and entered the hallway before anyone else could stop me.

Wax saw me immediately and rolled his eyes from his hiding place in the shadows of the staircase. However, he didn't protest. His attention went straight back to his father, now speaking at the door. I quickly joined Wax, behind the tall grandfather clock, feeling a weird mix of love and belonging. Like he was my older, sterner brother, or something.

I tried to decipher the conversation Jed was having. It was raining and I could hear a softer voice. *My mother.* 'Come in a moment, dear, out of the rain,' Jed was saying. He turned to the butler hovering nearby. 'Bring a towel, can you, Fredericks?'

The butler quickly turned on his heel, but I couldn't take my eyes off the sorry state of my mother. She was so thin and ill-looking. Her hair was plastered to her head. Her wet, inadequate clothes clung to her body and her mascara had pooled under her eyes, reminding me of a Day of the Dead skeleton. She was agitated and couldn't stand still. 'Have you seen her … my daughter? About this high,' she said, putting a bony hand out flat next to her face. 'I got up this morning and she wasn't there. Graeme hasn't seen her either.'

Oh really. My blood boiled. But I had to hand it to Jed. He handled my mother perfectly, with kindness, wrapping a towel around her and speaking to her with authority. 'Your husband, is he outside in the rain?'

She shook her head. 'No, he's still at work. It's just–it's the second time, you see. My first daughter disappeared like that. Exactly the same,' she said, breaking down into tears.

I'd always been so angry with her and I'd never seen this side of her. The devastated loss. I guess, the motherly side. She was shaking, possibly from the cold and shock, but more than likely from her alcohol abuse.

'You live in the cottage on the edge of my land, don't you?' Jed was saying, slowly steering her towards the door and grabbing his coat off the stand. 'I tell you what. Why don't we get in the car and drive around a bit and see if we can see her? At least you'll be in the warm and the dry.' He took a last look over his shoulder in our direction, making sure we'd heard and disappeared out of the front door.

I immediately materialised next to Wax and he started back towards the kitchen. 'What are we going to do?' I asked, jogging after him.

'We need to come up with a plan. The Ride comes in three days,' Wax said.

He was right. There was so much more going on here.

We talked long into the night. Tallulah couldn't understand why we couldn't just keep Trish with us, which was a lovely, oversimplistic idea so typical of Tallulah. But we all knew it would be no life for a young girl. She wouldn't ever be able to go out to go to school or see her friends in case she was seen. The one thing we all agreed on was that one way or another, Graeme had to go. Everyone came up with wild and outlandish ideas, like tying him up and dumping him at the police station with child abductor tattooed on his forehead. Until finally, we came up with a realistic plan: an anonymous tip-off to the police. Trish was missing and the body of the first daughter, i.e. me, could be found in the crumbled, abandoned well. Then, when Graeme got arrested, we would take Trish home with some sort of careful supervision of my mother. It sounded like it could work.

It was late by the time we agreed on a plan and Trish had fallen asleep with her head on my lap. I could only guess at the last time she felt relaxed enough to sleep like that. Joe carried her for me up to bed. I thanked him and got into bed next to her. I felt sad but wired with nerves. *Could it all work out? Would it?*

I quietly called out to Helix. He'd been noticeably absent again today. I missed him and needed to let him know our plans.

AT SOME POINT during the night, the fatigue must have come over me, and I slept. I found myself in my dream place. It occurred to me that it was always daytime and sunny there. Helix came moments after I became conscious of my surroundings, but something was different about him. He seemed distracted and troubled about something. More than that. Something physical was happening. He seemed even taller. Broader. More manly looking. Literally over night, he seemed no longer a boy.

Something stirred deep within me as I watched him stalk into the garden, confident and purposeful, like a large cat. It was then that I was reminded that he wasn't even a man, he was a demon, an apex predator.

Then why were my insides melting simply at the sight of him? Remembering his words, *we are a pairing, you and I.*

It seemed suddenly too hot, when my mind drifted to what it must be like to actually be with him in the true sense of the word. I got to my feet and didn't stop walking until we were standing right in front of each other, and he was looking down and searching my eyes intensely.

I was struck by the set of his jaw that clenched as his eyes dropped to my body and back up again. It was a shock because I could never remember him looking at me like that. 'I can't stay long. This close, I'm draining energy from her as well.'

I felt terrible. I hadn't thought of that. In the real world, he was next to the sleeping bodies of me and Trish. He wouldn't be able to help himself.

His face softened. 'She's happy,' he said, telling me exactly the emotion coming off her.

I smiled up at him sadly. This thing with us was so much more complicated than I imagined. However, I bit it back and explained the plan we had come up with to get rid of Graeme.

He picked up both my hands, sending electricity the whole length of my arms. It almost made me lose my train of thought. It was so distracting. I wondered how his whole body might feel. I felt instantly disloyal having these X-rated thoughts at a time like this. I swallowed and continued, shaking my head to clear it. 'So ... while we have Trish and the police have been notified, the anonymous tip-off should send the police to my body in the well. It's still in there, isn't it?' I asked, suddenly alarmed that he could have moved it.

I watched enraptured and my heart skipped several beats as he brought one of my hands to his mouth and gently kissed my knuckles, one by one. It was slow and deliberate and I'd never experienced anything like it. The whole of my insides melted away, leaving my knees weak and ready to buckle. He nodded. 'I covered you. Make sure you tell them to dig.'

By then I'd forgotten what we were talking about. I was fixated on his full lips. My chest ached. My stomach ached, right down to the juncture of my thighs. I had no idea what was happening to me. I was literally dissolving. I wanted and longed for nothing more than to feel closer to him. Vaguely, a nagging voice was warning me of what he was, willing me to push him away, but another, stronger part of me wanted to pull him closer to see what would happen. 'What's happening, Helix?'

I moaned in frustration as he woke from his trance, pushed my hands away and took a step back. He was breathing heavily and so was I. And hot. So hot. My clothes felt too restrictive and sweat was trickling down my temples.

He ran a shaking hand through his hair and he said something under his breath. As if he'd only just come back to his senses. His eyes darted, wild and scared, like he'd had some sort of close shave.

'What is it?' I asked, suddenly unsure whether to go closer to him or not.

He put up a defensive hand between us and took another step back.

'What's the matter, Helix? You're scaring me,' I pleaded, confused. Disappointed. Suddenly I wanted to cry.

His head hung low with hopelessness. My whole body

prickled in fear. I'd never seen him like this. 'Are you sick? Tell me, Helix. Let me help you.'

'He shook his head exaggeratedly, backing up his steps, as if he needed space to clear it. 'You can't … there's nothing you can do. I have to go.' He went to turn away and walk off.

'Please, Helix!' I wailed, starting to cry. I couldn't help it. My hands dropped hopelessly to my sides. 'Trish has to go tomorrow. I can't lose you too.'

He turned back to me with a face creased in agony. He took a cautious step closer, watching me intently with bleary, devastated eyes. He towered over me, but I was conscious of the space he deliberately kept between us. A creeping suspicion was now becoming startlingly obvious: he was frightened to touch me. Tears were filling my eyes and a hard knot was growing in my chest. 'Tell me,' I demanded, barely able to speak my jaw was so tight.

His brows drew together and his yellow eyes dulled with sadness. 'My time to be an adult male is almost here. I can feel the vibrations pulsing through me. Can't you?'

I swallowed hard and tried to clear my tears to think. Then I understood. My strong physical reactions. He always affected me deeply, but this was way off the scale. 'What happens when you become an adult?' I asked, searching his agonised face, fearfully.

He took a beat and shifted his weight uncomfortably. 'When I visited my uncle earlier, he explained to me why it is so important that I leave with The Ride.'

I shouted, 'No!' and went to cling to him, but he took a step back out of my reach.

I blanched in horror. He'd never rejected me so harshly.

'You have to listen to me, Sam … to become a male, I need to be with a human.' He looked away for a moment as if he was uncomfortable with what he was telling me. 'I need a particular kind of energy to survive the change.' He closed his eyes and rested on a hip as if there was no good way of saying what he had to say. 'And if I stay here ...' He left his last word trailing in the air. 'After everything that has happened to you.' He could barely look at me.

I found it difficult to swallow, now understanding what he meant. What Wax and Ollie had meant. It was all true. But most of all, I was horrified that he'd somehow linked the two. My blood surged and heated my face. I was furious. Hurt. Hopeless and bewildered in a two-second storm. I shoved him in the chest to walk past him to go somewhere. Anywhere. As long as it was away from him. But he caught me by the elbow and swung me back around. 'I'm not saying never, I'm just saying not now, while I'm not in control of it.'

I was speechless. All I could do was stare at him.

He continued a little more gently. 'When you're older ... ready.'

I narrowed my eyes, hating and knowing deep down that he was thinking of me. That it was coming from a place of caring and love. But he didn't understand that he was allowing Graeme to still affect me even in death. I still wasn't free of him. That son-of-a-bitch was still dictating my existence. 'So you have sex with some random girl and then what?' I asked with a rasp in my voice, where I could barely get out the words.

The corners of his mouth quirked into a small smile, that widened my eyes in indignation. But even then, I was struck by how gorgeous and completely adorable he was. Anger was hopeless as I was already imagining kissing that smile. I scowled again, to keep hold of my anger, which made him laugh.

Seeing his mistake immediately, he schooled his features and sobered again, standing a little straighter. 'Apparently, it's sudden. It happens very quickly and it's very painful. Energy from sex is very strong. Like a charge that fuels the change. My bones will break and grow and my muscles will stretch around them. I won't look the same,' he finished uneasily, as if he wasn't sure of my response or whether I would still like him.

It broke my heart to watch the insecurity ripple across his face. 'Yeah, but it will still be you. Like I'll still recognise you, won't I?' I couldn't help a slow meander down his body. Tracing his fantastic shape with my eyes and wondering how it could possibly improve upon what was already there. Wrapped in his trademark black that fit him to perfection.

'So I can't get near you, because I might …' Helix was saying, to try to bring my attention back up to his face.

He was half frowning, which morphed into slightly amused, when I finally looked back up into his eyes, with a distracted, 'What?'

His smile grew and my heart fluttered along with it. I sagged hopelessly but resigned. This was never going to work, staying apart. Surely he could see that.

He attempted to be serious again. 'Please listen, Sam. This is very serious. You won't stop me because I will radiate some sort of drugging hormone.'

'A pheromone,' I corrected. 'We learned about them at school.'

He smiled, a little exasperated with me.

'Don't you do that already?'

He shrugged, conceding I was probably right and smiled adorably. 'I don't know. Do I?' Then he laughed and I went to punch him in the arm, which he caught easily in his larger hand.

I was in the circle of his arms before I knew what happened or even took a breath. The smell of winter spice surrounded me like a warm blanket. Then I understood that it was the smell he was talking about. He was looking down at me, but his intense gaze was different. It held something else. Something smouldering under the surface. It dropped to my mouth again and again as if he was at war with himself. 'It will get stronger and stronger until I finally do it.' His voice seemed deeper and far more raspy than usual. 'I won't be able to help myself.'

I was inches from his mouth. Centimetres. Millimetres. Then we were kissing. Wild, wonderful, tasting, drugging, lost to the world, rolling in the grass, kissing. My hands were in his hair, clawing his back, pulling him to me in a burning hunger that came from so deep inside me it would never be sated. Not in a million years of knowing him.

Somehow, someway, he broke the seal of our mouths to breathe. He rested his fevered forehead on mine. 'Not yet … not like this. Trish is in the bed.'

I'd been so hopelessly swept away that I'd forgotten this was a psychic representation of ourselves. For a brief second, I wanted to see what we looked like together, real and in the flesh. However, our physical bodies were in my bedroom, on my bed with Trish. It was a huge bucket of water to my senses. I gave him a shove and he immediately sprang off me and helped me to my feet. I exhaled an exhausted breath and nodded in understanding. 'Soon though,' I said, taking in his messy hair and weary, bloodshot eyes. 'But I want to be your first, Helix,' I said, absolutely categorical on that.

He studied my face for a long, loaded moment, unmoving.

'I don't want you to have to leave with The Ride.'

The smile that came was regretful. 'That will happen regardless.'

Before I could complain, stamp my foot and rail against it, I found myself back in my bed next to Trish. I was breathing hard and my body still thrummed with the memory of him. Trish was still sound asleep and I allowed my breathing to return to normal. It was strange that I should think of it right then, but there was no sign of the goblin. The room was as it should be, I was relaxed and there was no more fear. Helix had chased the goblin away.

ALL OF US were up early the next day. For me it was doomsday. Wax had taken charge and no one argued against it. He was our undisputed leader. We gathered around the island in the kitchen, which was now our hub of operations and watched as he ripped open the plastic packaging around a small oblong object. 'A new phone?' I asked, not fully understanding why it was needed.

Wax plugged it in the wall to make sure it was charged. 'A burner phone that can't be traced,' he said in way of explanation.

I didn't fully understand how that worked, but I understood that we wouldn't want to use one of our own.

While it was left to charge, Wax got on a stool and went over the plan. 'I'll call the police, disguising my voice and give them the coordinates to the well.'

I had perfect recall now and remembered it exactly. 'Make sure you tell them that it's really hidden by brambles and the wall around it has crumbled away. Oh and there is a thick rope tied around a tree next to it. That should help give them its position. I'm covered in rocks and earth at the bottom.'

There was a moment of silence where everyone just stared at me. Wax looked deeply into my eyes for a moment and then nodded as if he was satisfied I was OK. 'The rest of you must keep Trish here. Don't go out. She mustn't be seen. I'm going to say I'm a concerned neighbour as it's the second daughter gone missing from that house. As soon as they make the discovery in the well and Graeme is arrested, we'll take Trish home. We don't want them doing a house-to-house and finding her here. Too many questions will be asked.'

It sounded like a good plan. 'What about Graeme? How will the police tie it to him?' I asked.

'I'll just say to start their enquiry with him and hope they find holes in his story. With Trish missing and actual evidence of a dead body of another daughter from the same family, he should be the prime suspect.'

I hoped he was right. There were a lot of assumptions there.

Wax pulled the charger out of the phone, tapped 999 and put it to his ear. 'Police please.' Then he rested his gaze on me while he waited to be put through.

My heart raced as I stood in absolute silence with the others. But his hard stare grounded and held me. It said he'd got me and we were finally doing it: making the call I'd waited a lifetime to make.

'Yes, I want to report a dead body,' he began. 'My name is Fred Smith.'

ax's gaze stayed locked with mine while he described the exact location of the well to the police in a deep cockney accent. It would have been comical if my throat wasn't slowly closing with fear. He also remembered to add the rope around the tree as extra evidence to mark the spot. Then I grabbed Trish's hand as he delivered the final piece of information that I prayed would end my nightmare for ever. 'Investigate the stepfather, Graeme Payne. Yes, Woodlands Cottage. The younger daughter is missing now as well.' Then he quickly clicked off the phone. I was still stunned, watching him as he popped the phone back in its carrier bag, opened a drawer in the island and pulled out a rolling pin. I blinked three times as he hit the phone hard through the bag on the countertop, making sure it was completely destroyed before he threw it in the bin.

Everyone seemed to let out a collective breath and moved for the first time. We all looked at each other with wide, dazed eyes, 'What now?' Ollie asked.

'We wait,' Wax said. 'In about half an hour I need you three to dematerialise and go to the cottage and keep an eye on what's happening. We have to make sure they find the well and arrest Graeme. Are we clear?' Wax looked intently at his brother, then Joe and Josh either side of him. They all turned to each other, nodded and shrugged.

'Not fair, why do they get to go and have all the excitement,' Tallulah whined.

'We need to stay with Trish,' Nicola said, ruffling her hair good-naturedly. I wanted to tell her to shut the hell up. This wasn't a game.

Tallulah flounced off to sulk and Trish remained quiet next to me, alert and taking it all in. This meant everything to her too. If today went wrong, she could end up back with a severely pissed off Graeme and even if it went well, she could end up in a children's home. This must be terrifying for her.

'Archie, you watch them like a hawk. No one is to go out,' Wax ordered. 'And, Dad! Only you answer the door if anyone knocks.' Wax flashed an apologetic glance at his mother.

She just rolled her eyes and said on an exhale, 'OK, I get it. Tea girl, in case I put my foot in it.' I loved her for that. She knew what rested on today. She was everything a mum should be.

'What are you going to do?' Ollie asked, his eyes straying doubtfully to the Whitelys.

They just looked at each other bemused, as if they'd entered some kind of parallel universe. Wax picked up Beccah's hand, who'd been quiet throughout the whole thing and gave it a squeeze. 'We're just going to be a couple out walking their dog,' Wax said with an intense gaze into Beccah's eyes that plucked my heart strings.

There was no time to dwell on that, as there was a light tap on the back door. We all turned our heads as Burt pushed it open and put his head inside. 'Can I come in?' he said, already coming inside and wiping his feet on the mat. He beamed his friendly smile and pushed his flat cap to the back of his head. He was dressed in green tweed like a gamekeeper and made sure he kept his green wellies on the mat. 'Morning, folks. Your lady, lordship,' he said with a nod to Jed and Olivia, doffing his cap a little. 'Like bloody Chicago out there, it is. Police sirens are going all over the place.'

We all looked at each other nervously. Thankfully, our attention was taken immediately by Brutus the Jack Russell, that Burt had let in the back door behind him. Trish crouched with delight to pet him when he scooted in with his nose to the ground. He rewarded her by wagging his tail furiously and offering his belly for a tummy rub.

Burt put his hand on the doorknob. 'Just drop him back later when you're done,' he said, nodding at everyone again and quickly left. Brutus sat looking up at us, wagging his tail, waiting for whatever fun we had in store for him. The little terrier would be Wax and Beccah's cover out in the woods to get close to the scene.

They immediately began heading for the door. I flashed a glance at the Whitelys, who still said nothing. They seemed traumatised, maybe making the connection to the constant barking they'd heard.

We congregated on the front porch ready for the boys to set off. Burt was right. We could hear sirens in the distance. The air was dank and still, like the natural world around us was waiting. The plan was working. Everyone was coming and coming fast.

I put my arm around Trish's shoulder and watched the boys and Beccah head off down the pathway in the direction of my old house. We all wished them luck and Ollie put up an arm in thanks before they disappeared into the trees. We were left there, looking at the empty place where they'd been.

Something caught my eye just coming into the circle of

the driveway. *Tallulah.* Where had she been again? She was definitely up to something. I looked back where Ollie had gone. Luckily he hadn't been here to see it and had no idea.

She approached us and immediately livened up. 'Why don't you go, Sam? I'm here to help watch Trish,' she said a little too brightly.

A large part of me suspected it was to avoid me asking questions.

I looked doubtfully at Trish.

'Go!' Trish whispered, next to me, stepping out from under my arm and shooing me with her hands.

I was conflicted, not sure if leaving her was a good idea. But she was almost as tall as me and sensible way beyond her years.

'You won't rest until you know he's gone for sure. None of us will,' Trish finished with a shrug and a half smile.

I looked doubtfully at Tallulah and then Archie and Nicola, sure there was no way the two of them would go for that. I was amazed when they looked at each other and Nicola nodded. 'It's OK. We can watch over her. Stay invisible … but come back and tell us what's going on!'

I had another wobble of indecision where I didn't want to leave Trish, but she was right, I had to know. We both did. I finally made up my mind and after a fierce hug, I was sprinting through the woods after the others.

I SLOWED down when the stillness of the forest started to seep through to me. I needed my head on straight for this. I couldn't rush in. In my haste, I hadn't even dematerialised yet. I remedied that right away.

I looked up through the bare trees at the red, angry sky bleeding into the grey treetops like a portent of what was to come. The forest seemed to know. The air was still and waiting. Everything sounded hollow and dull, as if the layers of decayed leaves were soundproofing the world. Nothing moved. Nothing even breathed.

The path narrowed, eventually, and I had to pick my way through the nettles and brush. The nearer I got, the more the air seemed electrified. Charged. Anticipating. My whole body felt on overdrive. My eyes and ears strained. My heart jumped at the slightest thing. Then my blood soared through my veins, making my temples thump. Even the break of a twig sounded exaggerated and weird. In fact, if I stood really still, I realised it wasn't quiet at all. The whole forest floor seemed to creep and crackle as if it was moving.

Then I felt it.

The punch of fatigue that made me sway and grab my mouth like I would be sick. I was forced to lean against the trunk of a tree to stop myself from falling.

Whispers, 'She's going. Quickly. Catch her.'

Helix? Left me on a soft murmur as I felt gentle hands catch me. But it didn't feel right. It seemed twice as strong and frighteningly unfamiliar.

'Don't put her to sleep yet,' a stern voice ordered.

I tried to force open my eyes to see where I was. I was still in the forest, but my gaze was swaying from side to side. Swinging and landing on a beautiful boy with yellow eyes, but before my heart could leap, it sank away. He was dark-skinned but had blonde, curly hair. I recoiled. It wasn't Helix.

She's seen you,' a voice came from behind me. The one holding me up.

I swung my head around to look up into his face, exaggeratedly, like I was drunk. Something was very wrong here. 'Who are you?' I asked, looking up into strange, green eyes and smelling a delicious smell I couldn't place.

He smiled slowly and turned me in his arms to face him. I became acutely aware I was flush up against him and his smile grew as if he knew. The other face peered at me over his shoulder. 'She is beautiful,' he said, in wonder.

I fought the almost overbearing urge to relax and succumb to them. Even that feeling felt odd to me, until I finally sifted my jumbled thoughts and pushed out of their arms and shouted, 'Get off me. I know what you are?'

I staggered and lifted my head to try to get a good look at them. They were tall, skinny youths, astonishingly hand-some. Standing shoulder to shoulder, watching me, as if intrigued with growing smiles on their faces. 'What are we?' the blond one said, laughing.

'Inc-incubuses.' It sounded wrong. I felt drunk and irri-tated by it. 'Energy-suckers!' I shouted, relieved I'd got there. 'And you have to leave me alone because I have something important going on today and my boyfriend will kill you if he knows you're here with me like this.'

They looked at each other and laughed. 'We can just put you to sleep?' the one with darker hair said, smirking.

Fear was breaking through my fog, that they would actu-ally do what they threatened to do and stop me getting to the well to see what was happening. I used all my strength to stand up to my full height. 'You could, but would you want to cross a paired demon?' I said, putting my chin up in the air proudly.

They looked at each other, wary for a second. 'Why isn't he here guarding you, then?' the blonde one said, eyes narrowing, slyly.

The other one began to smile, like they'd caught me in a clever lie.

I knew this could go one way or the other at this point. I had to be brave and, above all, I had to stay awake. Other-wise, I knew I'd have no resistance against these two crafty demons. So I did the only thing I could think of; I brazened it out. 'He is with The Ride.' I swallowed hard when they remained frozen and didn't seem to react. 'He is not here today because he is going through his change.' I inwardly flinched at revealing something so personal.

However, that seemed to do it, as they looked at each other again. 'The Ride *is* close,' the darker boy said to the other one. The pair now acting a lot more sober.

I nodded. 'It's coming here in two days' time.'

That seemed like all I needed to say. Something had rattled them. 'Be careful,' the blonde one said as they went to turn and walk away. 'Energy is strong here today.'

'The sort that fuels the change,' the other said with a final smirk.

I knew what that meant but didn't reply. They weren't wrong, that was for sure. It was probably what had brought them here in the first place. I should have asked them where they lived to tell Helix, but it was too late now.

I started to feel better as soon as they walked away and gradually blended in with the trees. The tiredness went and my breathing returned to normal. I couldn't help feeling a sense of relief at what a close shave that had been. They were undoubtedly incubus demons. Probably younglings like Helix, but certainly wouldn't have the same respect for me that Helix had.

I shuddered at what could have happened and pushed on in the direction I needed to go. My encounter had left my senses alive and buzzing. I couldn't afford to be side-tracked again. I was soon sweating; the air was so thick and damp. It wasn't cold and there was no wind at all. I kept going until the trees up ahead began to thin out and I saw blue flashing lights and heard voices.

I slowed down, even though no one could see me. There were several police vehicles parked in the driveway of my old house. I went closer, looking all around me as I went, in case they were searching the forest nearby.

As I came nearer, I could see my mother outside with a policewoman, crying. 'I don't know where he is. I swear. He didn't come home. What's happening? Have you found her… Have you found my baby?' She began to wail and the policewoman was forced to lead her over to a police car, where she sat her down in the rear seat. The policewoman stooped and continued to speak to her. My interest quickly waned. My mum was drunk. They'd get no sense out of her today.

I made my way to the fence that had always stopped me and slid easily between the rails. I headed purposely across the overgrown lawn, at the back, in the direction of the well. Then slipped through the fence again and into the trees, where the woods continued at the end of the garden.

It was at its thickest here. There were angry brambles scratching at my thighs and weeds hooking around my ankles. Navigating was difficult, but there was no way I'd give up now. I'd been delayed enough. I was just about to backtrack and go another way when I was yanked to the side and into the furious glare of Wax. I'd managed not to scream but I shrank a little under his glare. Beccah and the boys were behind him. Without a word to me, Wax motioned for Joe: 'Go with Josh and keep an eye on what's happening at the front of the house.'

Joe nodded and went off right away, with Josh following closely behind him.

Voices were nearby, so Wax pulled me behind the thick trunk of a tree. 'Why are you here?' he hissed.

I gave him my best dumb look, like he really didn't need to ask me that question. 'It's OK, Wax. Archie, Nicola and your mum and dad have Trish. I had consciously left Tallulah off that list and flashed a guilty gaze Ollie's way.

He hadn't appeared to notice. Wax exhaled, defeated, and eventually nodded in understanding. 'OK then. Go with Ollie and get a little closer. I'll come along with Beccah in a few minutes as nosey passers-by.'

Beccah smiled at me, holding the alert, panting dog in her arms. Ollie tipped his head in the direction we should go and I followed after a final nod of thanks to Wax. The silence was heavy, and not just from the gravity of the situation. Ollie had something on his mind, it was obvious.

The going was tough, though, so I had to match Ollie's footsteps behind him, picking an intricate path through the tree roots and brambles. I was surprised when we got to a clearing that hadn't been there before that morning. The police team had chopped everything back and cordoned it off in yellow tape in a huge rectangle. A metal frame was being erected over what was now clearly a large hole in the ground, about three feet across. A pile of mud and old stones, I guessed were the remnants of the wall, lay in a pile nearby. When a pulley was put in place, it was clear the frame was to lower someone down. I shivered when it dawned on me it would also bring someone up. *Me.*

Ollie had stayed quiet and looked at me sadly. He understood perfectly. He put a supportive arm around my shoulders and pulled me into a hug. He was such a nice guy, I really hoped Tallulah wasn't messing him around. My gaze tracked to the old oak and the thick rope that was still tied around it. Helix really did think of everything. It had stained green over time. I wondered where I'd be now if I'd used it properly.

I was jolted by a loud flash as someone took pictures of the scene. Ollie and I inched closer. They were pulling out a hose, which became clear was some sort of camera. A guy in white paper overalls nodded to his colleague. 'If we shore up the sides, there's enough space for someone to go down.

Ollie and I watched in silence. I felt numb. Detached. Like you would at a funeral after a tragic death. The bit when you watch the pallbearers do their job, solemnly. Quietly. Efficiently. I couldn't even pretend it was one of Helix's dream walks. It was real. I was a spectator, but this was my life. This was my death. A front row seat at my own grave.

Something struck my thoughts and brought me up sharp. With everything that had happened, I hadn't thought of it.

I looked around me. *Helix?* The two demons had been right about that. My heart thudded because he was nowhere around, which never happened. Not out here, at this place. I had flung the explanation of The Ride at them to scare them off, but I didn't really know where Helix was. He should be here. There was no way he'd let me face something like this on my own.

'Are you OK?' Ollie whispered.

I swallowed and nodded, but my heart was still fluttering. I couldn't let my fears distract me. 'I'm OK. It's just … you know.'

Ollie put his arm around me and squeezed me to him again.

They were putting long planks down the hole at intervals to stop any more earth from falling in. A rope was threaded through the pulley on the frame and a man, who looked more like a frogman, stepped into a harness and was slowly lowered down the hole.

I remembered the cloying air and how claustrophobic that felt. My breaths felt too shallow, just watching it. Maybe it was a lost memory of the air being crushed out of me. I couldn't be sure. That day was still a blur.

Ollie's arm squeezed harder as the frogman's head disappeared below ground.

'Excuse me. Stop! You can't be here,' a loud female voice said.

I looked up, guiltily, and caught sight of Wax hand in hand with Beccah, on the other side of the clearing. Brutus immediately ran up to Ollie and me and yapped. I crouched down and stroked him before he gave us away. I couldn't exactly pick him up, the little traitor. I could hear Wax's clear voice. 'Just walking our dog, officer. He caught a scent.'

'This is a crime scene. You need to keep back. There's nothing to see.'

'Brutus! Here! Sorry, officer. We'll go around and make sure to tell others not to come this way.' Wax looked right at us, widened his eyes and touched his ear. It was a clear message to be his eyes and ears.

'Thank you. Much appreciated,' the officer said.

'Is it OK if we get out at the path at the front of the house?' Wax asked just before he left.

'Yes, quickly,' the policewoman said, eager to hurry them along.

Wax made sure he walked directly past us. 'We'll check out the front,' he whispered. 'Stay hidden.'

Ollie patted his brother's back and Wax and Beccah disappeared into the thicket.

The rope and pulley system were proving useful. Several buckets of earth and stones had already been pulled up. Quite a pile was forming to the side.

'Hold it!' a voice came from down the well.

'Hold it!' an officer at the top repeated.

Everyone went quiet to listen.

He held his radio to his ear. 'Found anything, Jim?'

The radio crackled and then his voice came through clearly. 'Yeah ... there's something down here.'

CHAPTER 19

My blood froze and I looked up into Ollie's sympathetic eyes. He squeezed me closer and I faced the scene again. My eyes burned and my chest felt like it was filled with stones. Ollie's grip tightened, like he was holding me together, but I couldn't look away. I had to see it through to the bitter end.

A large canvas sling was being clipped to the pulley and slowly lowered down.

'Nothing changes. It's just closure,' Ollie said quietly, next to my ear.

I looked up into his kind brown eyes.

'Nothing more than that. You're loved. You're here. You're kind of alive,' he said with a rueful smile and a bob of his head. 'Now you'll be able to put all this behind you.'

I couldn't answer. The lump in my throat was just too big, but I snuggled into his warm arms as a thank you. He smelled of home, his favourite cologne and safety. We stayed that way for what felt like a very long time.

It took a while to load my body into the sling. I guessed it must be pretty decomposed by now. But I wasn't prepared for what came up. There was nothing recognisable from what I could see. Just a pile of slimy twigs. A gnarly tree stump dipped in wet mud. Or a petrified swamp monster pulled from the primeval ooze.

I edged closer, bringing Ollie with me, we were wound so tight. I must be cutting off his circulation.

Four officers unclipped the canvas sling from the pulley and lowered it gently to the ground. It opened like a giant leaf as soon as it was released. Then I began to recognise the mangled form of what was left of a human body. *Me.*

My mouth was distorted and open, set in a silent scream. Worse still, my eyes were gone. Just hollowed-out holes. My arms and legs that had first looked like twigs were frozen at weird angles because they had been broken and dislocated. I hoped that was after death from the weight of the landslide. There were no shoes.

Weird I should be struck by a detail like that. Of course. There were no clothes. Just my pink rainbow and unicorn nightshirt. The last remnants of childhood, reduced to a torn and muddied rag. You could just about make out the design, peering through the wet sludge. I'd been woken from sleep and ran, only to become a rotting mess in the ground.

Ollie must have sensed me unravelling, because he hugged me to him tighter if that was possible. 'You're OK. I'm right here,' he whispered a few times.

I couldn't take my eyes off my body. No wonder The Ride wanted me. I was grotesque. An abomination. I should not be walking the earth. I was so fixated; I hadn't even realised I was crying.

Ollie turned me into his chest and I finally released my gaze. 'Shh. It's OK,' he said, swaying. 'I've got it from here. Go home and be with your sister.'

I nodded next to the smooth fabric of his sports jacket, leaving a patch of wet from my nose. I pulled out of his arms, only half aware of what I was doing and stumbled off blindly into the forest. I didn't look back. There was no need. That part of me had gone. It was over. I was dead. Now I'd be buried. Have a grave in the graveyard and appear in the columns like everyone else. I breathed for the first time in what felt like an hour. I felt mildly better and began to recognise where I was.

'Trish! Trish,' a familiar voice was calling. Two voices.

Nicola and Archie? Even with my head fog that didn't sound right. Voices all calling my sister's name. I sped up. Then I started to run. My heart hammered. There was only one reason they'd be calling for Trish like that.

She must have gone.

I was now running. Bashing myself against the thin tree trunks and stumbling, almost falling a couple of times through scratchy jade evergreens. Until Waxley-Black Manor finally came into view and I flew into Nicola's arms as I joined the path. 'What is it? I asked immediately. 'Where is she?'

Archie joined us, then Olivia and Jed, looking wide-eyed and worried.

'WHERE IS SHE?'

Jed grabbed me and pulled me into his body like a strait-jacket. From his arms I saw the Whitelys approaching warily. They came to a standstill, traumatised and mute. Like they hadn't processed a thing and were being carried along on a wave of madness, expecting to wake up any minute. I wanted to take my fear and anger out on them. I wanted to scream and rail, welcome to the nightmare, but Jed kissed my cheek and I dissolved into sobs.

He released me when I was calmer and we all walked back in the direction of the house. Jed's arm was still around me, I guess to steady me as I wasn't looking where I was going. I was craning my neck to look in every direction. Nicola was at my other side as if they were scared I'd run off. 'We'll find her, I promise,' she kept on saying.

'I don't understand. How can she just disappear?' I asked no one in particular.

'She just went out into the back garden to put a bag of rubbish in the dustbin for me. She was there one minute and gone the next,' Olivia said, shaking her head miserably.

I stopped dead, making everyone stop suddenly too. 'I don't know why I didn't think of it before,' I said, dumb-founded with myself. 'Graeme has her … He must have lain in wait and snatched her as soon as he had the opportunity.'

I started walking again. Faster this time. Then I was running.

Archie and Nicola began running too and caught up with me. 'Stop, Sam. What is it? Where are you going?' Archie called breathlessly.

I burst into the open front door and ran up the stairs. Archie and Nicola stayed at the bottom, catching their breath. 'Keep looking,' I shouted. 'I need to find Helix. He's the only one who'll be able to find Graeme.' I had no time to explain.

I scrambled up the last of my little staircase to the attic and smacked open the door to my room. 'HELIX … HELIX! I shouted as loudly as I could. I hoped and prayed that he could tune into my heightened emotions from wherever he was. Surely he must know something was wrong by now. 'Please don't be too far away,' I prayed. Then I broke into desperate sobs when he didn't appear. *What can I do? What can I do?*

The police were busy digging up a body that was long gone, while Graeme had used the opportunity to take the only good thing left, *Trish. Oh my god, Trish.* I dissolved into misery.

I willed Helix to come, over and over. But even if he came, he'd put me to sleep and what use would I be. It was all hopeless. A wave of despair swept me down flat on the bed.

Then my stomach rolled. I was flying. Sucked into a vortex of blackness. Dark shapes. Feathers. Black wings enveloping me like a cloak. Warmth. The soothing aroma of winter spice. My whole body eased into it and relaxed. *Helix,* I sighed.

I had to fight the feeling. I shook my head. I couldn't succumb to the blissful sleep that was sucking me down. 'Helix … she's gone … he has her,' I croaked as the air whizzing past caught in my throat. It felt like the tops of the trees were zipping past fast below us. A blur of toy town houses and grey snaking roads. I wasn't scared because I was with Helix now.

'I know,' echoed through my head like a harsh wind through leaves. 'His energy is strong. I can easily follow it.'

I knew he would. My spirits rose with hope. I began to cry in relief. 'Where were you when I needed you?' His arms tightened around me and I strengthened my grip around his neck.

'I'm sorry, Sam. I had to meet The Ride. It is almost here.'

I couldn't even think about that right now. I could only deal with one catastrophe at a time. It was sapping my strength to remain awake as it was. I knew I was being carried and we were moving fast. Flying. Wind taking my breath. 'Where are we going?' I managed to get out between gulps.

'I know where he is.'

Everything began to go fuzzy. I felt woozy and sick. The world started to spin and I knew I was losing consciousness. 'Helix … Helix.' My pleas became weaker. Quieter.

The next thing I knew, I opened my eyes and was looking up into Helix's determined face. I was lying across his arms as he carried me. He gently put me down onto my feet.

I blinked. Looked down at my hands, opening and closing them, as they tingled. 'I'm awake. How can that be? Am I dreaming?' I asked, looking around me, desperately trying to get my bearings.

Helix smiled a nervous and crooked smile. 'It's the necklace,' he said, nodding his head towards me and raising his eyebrows for me to look.

My hand went up immediately and bumped into the small stone hanging around my neck. I picked it up and studied it. It looked like a yellow crystal of some sort, about the size of a penny.

'I will explain it properly later. We don't have much time. Just know while you wear it, no incubus can put you to sleep.'

I blinked while the implications began to hit me. My mind shooting straight to the strange encounter I had earlier. I didn't want to get into that now as I knew there was so much more to this than the obvious. Right then, I felt simply overwhelmingly grateful. The emotion was so strong that Helix closed his eyes in ecstasy to absorb it. He felt it from where he was standing. Then he opened them again with a slow smile. 'Come on,' he said, sounding like he'd like nothing more than to stay. He gripped my hand and we picked our way through the forest, this time more slowly, on foot.

Soon, the trees thinned and a small, single-story cottage came into view. Smoke was coming out of the chimney. A dirty white van was parked outside. *Graeme's.*

I surged forward as if to run, but Helix caught my arm and pulled me behind the cover of a tree. 'Stop, Sam!'

'What? Trish is in there.' I went to shout but adjusted my volume to a whisper.

'What are you going to do when you get in there?' Helix's expression was stern. It sobered me instantly.

'I'll materialise and throw him off balance.' As I said the words, I knew I hadn't thought it through.

Helix tutted and shook his head. 'What then? He'll have both of you.'

I felt suddenly angry and wanted to shove him in the chest, remembering our desperate measures as children. 'Well, what can you do, either?' I felt mean as soon as I threw the comment at him.

He didn't seem angry, in fact his face softened and then hardened with a bitter smile. 'Trust me. This time I have it covered. He will see me and he won't escape.'

I wanted to ask how, but he put me away from him, purposefully. There was something in his implacable expression that made me believe him. His look was dark and his eyes shone brighter. He started to scare me a little. There was something far, far deeper going on here. I had to trust him. So I nodded and finally let go of his arms.

'Please stay here out of sight. I will save your sister and put the balance right.' He pulled me back to him in a tight hug and kissed me for one combustible moment and walked away.

It left me bewildered. Stunned, dishevelled, and reeling. All I could do was watch his tall frame stalk right up to the front door. He tried the handle, stood back, gauged it for a second, then used his full weight to kick it in.

I was shocked at the violence of it and also his strength. The door splintered and opened easily, hanging off one hinge. Then he disappeared inside. I was beginning to understand that he was no longer the same boy as when we were children. Small in stature and making noises for distractions. Helix had grown up and so had I.

I heard Graeme's harsh voice shouting, 'Who the hell are

you?' For a moment my mind scattered, terrified for Helix. *What did Helix mean about putting the balance right?*

My heart was in my mouth as I trotted to the next tree, the last piece of cover before the house.

Then an ear-splitting scream.

Trish?

That was it. Hiding was forgotten, and I ran flat out to the house. I only just remembered Helix's warning for caution at the last moment. I didn't want to cause him more trouble. So instead of rushing in, I crouched to peep through the front window. I couldn't see anything with a layer of thick dust on the glass and the light behind me. I crept to the front door next and became even more worried when I couldn't hear anything at all.

I stood there for a moment, listening. My eyes prickled with sweat and my pulse raced when I heard a wail and then a whimper. *What to do. What to do.* I couldn't think beyond running in there, screaming.

Instead, I took two deep breaths and edged inside, my heart banging painfully on the walls of my chest. My legs were now shaking as I tipped forward slightly to peer inside a room. An empty bedroom. Simple bed, dark-wood side table and wardrobe. It didn't look used.

I rested back against the wall to gather myself. The back of my throat was too dry to swallow. I don't think I'd ever been so scared, not even when I was a kid.

To the right of me was a bathroom. That just left the open door in front of me. Kitchen and living room. *Must be.* I crept along the whitewashed hallway. Past framed yellowed photos of fishermen holding up large fish. Until I reached the door that opened inwards and I could peer through the crack between the door and the frame. I was right. The basic kitchen consisting of fridge, cooker and oak cupboards were at the end I was standing, and at the other, was like an old-fashioned sitting room, with a large open fireplace of red brick.

I moved to the edge of the door.

Trish was cowering on a small red leather sofa. I almost ran right to her, but I held myself back just in time. Helix had Graeme by the throat, pinned against the exposed brick wall.

Trish turned her head, her eyes widening when she saw me. Her sudden movement distracted Helix long enough for Graeme to draw back his fist and land a punch on Helix's jaw.

I screamed.

Trish leapt out of the way and squealed into my arms as Helix landed heavily where she'd been sitting. We clung together while Helix picked himself up. 'Get her out of here,' he growled.

I was shocked at the change to his voice. I couldn't move. My legs had taken root. Graeme now had a poker in his hand and was circling Helix with it.

I froze, terrified of distracting Helix again.

Graeme grinned and flicked his gaze at me. 'I knew you'd come crawling back sometime.'

My hatred bubbled up in my chest and I took a defiant step closer.

'Get out, Sam!' Helix shouted again. This time, keeping his eyes firmly fixed on Graeme.

'No!' I snapped back. 'Graeme needs to know who he's dealing with.'

Graeme laughed and threw the poker into his other hand to toy with Helix.

'He needs to know it's his fault I'm dead.'

A brief flicker of confusion rippled across Graeme's face.

I dematerialised.

Trish gasped.

The surprise made Graeme look twice, giving Helix the

valuable moment he needed. Before Graeme had time to think, Helix knocked the poker out of his hand and had him by the throat at the wall again.

I materialised, stooped, and picked up the poker.

Helix was transfixed with hatred, staring straight into Graeme's face, going a nice shade of purple.

'What are we going to do, Helix?' I was already looking around for a phone to call the police.

'Take Trish and get out, NOW!' Helix shouted, making me jump with the ferocity of it. He turned his head towards me and I hitched in a breath.

I took a step back and Trish clung to me again. I was shocked at the change in him. He looked so different. Not only was his voice several octaves lower, but his eyes shone bright yellow like a lantern. They more resembled a serpent and his features had become more angled and fierce. 'Please, Sam,' he said in his strange rasping voice. 'The Ride is on its way and I must fulfil my end of the bargain.'

I felt undone. Confused. Unsure what he meant. Any mention of The Ride terrified me. Somehow, I managed to shuffle the two of us towards the door, but I couldn't leave. Instead, I hovered and spied around the doorjamb. I couldn't help myself.

Helix had returned his full attention back to Graeme. He was slowly closing the distance between their two faces. My stomach rolled in horror and my throat was closing up, as I thought he was going to kiss him.

Graeme began to scream and struggle. Louder and louder. Scrabbling frantically, clawing at Helix's arms.

I covered Trish's ears instinctively, but I didn't move. I couldn't take my eyes off the grisly sight.

A flow of something; colour, vapour, spirit, whatever it was, began seeping from Graeme's mouth into Helix's. It became stronger and stronger until it gushed. Air began to rush around the room. Pictures were sucked from walls, ornaments from shelves, kitchen utensils from hooks. All were sucked into the vortex. A rumble began underfoot and the whole cottage began to shake. Thunder clapped overhead. Noise built until it was deafening.

Trish clung to me tightly. It was no use, we had to get out. I took one last desperate look at Helix, fearful that the roof would cave in. Graeme looked a grey and limp husk, as if the last of his life force had left him. The ceiling above us creaked and strained. I grabbed Trish and we ran for our lives. Out of the front door, across the shingle driveway until we were behind the cover of Graeme's van.

But we still weren't safe.

Something else was happening.

I looked up after another clap of thunder. Lightning forked and split a tree, no more than thirty feet away from us, making us both scream. The sky was growing darker by the second until it more resembled night.

The ground started to shake violently. So much so that we cowered low to the ground and I covered Trish with my body. I looked around me for somewhere to run to, but the van was our best bet after what happened to the tree.

The rumbling was getting louder. So loud that I thought the earth would rip in two. Suddenly a huge sinkhole opened up in front of us and I launched backwards, pulling Trish with me. Graeme's heavy van ached and groaned until it fell right into it. First the front wheel, then the whole thing lurched onto its side.

Trish and I scurried further out of the way as more earth caved in around it.

Then the rumble started to take form and rhythm. It got louder and louder until it started to make sense. A pattern, beating over and over until it reached a crescendo.

Hooves.

Hundreds and hundreds of them. A mighty stampede.

'Sam, Sam,' Trish whimpered next to my ear, clamping her arms around me as if she would get ripped away.

All I could do was shield her. Pulling her into my body and sheltering her with my arms. I was desperately trying to work out the direction the horses were coming from. They were already so loud; it was as though they were right on top of us.

Then they came. Out of the ground.

Jumping. Leaping. Neighing.

One after another.

Horse after horse leapt out of the widening sink hole of brown earth and grey rock, bringing smoke and the strong smell of sulphur with it. Huge, majestic, foaming horses. Each one carrying a creature more grotesque and terrifying than the last. Skeletons, ghouls, ghostly apparitions, spirits, demons, some red, some black, but mostly a washed-out grey, like the state of Graeme in the last glimpse I had of him.

I could only gasp, struck dumb, at the scene building in front of me. Trish was screaming, 'What is it, Sam? What is it?' over and over.

My heart plummeted as I understood. She couldn't see it. Only I could see what was happening, because I was dead and she was alive. To her it was a typhoon or an earthquake.

'It's OK,' I said, clutching her and soothing her while I kept an eye on the horses jumping up into the driveway. 'It will be over soon.' Although it didn't seem to be abating. The sweating horses were still coming, darting this way and that, as their riders struggled to hold them. Some were rearing and spinning, all impatient to get on with the race.

My heart felt frozen in my chest and every muscle tensed, as a hooded creature carrying a scythe as tall as his horse rode right up to me. 'The quarry?' his voice boomed, crackling as if it was coming from a loudspeaker.

I had no idea what he meant. My eyes strayed to the open door of the cottage and my voice stayed strangled in my throat. I watched, terrified for Helix, as the hooded rider took that as my answer, flattened himself down against the horse's neck and rode right in through the front door.

Then came the screams. For a moment, I lost my mind to panic. 'Helix!' I shrieked.

Trish had her head burrowed into my chest so I couldn't move and I couldn't leave her. My gaze remained riveted to the door. I didn't have to wait long.

The rider rode straight out, holding Graeme, kicking and screaming by the shirt collar, next to his horse. Then with a simple flick of the wrist, he sent Graeme flying up over the front of his saddle, like an old saddle bag.

Graeme looked grey and withered, as if he'd been dipped in a blue vat. The whites of his eyes and his teeth looked a hideous yellow. Blood oozed from the corner of his mouth. I wasn't sure if he was alive or dead.

My heart thrashed erratically as I tried to spot Helix, then sagged in relief when he came out casually after him. Another rider, a huge muscled being, with ruddy brown skin and twin axes crossed at his back, rode up to him, leading a spare horse. It gleamed, midnight black and pawed the ground, neighing loudly to the air.

I watched, amazed, as Helix vaulted easily onto the horse. I never even knew he could ride. The other male clapped his back loudly as if congratulating him. *Oh my god. The uncle. The man on the chestnut in the woods.* He was immense and terrifying this close up, like a huge, bearded Viking.

Hooves were still clattering and crunching the gravel

around us, but it was clear they were on the move again as they revved up their speed. I turned my head to see a line of them galloping off down the lane. The one with the scythe laughed heartily and smacked Graeme's behind across his saddle to torment him. 'I shall have great mirth with you,' he bellowed, laughing loudly.

Graeme pleaded to get down. I watched *him* helpless for a change, feeling nothing but gladness. I wondered briefly if that made me a bad person, but it didn't last long when I remembered why we were there in the first place. The hooded rider put a single bony finger to his bleached-white lips, as if to keep a secret. I had no idea what he meant. He simply laughed and galloped off after the others.

Their numbers were quickly dwindling and Helix rode towards me. My gaze tracked to the huge male riding next to him, who inclined his head as a greeting and rode off after the others.

Another rider. A beautiful woman came up behind Helix, riding an elegant grey. She said something and caught his attention. Her hair was long, black, lustrous waves to her waist and her flowing gown was blood red, almost completely covering her horse's back. She was stunningly beautiful. Ethereal. Pale.

I felt a fresh stab to my heart as Helix leant across and the two of them embraced for a full minute. I watched, enraptured, as she touched the side of his face and looked lovingly into his eyes. They said soft words to each other I couldn't hear and he nodded. I wanted to cry until the two both turned their heads to look at me.

The eyes. They were exactly the same. Same nose. Same full, sensuous mouth. *His mother.* It was so clear to me then. A cautious mix of fear and relief flooded through me.

She squeezed her horse nearer. I stiffened as she eyed me up and down and took a closer look. Then I hitched a breath as she bent down and touched a forefinger down the side of my face. Her eyes dropped to my chest and I instinctively put my hand up to protect the pendant Helix had given me. She smiled and sat back up in her saddle as if satisfied and looked back over her shoulder at Helix. 'You have done well, Helix. She is completely yours.' Her voice was warm and seductive, like soft wind chimes.

Helix's horse reared dangerously, eager to follow and then it hit me. This was it. Helix would be going with them.

'No!' I wailed, trying to get up on my feet, but Trish still clung to me, frantically. I wanted to talk to him. Decompress this. Meeting his mother, his uncle, what was going to happen to Graeme. Everything was unanswered. I needed more time.

'What is it? What's happening?' Trish screamed, gripping me tighter. Of course she had no idea what was going on.

Helix's horse pranced. He looked down at me sadly, but I knew there was no swaying him. This was the deal he'd made. Graeme's soul for mine and for him to join The Ride. Everything seemed obvious now. Helix had released me from the terror of Graeme and sacrificed his freedom. For me.

Helix managed to settle his horse a little to talk to me. He pointed at my chest. 'Never take that off.'

My hand instinctively went to the stone pendant he'd given me, around my neck, and I looked up at him pleadingly.

'I promise, I will be back.'

'Don't go,' I said, starting to cry. But my pleas were drowned by the crunch of hooves on gravel. Helix turned his horse, nodded at his mother and the two of them finally let their horses go. My eyes remained glued to him. He flew faster than I'd ever seen a horse run, down the lane, until he disappeared into thin air.

. . .

It was a long, slow walk through the woods to get back to Waxley-Black Manor. Neither of us could risk being seen. We found a dog walker's path and avoided most of the thorns and nettles.

The Ride was still a distant rumble, like a bad storm having passed. The sky was getting brighter, like the beginning of a new day, with the odd ray of sunshine breaking through. The air smelled clean like after fresh rain and the leaves seemed greener in this part of the forest. I realised I felt the safest I'd felt in my whole lifetime, but it was bittersweet, not knowing if I'd ever see Helix again.

Trish was quiet. I guess traumatised and thoughtful as well. Her future was more uncertain than mine. 'Was that the boy?' she asked, completely throwing me off guard. Up until then, I had no idea she'd seen him.

I let out a ragged breath to hide my emotion. 'Yes, Helix,' I said, simply. My face blank, with a lead weight pressing the centre of my chest.

Trish nodded and accepted it easily, not bombarding me with a million questions, which surprised me.

'OK?' I had to ask; it was so out of character.

'The same one who looked after you when we were kids,' she stated, nodding to herself as if it all fitted a picture she was building.

'Yes,' I said, watching her closely. 'He made sure Graeme went to Hell.'

Trish nodded again, absorbing it all. Surprisingly, she didn't seem scared at all. 'Is Helix your boyfriend?'

I let out a small blast of laughter, like a pressure cooker letting out steam. She looked at me and grinned. It was such a wonderfully ordinary, sisterly thing to ask. A conversation I thought we'd never get to have. My heart suddenly felt lighter and I wanted to laugh. Tears filled my eyes as I answered joyfully, 'Yes, we are a pairing,' echoing Helix's exact words. 'Incubus demons sometimes pair for life.'

I swallowed down the urge to bawl my eyes out and picked up the pendant he'd given me to examine it. It meant something far more than warding off amorous incubi.

Trish linked her arm through mine, giving me a knowing look. 'I'm glad, Sam. You deserve a love like that.'

We stopped and hugged right there in the middle of the forest. It felt suddenly alive with birds and new hope. A sob escaped me at the thought of where Helix might be and whether he would be safe. We patted each other's backs and laughed at our tear-stained, dirty faces and trudged on.

We hadn't gone far when I saw two boys, lounging back against the trunk of a tree on each side of the path, as if they had all the time in the world. My nerves instinctively ignited and prickled. It was the same two incubus boys I'd had a close escape from earlier.

I gripped Trish's hand and stopped dead in my tracks. They both pushed off their perch to face me. 'Don't come any closer,' I said.

The blonde boy looked at his friend and grinned. 'We mean you no harm. We just came to see what all the fuss was about.'

The Ride was now just a distant rumble and I was acutely aware that Helix had gone and we were two girls alone. I glanced down at Trish to check she wasn't affected by them. She was surprisingly awake. My hand went to my pendant and I wondered if it was extending its power to her as I held her hand tightly. 'Just The Ride,' I said, putting my nose up in fake bravado.

Both boys grinned and moved closer. I readied my stance. My heart began to beat hard, ready to run. 'Just The Ride?' the darker one mimicked.

'Yes, we were just seeing my boyfriend and his family,' I

said defiantly, not knowing whether I should give away that Helix had gone.

They were close to us now and I checked Trish again. She looked wide-eyed and curious. The pendant was working.

Both boys looked at it cradled in my hand. The blonde turned to the other. 'She was telling the truth.' Then they put their heels together and bowed their heads. 'Forgive us. We didn't realise.'

I swallowed, slightly bewildered but relieved. Not exactly sure of what just happened to change them, I gave them a stiff nod in response. 'Well, thanks. Excuse us, we have to get home.' I was already edging between them, dragging Trish with me as I went. However, I didn't miss Trish's goofy grin as she looked into the big green eyes of the darker boy. 'Sheeshh,' I said, under my breath. She was obviously not immune to their attraction. I had to yank her along.

'Be careful out here,' the darker one called. 'Keep your wits at all times.'

Trish was still craning her neck to see them as I pulled her along. The boy blew her a kiss and they both laughed and moved on in the opposite direction. It was a relief.

Thankfully, we arrived back before I could dwell any more on it. We should be happy. Graeme was gone and I had my sister back safe and well.

Archie and Nicola were out in the driveway and noticed us first. 'Hey! Here they are!' Archie shouted. 'They're back!'

Tallulah came running out of the woods on the opposite side of the drive. Olivia came out of the front door with Jed. 'It's OK, they're back. They look fine.'

All of them surrounded us, hugging and questioning us at once. We were bundled into the house, through the hallway and into the kitchen that felt warm and smelled of freshly baked bread. Trish looked alive and was smiling while the hugs continued. I felt numb and apart, right up to when Wax walked in with the others and pulled me to his chest.

My eyes remained open, in shock, as they tracked to Beccah smiling next to him. Her look of understanding was the final drop in an already overfilled cup of pent-up feelings and the tears finally came. Ugly, fat tears of heartache and relief. Everything just came pouring out like a mighty river. It was delayed shock, I guess. Happiness to have made it back with my sister in one piece, to the people I loved best in the whole world. The fact that it was Wax comforting me, making me feel safe, the one person who rarely showed affection, made it all the more raw. I sobbed my heart out in his arms.

'Come on now, you lot,' Olivia said, breaking up the grizzle fest. 'Hot soup and fresh bread to warm you.'

Wax let me go and gave me a single nod of respect that said infinitely more than words. Beccah kissed my cheek. 'Well done, brave girl,' she whispered.

We found our places around the kitchen table and we switched back to being a normal, happy family. My heart felt too full. Only the Whitelys were missing, but I was just too grateful to be home to ask where they were.

'Your mother is OK,' Wax said. 'She's still at the cottage.'

I nodded, flashing a look at Trish sitting opposite me. She just swallowed down the information, no doubt scared to contemplate what happened now.

'The well is still cordoned off for forensic investigation. The bo— the remains,' Wax amended after a quick glance at Trish, 'have been taken off to the morgue.'

I nodded and smiled wanly, in thanks.

All eyes went to me, waiting. I shared a look with Trish, which said she was OK with it. So I caught them up on everything that happened with Graeme. About Helix and about The Ride that took them both with them.

'Wow,' Nicola said, when I finally finished. 'How romantic, Sam. Helix saved you from The Ride and your stepdad by giving him to them. That's amazing. So brave of him.'

I felt the now-familiar lump come up into my throat at the mention of Helix and that last memory I had of him riding away. 'He had to promise to go with them,' I said, swallowing loudly.

Nicola smiled apologetically for being insensitive. I returned it, knowing she didn't mean to.

'Well at least that means we don't have to worry anymore about The Ride,' Joe said, reaching for a bread roll.

Wax, who was sitting opposite me, frowned a little. That brilliant mind of his was still churning. 'What is it?' I asked. 'It was the deal he'd made before I saw him.'

Wax ate a spoonful of his soup.

'Wax, what are you thinking?' Beccah prompted from next to him.

'Nothing … it's just not the next phase of the moon yet, so they wouldn't have moved on.'

My heart spiked. It meant Helix was still nearby. Then it struck me. 'Are you worried Graeme might escape?' I reassured myself that he'd looked pretty secure with the scary reaper with the scythe.

Wax just bobbed his head, not committing either way. 'Not exactly. I was just wondering who else they might leave … or take.'

My heart stopped, painfully. Of course. He was right. Helix came that way and they took souls all the time. They had one more day to do their worst before the next phase of the moon. There was no telling what they would do. I quickly made up my mind. If they came to this house and Helix was still with them, the obvious choice would be me.

I was just about to open my mouth with what I'd decided, when John and Jean Whitely appeared in the doorway to the kitchen. They were wearing their coats and carrying their overnight bags.

'Mom, Dad?' Beccah said, sounding surprised. 'Where are you going? Olivia made us some soup. Come and have some.'

They didn't move, making everyone stop eating to look at them.

'Everything is OK now, we're all safe.'

While thinking that wasn't strictly true, I nodded along with everyone else to support Beccah.

Jean looked up at her husband guiltily, for him to take the lead. My heart was already sinking with unease for Beccah, knowing whatever it was, it wasn't going to be good.

'Beccah, darling,' John began. 'I'm sorry, but we have to go home.'

Beccah didn't appear to be listening and shuffled her chair along to make room. 'OK, well, come and eat and I'll come with you.'

I looked around the table at all the furtive glances where we all knew what he was trying to say.

John made no attempt to come closer but remained standing with Jean in the doorway. 'No, dear, you're not understanding. I mean home to California.'

CHAPTER 22

$\mathcal{E}$veryone seemed to let out a collective sigh of disappointment.

'We've tried it here, honey, and we just can't make it work,' Jean added, sounding genuinely sorry.

Beccah's face filled with horror as their full meaning sank in. She looked stunned at Wax. Who stared back at her, frozen. Then across to his parents, who were straight on their feet to try and smooth it over. However, before either of them could utter a word, John raised his hand to silence them. 'Despite being eternally grateful for everything the two of you have done for our daughter and our family, our mind is made up. Beccah. Finish up your lunch and meet us at the house to pack. We have a car coming tomorrow afternoon at five.' With that, the pair of them turned and walked back out.

The room was stunned into silence. I sat numbly, weirdly grateful that the drama was on somebody else for a change. I was really sorry for Beccah. And Wax. They'd be parted just like me and Helix. Life was so cruel at times.

Everyone was uncomfortably quiet after that. We finished up lunch and Wax decided to go with Beccah to try and talk her parents around. I didn't hold out much hope. They'd seemed pretty decided.

However, my mind was soon occupied with more pressing things. Olivia and Jed offered to drive us over to my old house to sort things out with my mother. Nicola came along for moral support. Despite the drama with Beccah, things still weren't over for Trish. The police would ask questions and if my mum didn't sort herself out, Trish would be taken away and we couldn't let that happen.

We pulled straight into the driveway. Two police cars were still there with their blue lights flashing. Every room was alight behind them and the door was open, spilling out its glow onto the front driveway. It strangely lifted my spirits. We cautiously got out of the car and Trish flew into my mother's arms, standing in the doorway with two female police officers.

It was difficult for me to process after all the memories of neglect. After all, she was responsible for bringing Graeme into our lives.

One of the police officers immediately spoke into her radio. 'Missing child located. Repeat. Patricia Payne has just turned up at her home. Appears to be unharmed.'

Olivia hurriedly explained that Trish had been hiding at their house. 'She's just tired, officer. We found her in one of our outbuildings. We fed her and brought her straight back as soon as we could.' It was a good excuse because their house was the closest and it also released them from getting into any trouble. 'It took a little while to convince her as she was pretty scared to come home,' Olivia added to cover their tracks. It was a plausible cover story. She couldn't exactly say Trish had taken shelter with her dead sister.

The police officer continued her conversation into her radio and the word 'Child Services' was mentioned. My gaze flicked to Trish's and we exchanged a worried smile.

'She's welcome to stay with us until everything is sorted,' Jed said. 'She knows my son and his girlfriend and she seemed quite relaxed there.'

My heart warmed watching both their hopeful faces as the officer relayed it onto her radio. They were such wonderful people.

Both Trish and I watched the police officer walk away, nervously. It was clear she didn't want us to hear the whole conversation. I just hoped that Olivia and Jed, being lord and lady of the manor, gave them a lot of social standing and weight to their offer.

An agonising few minutes passed. Trish still clung to our mother. My mind was already racing to what I would do if Trish was taken away.

THE POLICE OFFICER came back and exchanged a look with her partner. My heart leapt with hope that it could be good news. 'Might be OK,' she said, smiling at Olivia and Jed. 'Would you be OK with this arrangement?' she said, directly to Trish.

She looked up at her mother, who smiled back and then nodded.

'I doubt your stepfather will be back. He'd have been on the run as soon as he realised the well was being excavated. He'll want to put as much distance between him and this place as possible.'

Of course I knew he'd never return; there was no coming back from where he was headed. But they didn't. So when it was decided that Trish wasn't in any immediate danger, I finally let out a slow and even breath and took comfort from that.

Trish simply said the truth. That she'd run away because

she thought she was next, which set my mother off again in another round of tears.

The policewoman was still talking into her radio. Social services and an emergency placement were mentioned.

My heart shattered with panic and Trish grabbed and almost crushed my hand.

My mother wailed, but it was clear she was drunk and in no fit state to look after a child.

'We have ample room, officer,' Olivia offered again. 'Can't she stay close to home? At least until a more stable environment can be arranged for her.'

The policewoman nodded to her colleague. 'A social worker will have to come out and visit you,' she said, pausing her call and talking directly to Jed and Olivia.

'Of course,' Olivia said, looking up at Jed in relief.

'Surely if her mother becomes better, she might not need to go anywhere else at all,' Jed said hopefully.

The policewoman smiled, not committing either way. 'Go and get some things,' she said directly to Trish, who brightened immediately and she shot inside to grab them. I remained outside not wanting to miss anything important.

I wanted to materialise and say a lot of things to my mother. I wanted to shout at her to pull herself together before she lost Trish and broke her heart. I wanted to show her I was still there, but I couldn't. She would definitely lose her mind and they would never give Trish to her, then. It would serve no purpose. I served no purpose here. Not anymore. It was a harsh fact, but I knew I would never live with my mother again.

However, while the police did a final check around the house, Jed did what I couldn't, with Olivia looking on kindly and was the perfect parent. They really were the best people in the world. He picked up my mother's hand and patted it. 'We'll do what we can to help you, Mrs Payne. If you get yourself sorted, counselling and all that, we'll do what we can to support you so Trish can stay with you.'

My mum was nodding gratefully and crying into an old hanky. Trish came back with her things and clung to our mother again. It shocked me how close they were. I guess I hadn't been around for quite a while. It stung a little. She'd always been the baby. I guessed with me out of the picture, they had grown even closer.

I motioned silently for us all to go. Jed shook my mother's hand, who hugged him instead. Olivia kissed her on the cheek and Trish was reluctant to let her go. We finally turned towards the car when the policewomen returned. What would happen to my mother next, I didn't know.

I turned for the car. It was now dusk and the air temperature had dropped. I let out a ragged, frosty breath and felt an overwhelming sense of relief. My past had gone and I was happy to let it go. I could finally begin again.

We got in the car silently. I sat in the back, next to Trish, who was waving frantically at my mother, still crying on the porch. I felt no emotion as we pulled away. Except strangely empty. I guess my heart had long left that place. It was now with Helix. My beautiful, perfect, demon boyfriend. Fear caught in my chest. I had no idea where he was, or whether he'd left yet.

THAT NIGHT we cleared out the spare servants' bedroom next to mine, so Trish had her own room. 'You can call it yours … for whenever you stay over,' Olivia said, smiling.

Trish immediately flew into her arms, her cheeks wet with tears. 'I'm so happy. Thank you, Mrs Waxley-Black.'

'Call me Olivia, please.' However, the look she gave Jed over Trish's head said they weren't out of the woods yet.

I was physically and emotionally exhausted, so, after

thanking Olivia and Jed as well, I kissed Trish and tucked her into her bed. Then I showered and slid gratefully into mine.

My mind wandered and tears inevitably came. I thought of all the years I'd spent with Helix and now he'd gone. It felt like a part of me had been ripped away. And what made it so much worse was that I had no idea when I'd see him again.

However, the tiring day, tears and the warmth of the bed, sent me into the deepest sleep I'd ever had and straight into my dream place.

Helix was sitting casually on the step to the pagoda. His long legs were stretched out, crossed at the ankles in front of him, and he was leaning back on his hands as if soaking up the sun. Which of course was me. All that upset and emotional energy was flowing straight out of me and into him. He reminded me of a lazy cat on a wall. I strode up to him. Faster, beginning to jog. I was so thrilled to see him, mixed with anger at the way he'd decided everything on his own.

I stopped just in front of him and he simply grinned and patted the space next to him for me to sit. I scowled but I couldn't keep it up.

He laughed and pulled me down, tumbling with me so we rolled into the soft grass. He ended up on top, searching my face with those beguiling lion's eyes.

I instantly relaxed and sighed into him. I couldn't help it.

His grin widened as he felt everything.

I became serious. 'Stop it, Helix. I'm upset with you.'

The smile dropped from his face and he looked contrite and soulful. 'Your stepfather is gone. You're free and you have your sister,' he said with a frown as if I should be happy.

'But I don't have you,' I said simply, swallowing, trying not to cry. 'You should have talked it over with me, Helix.'

He studied me for a moment, like he wanted to try to argue but couldn't. 'I'm sorry,' he said, eventually. 'But the outcome would have been the same,' he said, sadly. His eyes dropped to my hand as I picked up the loose pendant lying on my chest between us. I was surprised that it was even in my dream. 'What does it mean?' I asked.

Helix paused for a beat, rolled off me and leant up on an elbow. 'It means you can see all the creatures from the underworld, even if they don't want to be seen – particularly other incubi.'

I studied it, frowning. I totally got how that could be useful. Wax would definitely be pleased. It would certainly alert me to any of Helix's amorous relatives who happened to pass by. *Or those crafty demons in the woods.* 'Is that all it means?' I asked, knowing I sounded a bit ungrateful, but I couldn't help the disappointment landing in the pit of my stomach.

I reached over and pulled out the one that hung around his own neck, just tucked into his black t-shirt. It was the same colour as mine, just smoother, like a pebble.

'Mine is a moonstone, cut from the exact same piece of rock as yours. It means I can be seen when I want to be. But it also means that my powers can be held back from you.'

My eyes shot to his. It explained why we'd stayed awake with him earlier today. The benefits of that began to hit me. If only he was staying around to use it.

'You still don't get it, do you?' he said, laughing a little. 'The two stones are joined, as we are.' He was studying my face lovingly, as if he was waiting for me to fall in. 'The pairing is official. Everyone in the underworld now knows we are paired.'

My heart stalled. My mind went straight to the two demons, bowing. They must have recognised right away what it was. I was kind of in shock. 'Like a proper couple, you mean?'

He nodded solemnly. 'It's protection, but it goes far

deeper than that, Sam. It can never be broken.' He looked a little cautious as he said the last part.

'So I can see you in the real world, any time I like … like today?'

He smiled and nodded, looking relieved.

'And you don't have to put me to sleep?' I said, starting to smile as well.

He was now grinning, watching all the cogs fall into place.

'So we can—'

He laughed loudly and rolled right on top of me again. We were kissing. Long, deep, inhaling kisses. Rolling together, over and over in the grass. I was swept up in the wonderful taste and feel of him. Until I finally pulled apart for air. 'Take me back, Helix,' I said, breathily. 'Now please. I want this to be real.'

We were back in my room in the blink of an eye, but it was in complete darkness after the bright light of my dream. Then, as my eyes adjusted, I saw the bluish light from the moon shining over Helix through the small loft window. It was the stark reminder that he would be leaving me soon.

Helix was sitting on the edge of my bed and the moonlight caught the right side of his face. I had a perfect view of him. He pulled his shirt off over his head and I was rewarded with a perfect view of his smooth, perfect skin. 'Are you sure?' he asked, quietly.

I nodded. My heart was beating so fast, I could barely speak. 'And no powers.'

He shook his head. 'I promise.' He held up his necklace, which seemed to glow as if it was lit up from within. 'Not even the ones that come by themselves.'

He lost the last of his clothes and shimmied down on the bed next to me.

I could barely breathe as he helped me pull my nightshirt over my head.

We lay facing each other, searching each other's faces. The moonlight was behind him, so his face was now in darkness, but his eyes held a subtle glow. I was immediately transported back to when we were kids and we would huddle together for warmth and comfort. I knew then that we were always meant to be together. 'I love you,' I said, simply. I always had. Right from the angry little imp who threw things and ran through the house to distract Graeme. He was so brave. Everything he did was to care for and protect me.

'And I you,' he replied solemnly. His hand threaded through my hair and before I knew it, we were kissing again. 'We will be together whenever I can,' he whispered.

My heart broke when I realised this was his goodbye. A physical pain shot right through me. Silent tears fell as my whole body tingled, his warm skin against mine and I became lost in him. With him. For ever him.

Thoughts of Trish, happily secure in the bed next door, were rocked and eased away, with the gentle creaking of my bed, way up in the attic, while the rest of the house remained quiet and blissfully unaware.

CHAPTER 23

I woke deliciously warm, my skin sensitive and feeling the softness of the sheets around me. However, when I turned my head, Helix had gone. All I was left with was a wonderful memory and a hole in my chest where my heart should be. Because he'd taken it with him and I would never be the same again. He'd been everything I thought a love should be and then simply disappeared. It was heartbreaking.

Tonight was the new quarter moon. The Ride would leave and I didn't know whether I'd get to see Helix again before he went with it.

I wanted to talk about what had happened between us. I felt excited and exhilarated, punctuated by a bone-deep sadness that he had to go away. It felt like he was a soldier going off to war and I was the soldier's wife being left at home wondering. Worrying. He promised to come back. I had to cling to that, otherwise I'd go mad.

It was noon by the time I showered and ventured downstairs. I was nervous someone would notice the difference in me. However, as soon as I stepped into the kitchen, I knew something else was going on. No one was talking. They seemed agitated and snappy with each other. I sheepishly went and helped myself to coffee at the counter. Then I joined Trish already sitting at the kitchen table. I was about to ask her what was going on when I saw Wax at the far end, with his head in his hands. Ollie was next to him, talking quietly and rubbing his back, with Olivia doing the same on the other side.

I looked at Trish. 'Beccah has to go today, I think,' she said quietly.

Oh no. Wax must be devastated. He dropped his hands and his eyes looked ruined. Like he hadn't slept for a week. Or, he was drunk. I remembered how dangerously unpredictable he could be before Beccah came. He clenched and unclenched his fists as if he was fighting back the urge to explode.

Jed appeared to be standing by, nervously, just in case he erupted into one of his murderous rages. It felt strange because he'd changed so much and it felt like such a long time ago. I think we'd all forgotten how unstable he used to be.

I think I understood now. After Helix and only just discovering what we were to each other, I totally got it.

'She will come back at her first opportunity. She's an adult now, darling,' Olivia was saying.

Wax stood suddenly, shoving the table roughly and pushing his chair over behind him. The unexpected shunt and loud scrape almost pushed us off our chairs.

'Wax!' his father bellowed. 'Get a hold of yourself, there are children present.'

For a moment, Wax looked at me and Trish, bewildered. His eyes desolate. But then his face clouded over like a winter storm and he turned and kicked his chair so it crashed against the wall and he stormed out.

Olivia went to follow, but Jed held her back by the arm. 'Leave him. He'll calm down.' Then he pulled her into the shelter of his arms.

Trish was wary, but relatively calm about the whole thing. I guess she was pretty accustomed to violence. Nevertheless, I pulled her over to sit on the sofa, out of the way. We were soon joined by Tallulah and Nicola.

'That doesn't bode well,' Tallulah said.

'You can't blame him for being upset,' Nicola said.

I smiled at her. She always saw the good in people. However, they were both right. 'She was the one thing that grounded him and made his life tolerable,' I said wistfully, thinking of my own situation.

I became suddenly aware that no one had spoken for a full minute. I looked at them on either side, staring at me as if I'd said something profane. Trish in amazement, Nicola in wonder and Tallulah in shock. 'What?' I said, starting to feel uncomfortable. 'I didn't say anything.'

'You didn't need to,' Tallulah said, now laughing.

Trish frowned as if she couldn't quite believe something. 'Did you …?'

'Did I, what?'

'She did,' Nicola said, nodding sagely, like it was the most obvious thing in the world.

'The dirty deed,' Tallulah said, putting on a dramatic voice and then laughing. 'It's all over you like a glow.'

I put my hands up to my cheeks as if she was being literal. They felt hot. I looked at my sister guiltily. We were supposed to tell each other something like this, first. 'It only happened last night,' I said quickly, waiting for her disappointment, but her eyes sparkled with mischief and she was grinning widely.

'What was it like?' Tallulah asked, reducing her volume, conspiratorially.

'He's an incubus, Tallulah, what do you think?' I said flatly. But my stomach fluttered at the memory and I became caught up in their excitement. I had to admit I was really starting to enjoy myself. I wanted to tell people. I wanted to shout it to the world.

'Oh, I bet,' Tallulah said, wide-eyed. 'I wish we could see him, so we knew what he looked like.'

'He's beautiful and fierce, like a dark angel, or something,' Trish said.

We all studied her, amazed. I'd forgotten. Of course she'd seen him. At the cottage, when Helix wore his pendant. He'd killed Graeme right in front of her. Not exactly a great introduction.

I nodded with a sigh. 'He doesn't always look that scary.'

'How come she can see him and we can't?' Tallulah asked in her annoying, whiny voice.

'I think you will now if he's around. He got us these pendants,' I said, picking mine up and holding it out for her to see. 'It means we can see him without his powers putting us to sleep.'

I turned the stone over and looked at it lovingly. 'It means we are together. He said they're cut from the same rock.'

Trish reached out her hand to look at it more closely. 'In his language, that means you're like, married, Sam.' I looked at her enraptured face, stunned. She was so insightful. She was also right. That was exactly how it felt. I felt so painfully happy, but then I became swamped by an overwhelming sadness. My life had only just begun, only to have the lid slammed down hard on it before it even got started.

'Excuse me,' I said, getting to my feet. I needed to be alone.

They seemed to understand and looked up at me sympathetically, letting me go without protest.

I walked quickly out of the kitchen and ran all the way up the stairs until I got to the first landing of bedrooms.

I paused, hearing hard metal music blaring from Wax's room. I wasn't the only one upset and cursing how unfair everything was. I turned and walked towards Wax's door, coming to a standstill right outside.

I knocked.

There was no answer, so I tried the handle. It opened, so I pushed it slightly and peered inside. My heart raced, knowing I could be entering a wild animal's cage. However, when my eyes adjusted to the dimness of his room, I saw him sitting on the end of his bed, looking at his phone.

I ventured inside and closed the door. He looked up and saw me. I froze, expecting him to yell at me to get out, but surprisingly, he went back to scrolling.

His lack of response gave me the confidence to slowly walk into his room, until I sat quietly next to him. He was scrolling photos. Every one of them of Beccah, or the two of them together. Many were selfies. Looking happy and carefree.

He picked up his remote from the bed next to him and turned down the music.

'She will be back, you know.' *A lot sooner than Helix*, I finished in my head.

'It's not the same,' he said, clenching his jaw. I realised then just how close to the surface his anger was.

I let out a sigh. I agreed with him there.

He looked at me sideways as if he was surprised I hadn't gone on trying to make him feel better, which was impossible. 'So you and whatshisname … you're a couple now?'

I felt the heat of his inquisitive look and wondered how the hell he knew so quickly.

He answered my unspoken question by tapping his

temple. 'Spirit realm telegraph, remember? Bloody gossip central.'

'What are they saying?' I asked, barely able to get the words out, I was so shocked.

He smiled slightly and looked at his phone again. 'What aren't they saying?'

Despite my mortification at being branded the new hussy of the spirit world, I relaxed a little, probably because Wax had. He seemed to have lost that sharp edge to his anger.

I let out a ragged sigh and thought about that. I could only imagine what it was like to be hounded by voices every minute of the day.

'She's the only one who quietens the voices,' he said miserably, reading my mind again. He threw the phone away on the bed behind him.

'I don't know when I'll see Helix again,' I said, mirroring his mood. 'The Ride leaves today and he will have to go with it.

Wax looked sideways at me again, but this time, frowning and curious. As if he was seeing me properly for the first time.

We really did have a lot in common.

He nodded to himself as if I'd answered some sort of internal question and faced front again. 'Beccah is leaving at five.'

Around sunset. The same time as Helix.

We both sat in silence after that. Neither of us feeling uncomfortable. We were both so lost in our thoughts. I finally stood up. I'd become stiff and restless and wanted to check on Trish. I slowly made my way to the door.

'For what it's worth, I'm glad you're here, Sam.'

Wax's rare words of praise made me pause with my hand on the doorknob. 'Thank you,' I said, my emotion threatening to come up into my throat.

. . .

TRISH APPEARED TO BE FINE, watching TV with Nicola and Archie, so I went back to the sanctuary of my room. I went straight to my drawer, which still felt like the start of it all, and pulled out my diary. I hadn't written in it for such a long time. I went to the last entries. The ones where I had left the messages for Helix, tracing his wonderfully childlike writing with my finger. I took out the pen from the spine, went and sat on my bed and began to write:

TO MY DEMON in the attic.
Thank you for always being there.
You are my rock, my heart and my best friend.
Even though you're going away, I know you're doing it for me.
You always think of me.
Please come back.
For as often and as long as you can.
And I pray that one day we will be together, for ever.
Lots of love,
Your Sam
XXX

MY CHEEKS WERE wet by the time I'd finished writing and placed it back precisely in my drawer. I remembered to tie the pink ribbon around the drawer knob and hoped he got to read it before he went.

Then I went and lay down on my bed, curling tightly into a ball, waiting for sleep. Praying that he'd need to charge his energy before he left.

I must have slept, because the next thing I knew, Tallulah

was rapping loudly on my door. 'Are you decent?' Tallulah said, giggling.

My heart sank at my being completely alone. 'Go away, Tallulah,' I shouted into my pillow.

'You have to get up. Beccah has come to say goodbye. The Whitelys are here before their car comes to take them to the airport.'

I hadn't realised it was so late. Helix hadn't come. I groaned and dragged myself to sit up. 'OK, I'm coming,' I said with a weary voice.

'No snogging. Get up!' she said with a final giggle and clomps down the wooden staircase.

I wanted to shout out I was alone, idiot, but I didn't have the energy and her footsteps had already receded. I looked at the ceiling and let out a long sigh. I had to pull myself together to say goodbye for Wax and Beccah's sake.

I hefted myself out of the bed, feeling double my usual weight. Then I grabbed the first pair of jeans and jumper I came to, quickly dressed and pulled my boots on. I did actually brush my hair, though, and pulled it back into a neat ponytail.

I went downstairs and spotted Trish standing in the doorway to the snug with Nicola and Archie. She smiled at me weakly to say it was awful, but she was OK.

The Whitelys were already there in the hallway. Jed was shaking John's hand, then he kissed Jean's cheek and pulled Beccah into a fierce hug.

My focus went straight to Wax, standing pale, withdrawn and perfectly still, nearby. He was an empty shell. There, but not there. Lost. Empty. Devastated. I went and stood next to him and gave his hand a squeeze.

He looked down at me with a flicker of recognition. As if he was trying to break through a haze, but it only lasted a second and he went straight back to gazing at Beccah, who was now hugging us all one by one.

'Are you sure you can't stay?' Olivia was saying, swapping a look with Jed, when she saw what I had in Wax. She was terrified at what would become of him if Beccah left.

Jean did the same with John, a little exasperated. 'It's the right thing to do,' she said as her only explanation.

'Not for me,' Beccah said, running straight into Wax's arms, knocking the air out of him. He tightened his arms around her and pursed his lips as if he'd fight anyone before he'd let her go.

Then there was a huge clap of thunder and the lights flickered and went out.

CHAPTER 24

*E*veryone stood still for a stunned moment while our eyes adjusted to the darkness. It was dusk outside, making the hall pretty dark but not completely.

'Quick, Jed. Grab some candles,' Olivia said. 'They're in the middle drawer in the kitchen.'

Jed flicked on the torch on his phone and went to walk off in that direction.

'Wait … Listen!' Ollie hissed.

Jed stopped and turned.

I moved quickly, nearer to Trish and put my arm around her. 'What is it?' she whispered. My eyes were still adjusting, but I could hear it, rumbling. Louder and louder in the distance, like the approach of a train. The house itself began to shake. The floor was vibrating. Glass and china were clinking together in their display cabinets.

'Is it an earthquake?' Tallulah shrieked.

Trish and I clung together. 'It's them,' she whispered fearfully.

She was right. She'd been blind to them that day but had heard them perfectly. My heart was beating right out of my chest. 'It's The Ride,' I shouted. Terrified and elated at the same time that Helix could be with them. *Yes.* Hooves. Hundreds, clearly noticeable now.

'We need to go now, John,' Jean was yelling. Panicking, trying to pull John by the arm. Not wise at all, because I was sure they were coming right up the drive.

I felt a little braver and stepped out into the centre of the hallway. 'Please. Don't move,' I called out, as calmly as I could. 'You'll be OK, just don't panic and stand still.' I didn't even know where I was getting my bravery from.

There was a loud bang. I turned and the front door burst open to reveal the huge form of the Reaper. Hooded. Black cape. Scythe. Everything. I quickly looked around at the others to make sure they were seeing what I saw.

Jean faded into a faint in John's arms.

Tallulah let out a scream, which she quickly stifled with her hand.

I guess I had my answer. For a moment, my heart stalled and I faltered, thinking I'd got it all totally wrong and they were here for another soul, but he stepped forward and out of the way to reveal a stunning, fidgeting black horse in the dark porch. Its sweat gleamed on its twitching muscles in the rising moonlight. On his back was a huge male, with what appeared to be a boy on the front of his saddle. His horse pranced, but he managed to lower the boy as gently as he could by the scruff of his collar to the porch floor. He landed in a messy heap and scrambled up onto his feet. His clothes and his face were filthy, covered in what looked like soot. Under all the dirt, his hair appeared to be blond. He looked about thirteen or fourteen – thin and awkward, at that gangly stage.

I felt the others close in behind me as we all craned to see who it was. It was Beccah who came up to my left shoulder. She had a strange, entranced look on her face. She edged forward and Wax went to grab her to pull her back. 'Be careful,' he said.

My gaze shifted from the boy dusting himself off to movement from the large male on the horse behind him. He dismounted and let his horse go with a pat. It turned and trotted out to join the hundreds of others neighing and circling the driveway. None of us moved; we were all transfixed by the strangers.

'Pete … Is that you?'

I turned my head to stare at Beccah, leaning forward, her eyes brimming with tears.

'Beccah?'

I faced front to see the boy begin to run towards us, to be met by Beccah. Slamming into each other's arms. They cried, clinging to each other, rambling words of disbelief, love and fear of never seeing each other again.

I remained frozen in shock as it was clear who the boy was. I turned to see if the Whitelys could see what I was seeing.

They seemed reluctant at first. Not fully understanding. Or daring to hope they weren't dreaming. Jed and Olivia gave them a little nudge forward. The rest of us looked between them and Beccah and Pete, who were now openly crying in each other's arms.

The Whitelys remained wide-eyed and hesitant. Then Jean took a cautious step. It was like morning light when recognition gradually dawned on her face. I wanted to cry at the strength of it. 'Peter … my baby,' Jean cried and ran to him.

'Oh, my boy!' John said, quickly on her heels.

Beccah immediately opened her arms and pulled the two parents into one big, huddled embrace. I think we all fought the urge to join them.

I tore my eyes away from the heart-rending scene to look

at the large male still waiting patiently nearby. His eyes were on me, gorgeous, dark-lashed, citrine eyes, watching me closely.

Heat began to slowly rise through my whole body from my toes. A familiar pain stabbed me through my lower abdomen as an overwhelming attraction hit me. Another large male came and stood next to him and whispered something. The first one nodded.

My eyes meandered down his long legs and back up to the trim waist and huge, muscular torso, clad in black wool and leather. Then I stopped dead at the yellow pendant against his chest.

Pendant?

My eyes shot back to his face. Square jaw. Five o'clock shadow. High cheekbones. Overlong black hair. 'Helix?' came out as a tiny squeak. My breath left me and I flew across the tiled floor into his arms.

He felt bigger, stronger, but I knew his smell right away. I buried my nose in his shoulder and breathed him in. I was vaguely aware of the swirling movement and sound of horses receding behind us.

The lights flickered and came back on. I pulled apart and looked up at his face. Helix's face, but different. I swallowed down my emotion at seeing him again. 'You changed.' I clung on to him, not caring what a spectacle we were making.

Then he was kissing me and spoke in a rush at my ear, 'I'm sorry. I had to go. My change was upon me. I needed to get to my uncle.'

I looked up into those eyes. The same eyes, as beautiful as ever and remembered the conversation about him becoming an adult. Our night together must have triggered it. 'Are you staying now?' My heart lifted with hope.

He shook his head sadly. 'I have a week to regain my strength before I must catch up with The Ride again.'

A week. It was something. I began to smile. 'A week here. With me?'

He grinned his lopsided grin and lifted me into a bone-crushing hug that squeezed the life out of me. 'Well, I hoped.'

I kissed him shamelessly then.

We finally pulled apart and the absolute silence hit me. No hooves and no voices. Helix released me and I turned to see that all eyes were on me. Wide eyes and open mouths. I guess they'd never seen the quiet girl in this light before. I made sure I kept hold of Helix's hand. I gazed up at him and he looked adoringly down at me. 'This is my …' And I thought about it for a moment. 'My for ever partner, Helix.'

HELIX WHISKED me off to my attic room after shaking everyone's hand. They were too preoccupied with Pete and the Whitelys to take too much notice. Olivia gave them a room to be alone, to spend some precious moments with the son they'd thought they'd lost for ever. Olivia called after us all, 'Family dinner at seven in the formal dining room, please. Don't be late.'

I didn't care. I spent the next couple of hours acquainting myself with Helix's new body. I wasn't complaining. Although I was pretty fond of the old one. I soon relaxed into the same citrine eyes, same laugh and mannerisms that had kept me safe for a lifetime. When, at last, we lay in a crumpled heap in each other's arms, I don't think I'd ever felt happier.

The gong rang at seven o'clock, calling everyone in the house to the dinner table. We dragged ourselves out of bed and quickly showered and dressed. I put on the one dress I owned from the last dinner party, remembering ruefully the disaster that had been and stood in front of my full-length mirror. Helix stood behind me with his hands on my shoulders. He dwarfed me on all sides. 'Was it painful?' I asked, brushing my hair into a neat ponytail.

He nodded, absently, watching my every movement as if I was hypnotising him. 'Every bone must break and my muscles tear and expand.'

I flinched just at the thought and turned in his circling arms to gaze up at him in wonder.

'But it was worth it to finally be what I was born for with you.'

My heart fluttered and he stooped to kiss me gently. 'Are you ready to go and be part of the family?' I asked, dragging myself out of the kiss with effort.

He nodded and smiled into another kiss. 'I'd walk through Hell for you.'

'Hey, it's not that bad,' I laughed, playfully smacking his arm. Then I stopped at the genuine look of confusion on his face. He was being literal. The reality of that brought a lump to my throat. He'd bargained with The Ride to go with them if they took Graeme, which really did go to Hell. 'Will it be for ever?' I whispered, suddenly feeling like I wanted to cry.

He nodded next to my cheek. 'I'm a demon, Sam. But a paired one. I do get time off for bad behaviour,' he said, pinching my sides, making me dispel my sadness with loud laughter.

We kissed again. I just couldn't get enough of him. But as the gong began to bang incessantly, I picked up his hand and led him towards the door. It was too dangerous to stay a moment longer, or we'd end up in bed again.

We walked hand in hand into the dining room and everyone was already there chatting and laughing together. It was a happy din. I looked up into Helix's eyes to make sure he was OK. His smile was a little unsure, but he squeezed my hand. It struck me then that apart from the day we beat Graeme, he had only ever mixed with spirits, demons, or me.

He nodded his head in the direction of the table to make me move.

As everyone began to spot us, the room began to hush. Even the Whitelys looked over from their conversation. We just stood there surveying the faces, nervous of our reception.

Trish waved and smiled happily from her place next to a much happier and cleaner Pete.

'Come and sit down,' Olivia said warmly, pointing to two vacant chairs on the opposite side of the table. 'We've saved your places.'

I looked up into Helix's eyes and he looked startled for a moment. I guess he'd never had a place saved for him before. He'd been hidden since he was eight years old. 'It's OK,' I whispered, with my eyes misting over with tears. I squeezed his hand. 'Come on. Come and meet the family.'

We went to take a step forward, right into the path of Wax. He'd got up from the table to bar Helix's way.

My heart literally stopped beating in my chest. The atmosphere around us had suddenly become sub-zero and charged. Nobody spoke. Nobody dared to breathe.

Wax was tall, well-built and had an aggressive streak a mile wide, but Helix was at least six and a half feet and now he was packed with muscle. No one would be able to call it. It was a moment fraught with danger.

They stared into each other's eyes as if getting the measure of the other. Then Wax completely surprised me by saying one word: 'Thanks.'

The place was silent, with everyone still holding their breath.

'For everything. You're sacrifices for this family and for Pete,' Wax said, still not breaking the stand-off.

Helix narrowed his eyes, as if it was the last thing he'd

been expecting too. I felt his hand tighten around mine as if he didn't know how to respond.

'It's OK,' I whispered.

'Thank you for being there for my Hjarta,' Helix replied.

There were several 'ahs' from the females around the table. Wax stepped aside and held out his arm for us to take our seats.

'Come and sit next to me,' Tallulah called out to Helix, patting the seat next to her.

I rolled my eyes. Helix looked genuinely scared. I could just imagine the questions she would ask him.

We both sat between Tallulah and Ollie. Ollie immediately put his arm around my shoulder and gave me a brotherly hug.

Helix looked bemused as Tallulah pinched his bicep. Then she launched into an avalanche of questions that she didn't even give him time to answer. 'There are loads of things I've been dying to ask you, like how old are you? Like, do you live for hundreds of years? Where were you born? What I mean is, are you born or are you made? I have no idea. Oh and is it true you feed off sex?'

'Tallulah!' Olivia scolded, with an apologetic look.

Helix just smiled, looking a little bewildered.

'Sorry about her,' I whispered.

He looked craftily sideways at me. 'Don't worry, if she continues, I will simply remove my necklace and put everyone to sleep.'

I put my hand over my mouth to hide my laughter. He had such a lovely sense of humour when he got to show it.

'Hey! What are you whispering about?' Tallulah asked loudly.

My eyes were still glued to Helix's. 'I was asking him what a Hjarta was.'

Without taking his eyes off mine and without missing a

beat, 'It is from the ancient demonic tongue, meaning soulmate.'

It felt like my heart dissolved into liquid that flowed straight down to places I didn't dare think about at the dinner table. I had to tear my eyes away to look around the table to breathe.

Everyone was oblivious and back to chatting and grabbing food from the huge serving plates. The butler and the maid were busy pouring wine. Then I suddenly remembered that Helix probably didn't eat food. He hadn't said a word and was sitting with his hands in his lap, watching everyone else. 'Oh no, you can't eat,' I said, feeling suddenly terrible for him.

He smiled with a devilish look. 'Don't worry, there is enough joy around this table to sustain me till bedtime.'

I giggled, even more when I saw Tallulah's questioning look, where she was trying to hear what we were saying. I couldn't help remembering the blissful look Helix had when he was sunning himself in my dream place as he absorbed all my emotions.

'What? What are you laughing at, Sam?' Tallulah asked loudly.

I decided I'd had enough of her intrusive questioning and got serious. 'Nothing, Tallulah. I was just concerned that Helix felt the odd one out, not being able to eat.

'Oh,' Tallulah said, exaggeratedly, rolling her eyes and tearing a huge mouthful from a chicken drumstick.

I let out a sigh and shook my head. 'He said he's fine sucking the energy out of us, particularly those sitting close to him.'

She almost spat her food out. Ollie and a few of the others who'd heard laughed loudly.

Tallulah attempted to shift her chair a little further away from us.

'Mmm, fear,' Helix said, closing his eyes in mock ecstasy, making the table erupt into laughter at the look of horror on Tallulah's face.

'I can see he's going to fit in great here,' Ollie said, laughing.

I flung my arms around Helix's neck and kissed him.

'Steady on … children present,' Jed said, to a chorus of boos. 'Oh, I almost forgot Sam … and Trish. Your mother phoned earlier. She said she's accepted the regular counselling that the police offered to put her in touch with and she starts next week. So all looking really positive there.'

Trish and I held each other's eyes. She was glowing and looked so happy. My heart swelled for her. Then she looked at Pete. A strange look I'd never seen on her before and he returned it shyly.

'A budding friendship there,' Helix said quietly next to my ear.

I nodded, not daring to ask what energy was coming off them. I was scared but thrilled at the same time. It was such a wonderful, normal, teenage thing for Trish to experience. 'What is he though?' I asked before I got too carried away. I turned to look up at Helix.

He smiled ruefully. 'A Shade like you. Locked in this twilight world of neither the earthly nor the spirit realm.

I looked back at the two of them, happily chatting. I'd never thought about it like that. That we were sitting on some sort of nether plane where the humans in the room straddled both. 'So he did die in the accident, then. I wonder why he didn't come straight here like Beccah?'

Trish laughed loudly at a silly face Pete pulled whilst explaining something.

Helix nodded, watching the same thing. 'Beccah was something different, remember? The old uncle here needed her for his spell. It simply prevented Pete from crossing over.

The Ride just picked him up lost and scared. When you think about it, it was the best thing that could have happened to him.'

I looked up into Helix's eyes and he looked down at me sad and regretful. 'All Shades are viewed as an unnatural abomination by the underworld.'

I understood. It made sense. We were made and trapped by Wax's uncle Ainsley's spell. It was just Wax's fountain waters that kept us corporeal. Without it, I guess, we'd simply cease to be. No telling if we would even exist if it weren't for that. For all we knew, Ainsley could have robbed us of an afterlife.

I snuggled into Helix. No wonder he had to offer himself to The Ride in exchange. It wasn't just to get rid of Graeme, but to keep us all here. 'So you saved Pete as well,' I said more to myself, hugging closer into Helix's body.

Everyone seemed oblivious to a definite cloud still over us. All happily eating and engaging in lively conversation. 'I didn't do anything really. The Ride already had Pete. I just knew who he was and parleyed for them to bring him here. But that isn't the whole reason I ride with them, there is something more. I just don't know what it is yet.'

I looked up at him sharply, my heart spiking in fear. 'What do you think it is?

He shrugged, looking out at the table while he thought about it. 'They didn't just come here for you. They are rounding up all the Shades.'

I turned my focus back to the table, alarmed, just in time to see Beccah happily telling a funny story about her brother, making Trish laugh. 'Why have they left us alone all this time then?' I looked back at Helix. 'It must be because you're going with them.'

Helix smiled a little, not looking convinced. 'I'm not sure. I sense something bigger coming. The spirit world is ominously quiet, as if they dare not breathe a word. Like a storm building. Maybe they need the Shades now.' He let out a ragged breath. 'That's why I need to go, to find out more.'

How I loved him then. I kissed him on the lips and looked back at all the happy faces around the table. Just when everyone thought they could relax and be happy. Especially the Whitelys. I'd never seen them smile, let alone be this happy. They had their Beccah and their Pete. I had Helix and my sister. Wax had Beccah. It seemed so cruel to think something could come and mess all that up.

Ding ding ding. John slowly got to his feet, clinking his glass with his knife.

'Speech … speech!' Jed echoed.

'Friends … family,' John said, looking indulgently around the table at all the happy, rosy faces. 'I'd just like to say a few words.' He looked down at Jean next to him, who was already dabbing her eyes with a napkin. He took her hand and looked at us all again. I just wanted to apologise and convey my heartfelt gratitude to you all.'

'No need,' Jed piped up.

'I do, Jed.'

'It's OK, John. Truly,' Olivia said, smiling. Jed put his arm around her shoulders.

'Above all, I wanted to tell you how eternally grateful we are that you brought our lost son home to us.' John's eyes finally rested on Helix, who acknowledged him with a small nod. 'Thank you all, from the bottom of our hearts.'

There were several 'ahs'. Then people took sips of their drinks.

'Happy to have you,' Olivia called out.

'But I do need to apologise,' John continued.

Jed put his hand up to protest, but John raised his own hand to stop him. 'No, Jed. I need to do this.' He looked out at us all again and we all went quiet. 'Because we judged you,

Jean and I. Out of ignorance and fear, but we were rude and dismissive, nonetheless. Whether you are human, shade, ghost, or moaning, malevolent spirit,' he said, pulling a scared face, making us laugh. 'We will no longer shy away from you but welcome you with open arms at Blackwood House.' His eyes fell on Beccah with those last words.

'What?' Beccah shrieked and sat up straighter. 'We're staying?' Her eyes were shining as she looked at Wax, excitedly, next to her.

'Yes, we're staying. There's nothing for us in California. Everyone we love is here.'

Beccah leapt to her feet and threw her arms around his neck. Wax stood too and shook his hand. Jean was crying and hugged him too.

It was hard to stop my own eyes from filling up with tears. I leant back into Helix's chest and felt his warmth surrounding me. It was a new happy beginning for everyone. But while everyone filtered back into happy conversation, the dark cloud of what Helix had told me hung over my head.

I was dragged from my thoughts by a mobile phone ringing. I glanced absently at Tallulah putting her phone to her ear and walking away from the table. I did briefly wonder again who it was she kept talking to when everyone she knew was right here, but my thoughts were quickly swept away when Helix pulled me into his lap.

Someone else was clinking his glass. It was Wax. I briefly glanced at where Tallulah had gone and tuned back into Wax. He was happy and laughing. Giving playful speeches was so unlike him that I just had to listen.

'Thank you, John. It's pretty hard to follow that,' Wax said to a few chuckles. 'You've made me the happiest man tonight, for more than one reason.' Wax seemed choked up and lost for words. The mood instantly went sombre. It was so unprecedented, it made me sit up straighter. 'About three seconds ago I asked John a question and then I thought I'd better double-check with Beccah to make sure she agreed … Sorry, I'm making a complete hash out of this. Stand up, can you, Becks?'

Excitement was building in my stomach. Everyone was looking at each other, not daring to guess what it was, as Beccah slowly got to her feet and held up her hand. 'Ter-dah!' she sang.

It took me several seconds. It took everyone several seconds to fall in with what she was showing us.

'Oh, congratulations,' Olivia said.

'We're engaged,' Beccah said, leaping into Wax's arms.

The table all leapt to their feet, cheering, patting Wax on the back and kissing Beccah. I don't think I'd ever seen Wax look so happy. He'd gone from losing Beccah to asking her to marry him in a single evening.

Helix nuzzled my neck and put his lips next to my ear. 'Let go of your worries,' he whispered. I turned and kissed him, gazing into his bright, mesmerising eyes. He knew my every feeling. Everything about me. He was right. I needed to forget unpleasant things and concentrate on right now. Forget The Ride, the terrifying Grim Reaper and whatever it was he might want us for. That Helix had to go. That my mother was a raging alcoholic and Tallulah was talking to strangers. For now, I just wanted to be happy and together. Beccah was staying. Pete was staying. Trish was staying. For now, that was enough.

CHAPTER 25

We finished a happy meal and sat at the table and reminisced for hours. Everyone gradually filtered away and back again. We sat for so long that breakfast pastries were brought out. I was beginning to feel very sleepy.

I looked sideways at Helix, feeling a little suspicious and he grinned. However, no sooner had I laughed and thumped him in the shoulder than Ollie marched into the room looking anxious and scared. 'Has anyone seen Tallulah?'

I certainly hadn't seen her. I looked around the table and everyone was shrugging and shaking their heads too. 'Last time I saw her she went out to take a call,' I said, not sure why I felt so guilty. I guess I'd been concerned about her for some time and with everything else going on, I hadn't said anything about it.

'Who was she talking to?' Ollie asked, perplexed, arms outstretched, thinking the same thing I had.

I shrugged.

'She's always talking on her phone,' Beccah said.

I looked at her nodding along. We all did. 'Yes,' and,

'That's true,' came from several around the table, backing her up.

Ollie looked at me and I nodded again, feeling terrible for him. I could see the level of terror building on his face. He'd realised he'd seen the same thing and never really questioned it. We'd all taken it as a part of who she was.

A bellowing knock sounded from the front door. Everyone froze and went silent and looked at each other wide-eyed.

I grabbed onto Helix. His arms tightened around me and my heart constricted in my chest.

Surely this couldn't be another visit from The Ride in one day.

Jed rose slowly from his seat as the butler came into the room. 'Who is it, Fredericks?' Jed asked, looking at his watch. 'It's way past midnight.'

'Two gentlemen to see you, sir.'

Everything was sounding more mysterious by the minute.

'Stay here,' Jed ordered over his shoulder.

'Not a chance,' Wax said, already following.

Helix was already lifting me from his lap to stand as well. I was determined not to let go of him and jogged to keep up. In fact, as we passed the staircase, those who weren't at the table came to the bottom of the stairs as well. Everyone, except Tallulah that is. Maybe this was about her.

Then my heart stopped as I saw who it was. Trish flashed me a glance of alarm. I was astonished to see the two demons from earlier, no longer looking so sure of themselves. They were standing there right in our hall, fidgeting and looking really awkward.

Helix was glaring at them, his face shifting to the scary, aggressive version I'd seen with Graeme.

Jed was asking what they wanted at this hour, but their

eyes seemed to continually stray to Helix. 'We were hoping to speak to the prince of The Ride,' the blonde one said.

Prince? I think we all thought the same thing as we all shifted our focus to Helix. I looked at him, confused.

'Speak,' Helix said, his voice gone several octaves lower. I could tell he was a coiled panther ready to pounce.

'I am Asher and this is my brother Tomas.' The two boys bowed low from the waist.

Helix took a step forward and everyone parted for him. 'What do you want here?'

'Forgive us, Lord. We were passing through, drawn to the increased energy in this region. We met your heart out on the path yesterday and thought it our duty to warn you. Many will be passing this way for the same reason. It isn't safe for anyone to be out alone. There is a great power in this place that pulls beings to it from far and wide.'

Helix seemed to relax his stance a little. It gave me the courage to edge closer and stand next to him again. The one called Asher addressed me then, directly. 'Your friends need to be careful. There are more like you arriving here. Their numbers grow every day. A great clan is building.'

'Where is this clan?' Wax demanded, standing next to Helix on his other side.

'We're not sure where they live exactly, but we know it's close by. But they aren't peaceable like you.'

'These ones seem wild and angry and hellbent on trouble,' Tomas added.

'Many ride motorcycles in a great cavalcade through the village,' Asher said.

Wax looked at Helix, confused, and for a moment, they just looked at each other, sifting through what it meant.

All I kept thinking was *Hells Angels, here? In sleepy old Swineleigh Cross?*

'The curse is broken. Shouldn't they have all just died or

crossed over without the spell to keep them here?' Wax asked.

I certainly thought so. It was the fountain waters that kept us all here.

Helix considered that for a moment. 'Maybe it doesn't happen straight away. You are famous throughout the spirit realm as day walking survivors. Maybe they simply want what you have, before it's too late,' Helix said.

It certainly sounded feasible. They just wanted to survive.

'Then why haven't they just come straight here, peacefully? What are they waiting for?' Wax cut in angrily.

I was looking between them, agreeing with every good point they said. We all were.

'We only sought to warn you,' Asher said again, reminding us they were there.

Helix let out a slow breath and nodded. 'Thank you. You did me a service today.' But then he stiffened and took a menacing step closer, until he loomed over them. They shrank under his glare like a pair of adolescent boys, which I guessed they still were. 'But you will overlook the occupants of this house. Male or female.'

The two exchanged a fearful look and nodded, guiltily.

I glanced sideways at Trish and noticed the pink flush enter her cheeks. It gave me an uneasy feeling as I watched the two demons bow, take their leave and disappear through the front door.

We were all left stunned. Until Helix, after saying something to Wax, finally rested his eyes on me guiltily. 'You're a prince,' I said, flatly, more than a little thrown by the revelation.

'There are more of you?' Wax said to Helix, accusingly, narrowing his eyes.

'There are more of you,' Helix threw back just as aggressively.

My breathing slowed as Wax stood down, slightly. We all did. Helix was right. They were both right. This was huge. 'Go to bed,' Wax said, already grabbing Beccah's hand and walking away. 'We'll talk in the morning.' The discussion over, Wax needed to process.

HELIX and I undressed and got into bed silently. We were both lost in our own thoughts. He absently pulled me close so I comfortably nestled into the crook of his shoulder. 'Did you know all this time you were a prince?' I asked eventually. Not sure what I thought about it exactly. Stunned. Hurt that he hadn't trusted me. A little amazed. In awe, maybe.

I felt him shrug slightly. The underworld is full of principalities and queendoms. My uncle tells me they squabble and fight all the time. It is always changing. And in all honesty, it has never really affected me here with you on the earth plane, so it never came up.'

I let out a deep sigh. It made a weird kind of sense, I guessed.

'Why didn't you mention you met demons when you were out on the path yesterday?' he threw back at me.

'There was rather a lot going on in case you'd forgotten, Helix. I met them twice, actually. Once near the well and the second time I was coming back with Trish after you left with The Ride.'

His eyes narrowed and he searched my face to check me for half-truths. 'And they attempted nothing with you?' he asked, sceptically.

'Well, they tried to put me to sleep the first time, I think. The second time, they saw my necklace. To be honest, they seemed more interested in Trish.'

Helix nodded thoughtfully. 'That will be why then.'

I leant up to face him more squarely. 'What do you mean? I thought they were warning us about the others.'

He bobbed his head. 'That's true. But you have to remember who they are, Sam. What they are. They are new to the area. They need a source to feed.'

I was shocked when I fell in with what he meant. That they could be looking for someone they could go to regularly. Maybe young and impressionable. Someone just like Trish. *God, the world was a minefield, even when you're dead.* And Trish was very much still alive and I wanted to keep her that way.

Helix searched my face knowingly. He knew I was worried, but still wanted to make sure I got his point. 'More than that,' he said, softening a little. 'They are looking for a partner to facilitate their change. That is the real reason they were drawn to the area.'

I swallowed, understanding right away. I was the one who was gullible and stupid. I had to warn Trish to be careful. With everything she'd been through already, I knew she couldn't handle that.

Just then, there was a door slam and then voices. Loud, heated conversation. 'Tallulah's back,' I whispered, sitting up quickly. 'Should I get up?' I said, looking down at Helix, who hadn't moved. Ollie was now shouting as well.

Helix shook his head and pulled me back down with him. 'It is a lovers' quarrel. Believe me, you don't want to get in the middle of that.' I was about to argue when I realised what he meant. He could feel their energy and know right away what the emotion was.

He turned to face me and kissed me. 'Jealousy,' he answered, even before I could ask. I felt sad as we listened. Poor Ollie. Happy, cheerful Ollie was tearing his heart bare. The longing and desperation were evident in the strength of his words.

'Keep your voice down,' Tallulah hissed. 'You'll wake the whole house.'

'You think I care. Where have you been all night? I've been worried sick … You've been with him, haven't you? One of them.'

'You don't own me, Ollie … Don't push me!'

A door slammed and I guessed they'd taken their argument into Ollie's room. I couldn't hear what they were shouting after that. Just a blur of raised voices that made me sad. I hoped they worked it out. I really did.

THE NEXT DAY, Ollie and Tallulah hadn't come out of their room. Wax called time and decided we wouldn't wait. He wanted Pete to drink the fountain's waters right away. I guess he wasn't taking any chances with the stability of the Whitely family now that he had Beccah back. Plus, we all drank the waters regularly and he said we were about due.

We traipsed silently through the underground passageway from Waxley-Black Manor to Blackwood House. We were a sombre bunch after the visit of the day before. I suppose we were all still digesting it. That maybe we weren't the only Shades in our universe and what that would ultimately mean to day-to-day life.

It was as if we were filled with an overwhelming sadness. Which was weird considering the Whitelys had their son back and Beccah and Wax had just got engaged. We should be celebrating. But instead, it felt like we were in mourning. I guessed everyone must have heard Ollie and Tallulah's argument last night and come to the same conclusion that I did. That their relationship was nearing its end and that it would cause trouble in a group as tight-knit as ours.

Wax stopped about halfway through the tunnel and we all crowded around him. At the slight bend in the jagged wall, the spirit of Jedediah waited, hovering, next to the pale outline of the ghost of his wife, Lucinda. He didn't usually accompany us to take the waters. Something must be wrong.

We all seemed to sense it and bunched closer together as we watched Wax approach them. He seemed as unfazed and confident as always. I turned to check how Beccah's mum and dad were faring. They seemed OK. Just checking around at all of us, to see if they should be scared. Jean pulled Pete to her and he struggled to stand free. At least they weren't losing their minds this time.

Helix gripped my hand to ground me. We exchanged a reassuring smile. I had no idea what the problem was. The mine containing the fountain waters now belonged to Wax as the eldest living Waxley-Black son, but they were originally Jedediah's. He'd never seemed to have a problem with us going there before. He knew we had to drink from the fountain to stay materialised and real.

It felt like we were all nervously holding our breath as Wax spoke to the spirits in hushed tones. Jedediah looked fearsome with his black cloak constantly moving and billowing all around him in an invisible, cosmic wind.

Wax was speaking, the malevolent spirit nodded slowly and Lucinda's voice carried in the tunnel, 'Be careful,' like whispering leaves. Jedediah pointed at the wall and the two of them disappeared through it. The whole thing was bizarre and intriguing.

Wax reached for Beccah's hand but he didn't say a word about what had been said. 'We're going through the gap in the wall and following the path through the mine,' he said for the Whitelys' benefit. 'Stick together and no loud talking. I don't want the roof caving in on us again.'

The Whitelys looked at each other, horrified. Helix raised his eyebrows. He could be squashed as well as any human.

We went single file through the fissure in the cave wall. It was only just wide enough to fit through sideways. It wasn't difficult and we soon came out into a huge cave, lit by a line of torches alight with paranormal flames. Underneath the first was a tub containing a bunch of unlit ones. We each took a torch and lit it from the one on the wall and moved on.

The path was narrow, so I followed closely behind Helix. It smelled musty and damp and meandered this way and that and went up gradients and down. I had no idea of the way. It forked several times. We walked on for several minutes until Wax finally announced, 'We're here.' He stood at the small opening, ushering us all inside.

The cave we walked into looked like Indiana Jones after the Temple of Doom was destroyed. Huge dust-covered slabs of rock were lying at weird angles and piled-up rocks covered the sandy floor. I couldn't understand why we had to come here. Surely it would be safer to just fill up a plastic bottle and bring some back for everybody. But Wax always made us come like it was some kind of sacred pilgrimage.

He ordered us to wait and squeezed through a gap of two plinths holding each other up. 'What do these waters do, exactly?' Jean said, looking around her fearfully.

'They have magical properties,' Archie said.

'We discovered them last year,' Nicola added.

'They allow the kids to have a physical body for most of the day,' Olivia explained more fully. 'And we drink it to stay with them,' she finished with a sad smile.

John and Jean exchanged a confused look and John put his arm around Jean's shoulders. 'Are you saying it's a fountain of youth?' she said, holding onto Pete as if something would fly in and get him. He fidgeted irritably, but allowed it.

'Exactly,' Olivia said, nestling into Jed's side as he comforted her.

Before Jean could ask anything else, Wax crawled out of

the gap in the rock carrying a flask full of the water. He took out several plastic beakers from his rucksack and began handing them out. Wax looked Helix in the eye, who shook his head.

In a flash of panic, I thought he had to drink the waters otherwise I'd lose him.

He quickly pulled me into the shelter of his body, 'It's OK,' he whispered into my hair. 'Demon, remember?'

I pulled apart and looked up into his intense, burning eyes. 'You live for ever?'

He shrugged. 'Not immortal. We can be killed, but we don't wither and die like humans.'

I swallowed. Good enough, I guess.

'Couldn't we have drunk this back at the house?' Joe said, pointing at the flask and looking up warily at the unstable roof.

'Jedediah allowed me a tiny, charmed amount to take for Beccah in her coma as the last Blackwood daughter, but other than that, it only works close to the source. Which means—'

'No one can ever remove it to sell it,' I finished for him. It made perfect sense. It was exactly what Wax's late, evil uncle, and probably many before him, intended to do with it. I could just imagine all the creams and potions. You could make millions from the cosmetic industry alone.

Everyone nodded, satisfied, taking a sip from their cup. The Whitelys looked at Olivia and Jed, still unsure. 'Go on. It's perfectly fine,' Olivia said, making sure she took a big gulp.

'OK,' Wax said, bringing our attention back to him. I just wanted to say a few words now I have you all together. In light of everything that has happened in the last few days—'

My mind instantly shot to Ollie and Tallulah's argument.

Not everyone was here. I looked behind me. They still hadn't appeared.

'It seemed fitting, as we have so many new additions,' he said, nodding at the Whitelys, Pete and Trish. 'Some human, some Shade.'

I reached out and held Trish's hand. She squeezed it back.

'Some Incubi,' he added.

Helix gave him a single nod of acknowledgement. I hugged into his side.

'I wanted you all to know that despite everything that is going on around us: more demons and Shades, bringing their own dangers, that we are all now a family. And we should all stick together and continue to look after one another.'

Everyone nodded and murmured their agreement.

'We have a great gift here. From where it came, we have no idea, but my spirit uncle, Jedediah, found it and saw to it that it came down to us. I believe it was for a reason. We've been chosen for something. I like to think it's to do something great. So let's drink and appreciate the blessings we have.'

'Amen,' Jed said, downing his water in one.

'Let's go back and have a wonderful family day,' Olivia shouted, joyfully, to several cheers.

We were all relieved for the release of tension and eagerly turned to file out the way we came. 'What about a barbeque, Jed?' Olivia added.

'Why not?' Jed said, hugging her as they walked.

I watched Trish fall in step with Pete and registered again their budding friendship. Helix bent down to my ear. 'Everything you do revolves around food.'

I giggled. I suppose it did. I narrowed my eyes at him. 'Coming from you?'

He laughed and tickled my ribs.

CHAPTER 26

We came out eventually through the door under the stairs of Waxley-Black Manor. The Whitelys headed straight for the kitchen with Olivia and Jed. The rest of us turned in the direction of our rooms.

We all came to a standstill at the foot of the stairs. Sitting on the bottom steps was Ollie, leaning on his knees with his head in his hands.

'What is it?' I asked immediately, already dreading what he'd say.

He looked through his eyebrows at us miserably, his eyes red from crying. I rushed and sat next to him, putting my hand around his back. Nicola immediately went to his other side and did the same. 'The two of you will work it out,' Nicola said kindly.

'No we won't,' he said, snapping, making Nicola flinch away from him.

I swapped a look with her. 'Do you want me to talk to her? See if we can sort something out?'

He was so angry, pushing his fingers up through his hair, he reminded me of the old Wax.

Wax stepped forward and kicked his foot to get his attention. 'Hey! What is it?'

'You don't get it, do you. None of you do.' He got to his feet and turned to go back up the stairs. 'She's gone!'

'What do you mean, she's gone?' Wax said, his own anger starting to rise. 'Gone where?'

I looked between them, stunned. I didn't think any of us could leave here, either.

'How the hell do I know? We argued. We slept. I got up and the house was empty.'

We all stared at him blankly.

He threw his hands up in frustration. 'Well, have a look if you don't believe me. All her stuff is gone.' With that, his voice broke and he ran up the stairs.

'Ollie!' Wax called after him. 'Come down. We'll all help you look for her.'

'Leave me alone. All of you. She's gone for good. She's left me.'

A loud slam of his bedroom door made me jump and signalled the conversation was over.

We were left standing aghast at the devastating news. I didn't know what to think. Surely, even if she'd broken up with Ollie, she wouldn't have left us all like that without a word. It was unthinkable. 'What shall we do?' I said, looking at Wax, flummoxed.

Beccah cuddled into his side. He looked worried. This was uncharted territory, him quiet and settled and Ollie a loose cannon.

My mind shot to the phone calls. 'It sounds like she's got someone else,' I persisted, daring to state the obvious.

Wax just nodded, looking completely heartsick for his brother.

'Come on,' Helix said quietly. Pulling me with him to go up the stairs.

'Sam!'

I stopped and turned back to face Wax. His expression was strong and direct, already making me feel nervous. 'I wanted to speak with you. Be careful from now on. Your stepdad may have gone, but it isn't over.'

Helix stiffened immediately next to me. 'He has gone. I saw him off with The Ride, myself,' Helix said.

I nodded manically, my gaze going from Helix to Wax.

'No, it's not that. Remember my Uncle Jedediah stopped us this morning? It was to warn us about something. Something else we had no idea existed.'

'What do you mean?' My heart began to beat hard in my chest. I couldn't bear it. Not after thinking everything with Trish was sorted.

'Listen, I've got to find out more. It's not the time for it this morning,' he said wearily.

'What did he say?' Helix cut across him, his face becoming angry and fierce.

Wax shuffled his feet as if he didn't want to have to say it. 'He said you have a Shadow Man attached to you.'

I had no idea what that was and looked up at Helix to gauge his reaction. He just returned my gaze, shook his head, but looked worried.

'I don't fully understand it,' Wax continued. 'But that's what Jedediah said. Apparently, it's a separate entity but connected to Graeme. It comes directly from Hell. That's all I know,' Wax said, directing his gaze right at Helix. 'You might be able to shed some light on that.'

I looked up at Helix and he returned my questioning look with a shrug. 'I'll see what I can find out,' he said, looking back at Wax.

I could feel the ice crawling up my spine and my throat constricting. 'Why me … what does it want?' I asked in a cracked and broken voice.

Wax shrugged and shook his head slowly. 'That's all I know, Sam … Jedediah said it's an evil being who lives to cause trouble and toy with its victims. Its doorway to this world is through dreams, but when someone truly evil comes along, they can latch onto them and can sometimes cross over. Jedediah said the spirit realm is alive with talk. I have heard it myself, Sam. They're saying you have one because of Graeme.'

I was left so utterly shaken, I couldn't speak. My mind went to the Goblin, but I couldn't articulate the words. I knew the visions, or whatever they were, were connected to Graeme. They were my way of processing him. They'd disappeared with him. I shook my head, convinced that I hadn't seen the goblin since Graeme had gone.

'Have you seen something?' Helix prompted. Turning me around to face him, anxiously.

'No … I mean, nothing really. Just a nightmare. An ugly goblin that comes in my dreams… just a shadow.' My voice trailed off.

ACKNOWLEDGEMENTS

As always, sending a special thank-you to my team: Nicky Lovick, my Night Shades artist Daniela Owegoor and Jane Harrison. And, of course, my wonderful readers, without whom, getting up at the crack of dawn to write before work would not be worth it.

CONTACT T

To receive your two 21st Century Sirens Novellas, and be the first to know anything relating to T's books, leave your details here: https://mailchi.mp/d18c89c14f50/tstedmannovellas
And please don't forget to leave a review wherever you bought your book, I really appreciate the feedback.
Much love,
T
www.tstedman.com
Facebook
Twitter
TikTok

ALSO BY T STEDMAN

The Night Shade Novels

Demon in the Attic

The Blackwood Curse

Young Atlanteans

Two Tribes

Cross Heirs

21st Century Sirens Series

Soul Breather

Blood Sister

Shield Maiden

Tiger Lily

Night Goddess

Darkly Begotten

Dark Valentines Collection

Star Child

The Watchers

Diablo

The Novellas

Protector

Lost Moon

Non-Fiction

My Migraine Story